## MORE PRAISE FOR
## *QUICKLY, WHILE THEY STILL HAVE HORSES*

"Jan Carson is an essential voice from the island of Ireland. . . . There's something of the fable about each of these stories—troubling, timeless, wistful, and wise."

—Caoilinn Hughes, author of *The Wild Laughter* and *The Alternatives*

"Imaginative, whimsical, mischievous, and brave, but tender and curious too."

—Lisa McInerney, author of *The Glorious Heresies*

"Story after story glints with the strange, hard magic of the North. . . . This is a Northern Ireland at once uncanny and familiar, ancient and modern."

—Lucy Caldwell, author of *These Days*

"What an enormous pleasure it is to read Jan Carson. Each short story is masterful, brilliantly inventive, and moving. Every page reveals the mark of an extraordinary, original, and gifted writer."

—Karl Geary, author of *Juno Loves Legs*

"Utterly captivating . . . speaks to the complexity and emotional temperature of a modern Northern Ireland, real and imagined, without losing sight of the past."

—Olivia Fitzsimons, author of *The Quiet Whispers Never Stop*

# PRAISE FOR JAN CARSON

"A born storyteller, [Carson's] narratives are uncontainable, fizzing up out of her pages like soda and vinegar in a bottle."

—*The Guardian*

"Carson proves herself adept at making the familiar marvellously uncanny . . . Carson's writing—bracingly fresh, darkly funny, unwaveringly compassionate—represents such a direction in Northern Irish fiction."

—*Irish News*

"Her stories move effortlessly from reality to dystopia to surreal vignettes in a style that recalls the up-and-coming American authors Laura van den Berg and Diane Cook."

—*Irish Times*

# PRAISE FOR *THE FIRE STARTERS*

## **WINNER OF THE EU PRIZE FOR LITERATURE**

"Sound the siren: this novel truly burns bright."

—*The Independent*

"Jan Carson seems to have invented a new Belfast in this gripping, surprising, exhilarating novel."

—Roddy Doyle

"*The Fire Starters* succeeds in dramatizing the simmering volatility of a region that, with the looming post-Brexit threat of a hard border, could explode again."

—*The Guardian*

## ALSO BY JAN CARSON

**NOVELS**

*The Raptures*

*The Fire Starters*

*Malcolm Orange Disappears*

**STORIES**

*The Last Resort*

*Postcard Stories 2*

*Postcard Stories*

*Children's Children*

**ANTHOLOGY**

*A Little Unsteadily into Light: New Dementia-Inspired Fiction*
(co-editor)

# QUICKLY, WHILE THEY STILL HAVE HORSES

STORIES

JAN CARSON

SCRIBNER
New York London Toronto Sydney New Delhi

Scribner
An Imprint of Simon & Schuster, LLC
1230 Avenue of the Americas
New York, NY 10020

This book is a work of fiction. Any references to historical events, real people, or real places are used fictitiously. Other names, characters, places, and events are products of the author's imagination, and any resemblance to actual events or places or persons, living or dead, is entirely coincidental.



Originally published in Great Britain in 2024 by Doubleday



First Scribner trade paperback edition July 2024



Interior design by Jaime Putorti

Manufactured in the United States of America

10 9 8 7 6 5 4 3 2 1

Library of Congress Cataloging-in-Publication Data

ISBN 978-1-6680-5661-5
ISBN 978-1-6680-5662-2 (ebook)

*For Kristen,*

*who never fails to encourage me*

“At present I would prefer not to be a little reasonable.”

—HERMAN MELVILLE, “BARTLEBY, THE SCRIVENER: A STORY OF WALL STREET”

# CONTENTS


A Certain Degree of Ownership *1*

Grand So *7*

Fair Play *21*

Tinged *41*

Quickly, While They Still Have Horses *53*

Victor Soda *67*

Pillars *91*

Jellyfish *103*

Mostly People Just Throw Bricks *119*

Bat McElhatton Learns to Drive *141*

Caravan *159*

Troubling the Water *175*

In the Car with the Rain Coming Down *187*

One-Hander *211*

Coasters *231*

Family Circle *253*

A Note on Previously Published Stories *265*

Acknowledgments *267*

# QUICKLY, WHILE THEY STILL HAVE HORSES

# A CERTAIN DEGREE OF OWNERSHIP

Sean says it isn't safe, swimming alone.

"No one will notice if you're drowning," he says.

"If I'm going to die an undignified death," I say, "I'd prefer not to have an audience."

Sean does not think death is something to joke about. Sean is a worrier, the sort of man who takes a wet wipe to every apple he eats, just to be on the safe side. Sean would rather I didn't swim outdoors. If I "simply must"—Sean's own words—he'd rather I swam at the main strand, cautiously, in full view of the lifeguards' station.

Instead I swim here, in a tiny cove cut off by boulders on one side and a sheer cliff face on the other. A thick band of seaweed separates the sand from the sea beyond. In summer it smells like soy sauce and warm piss. The kelp flies rise in consternation when I pick my way through. In winter it is less pungent but slippier. I wear neoprene booties and step carefully. My feet are ludicrous: two fat slugs squirming at the ends of my shins. At high tide the seaweed swims with me. Its smooth tongues lap my arms and legs. I think about Jonah in the belly of the whale, all those slick intestines sliding against his skin. I feel small in myself and held.

I choose to swim here because it is always empty. The seaweed puts people off. It is a decent hike from the road, through fields and a small forest. Once I brought Sean with me. He was meant to read while I swam. Sean could not concentrate for watching me. I could not swim easily with his eyes on me. Afterward we had words in the car. We argued about what should be made for supper, aware that this was code for a much deeper frustration. Sean did not come to the beach again.

It is warm today. The beach hums in the heat. I leave my towel, water bottle, and book in a pool of shade next to the rocks. I slip my sundress over my head, heel my trainers off, and swim my usual six laps of the bay. Though there's hardly any wind, the sea is choppy. Toward the end of the fifth lap, my arm muscles begin to burn. By the sixth, I'm exhausted. The sun is loud in my eyes as I thrash clumsily through the shallows. I am thinking about the granola bar that I might have brought from home. I'm already on the beach before I notice them.

There are three of them or, rather, two and a half. Anything younger than sixteen counts as half in my book. Sean disagrees. Sean likes children. Occasionally, he raises the possibility of acquiring some. I've told him I'm not interested. I suspect Sean has no specific interest either. He sees children as something that should be done at our age. He has similar feelings about personal trainers.

I make my way up the beach, squeezing the water out of my hair. I stare at them. They haven't noticed me. She is leafing through a glossy magazine, pausing between pages to tip the ash from her cigarette into the sand. He is dozing on his front, one hand draped heavily across her thigh as if afraid someone will run off with her while he sleeps. Her thigh is the fake mahogany color of a flatpack desk. His swimming trunks are Barbie pink and printed with anthropomorphic pineapples. The pineapples dance across the hump of his backside, shaking their tiny maracas and tambourines like billy-o. The baby is wearing nothing but a white disposable nappy. It is stuffing sand into its mouth in greedy handfuls. The sand is stuck to the snot running out of its nose. I look at the baby's face. It reminds me of an ice cream dipped in sprinkles, but dirtier.

I should feel sorry for the baby. I don't.

The person I feel sorry for is myself. I shouldn't have to share my beach with them.

I could leave. If Sean were here, he'd say, *Just leave them to it. You're only going to sit there seething if you stay.* I am not going to leave. This is my beach. In the two years since I began swimming here, I have encountered no other human beings. I have assumed a certain degree of ownership. The beach is like that thin strip of flower bed between our garden and next door's. *Does it belong to us? Does it belong to them? Who knows?* Sean said we should consult the architect's plans. I said, "To hell with that," and stuck a couple of rhododendrons in. Now the flower bed is ours. The same principle applies to this beach.

I walk over to my things. I try to look unperturbed. I spread my towel out and lie down, then remember the granola bar. I fish around inside the pockets of my sundress and find two used tissues and a ballpoint pen. No granola bar. I glance over at the baby. The baby is looking hard at me. It seems to register my disappointment. Babies can be very perceptive. Sometimes babies look at me and they do not look like babies. They look like adults trapped in baby faces. I do not like it when babies look at me like this. I find it unsettling. I pretend to be searching for a tissue. I lift the less crumpled of the two from my sundress pocket and blow my nose dramatically. I am doing this for the baby's benefit. I do not want it to know I haven't found what I'm looking for. I smile at the baby. The baby goes back to eating sand.

I open my book and begin to read. I read the first paragraph four times and cannot remember anything I've read. I read on. The second paragraph makes no sense, divorced from the first. I return to the first paragraph. It is uncomfortable holding the book with one hand and shielding my eyes with the other. I think about my sunglasses sitting on the telephone table at home. I think about Sean shouting from the living room, "Your sunglasses are on the telephone table," and how I'd shouted back, "I'm grand without them. There's hardly any sun." I reposition the book so its shadow falls across my face. *You're grand without sunglasses,* I tell myself. I begin to read the first paragraph again.

Something shudders in the corner of my eye. I peer around the edge of my book. The baby has quit eating sand. It is shuffling down the beach toward the sea. The man and the woman have not noticed. The man is sliding his hand up and down the woman's thigh. Up and down. Up and down. Like she is a car in need of waxing. The woman has lifted her hand to her face in order to examine her fingernails. Her fingernails are such a vibrant shade of red I can see them screaming from the other side of the beach. The man's face is pressed into his beach towel. The woman is preoccupied with her fingers. Neither has noticed that the baby has now reached the seaweed trench.

The baby considers the seaweed. It glances back as if waiting to be stopped, then crawls on, hands and knees scouring through the scratchy kelp. Crawling forward, the baby makes a noise like scrunched-up paper. Surely the man and woman will hear. They will look up and see the baby moving toward the sea. I can hear the baby. I can see the baby. The white flag of its nappy blooming against the black seaweed. The black flies shimmering around its chubby shoulders. The clean cup of its upturned soles like a pair of parentheses plowing through the kelp. I can see the baby. But it is not my baby. I did not bring it here to this quiet beach.

The man has turned his back to me. He lies on one shoulder now, facing the woman. He pushes his mouth into her neck. He nuzzles her like a dog. The anthropomorphic pineapples on his swimming trunks stretch with him. Their happy, grinning faces distort as he throws a single leg over the woman's thighs. The woman continues to read, flicking listlessly as he clings to her side like a giant baby. It is ugly to look at them. Her distance. His neediness. Moments like this should not be seen. Sean and I only touch in private. Sometimes when we are out and about, drinking coffee or visiting a garden center, he will reach for me. I always stop him. I do not want anyone to see the way my face goes when he kisses me. The dreadful softness. The need.

The baby has reached the shallows. It sits at the sea's edge, its filthy white nappy beginning to bloat. I watch the baby from behind my book. I think, *This is the kind of setup people take photographs of: babies, beaches, sunny days.* I also think, *Someone should lift that baby before it gets any farther.* I hold both thoughts at some distance. I do not, for example, think, *I wish I had a phone with photo-taking ability so I could capture this beautiful moment*. Neither do I think, *I should rise from my beach towel and grab that baby before it crawls into the sea*. Sean says I am exceptionally good at removing myself from responsibility. Like when I say somebody should do something about the polar ice caps or the teenagers who stand about drinking at the end of our street, and what I really mean is somebody who isn't me.

I do not want the baby to crawl into the sea. But I do not think it is my job to stop the baby crawling into the sea. I did not make the baby. I did not bring it here to this beach. I certainly did not leave the baby to eat sand and crawl through seaweed while I read *Cosmopolitan* or dry-hump my girlfriend's leg. I do not want the baby to crawl into the sea, but a small, mean part of me thinks it would be quite proper for the man and woman to look up, seconds from now, and see the baby about to crawl into the sea and, in that brief, heart-stopping moment, realize—perhaps for the first time—that they are dreadful, selfish people who do not deserve the baby or this beach.

I have abandoned my book. It is impossible to concentrate with the moment tottering in front of me, like a baby up to its oxters in the rising tide. I have given up on my book, though I'm still holding it like a shield in front of my face. I am sideways-watching the man and the woman. I am waiting, waiting, still waiting for them to look up and notice the baby, when the wave comes crashing in. I do not see the wave until I hear it. The wave sounds like handfuls of pebbles dropped from a great height. The baby screams. Then the woman. Then the man.

I look up from my book. I arrange my face appropriately. This is the face of someone who has only just noticed a baby being swept out to sea. I rise to my feet. I sprint down the beach, through the seaweed, to the sea's edge. My mouth says all the right words. Mostly expletives. My head is much neater. It is already rearranging the last few minutes, moving me to the edge of the picture. Later, when I recount the afternoon's events to Sean, I will be almost absent. I will say, *It was so very sad,* in such a way that Sean understands the baby had nothing to do with me.

# GRAND SO

Nobody wants to buy luxury jam.

This is Northern Ireland. In the eighties. People have other things on their minds.

Granda and Granny have tried everything. Advertisements in the paper. An ad on Downtown Radio. A big sign next to the Banbridge turnoff—"Loughbrickland Country Preserves" written in curly letters next to a photo of wee pigtailed Ruth, nibbling strawberry jam off a spoon. When the sign first went up, Ruth hadn't minded being famous. Now that she's older, she's mortified. She's for the Academy in September. Every morning and afternoon the school bus will trundle past her big jammy face.

The car is Granda's latest idea. Granny will drive around with samples, rooting out potential customers. She'll target small shops in villages where the bus stops only twice a day. She'll be covering the whole province: Newry to Ballycastle, Donaghadee to Belleek. Coast to border. Border to coast. Skirting Lough Neagh's dismal shoreline. Circumnavigating Fermanagh's lakes. Through the moss-green Glens of Antrim. Round the skirt-tails of the Mournes. Four or five hundred miles per week. She couldn't manage without a car.

It's not the best time to be sending your wife out round the country on her own. There are army boys concealed in hedges, regular checkpoints and ambushes. It's not uncommon to come across a burned-out car smoldering on the roadside. There's a bomb on the news nearly every night. Granny and Granda don't have a choice. They've thrown everything into the jam. Their savings. The house. The money set aside for Ruth's education. Every bloody penny they have. Granda says it'll be grand. Loughbrickland Country Preserves is just going through a sticky patch. He tries to make a joke of this. "Sticky, ha ha, like the jam." Ruth can tell he's nervous. He isn't laughing with his eyes. If they want to hold on to the business, Granny needs to find new customers.

Granny's up for the challenge. "You know me," she says, "I could sell snow to the Eskimos."

"Never worry about the Eskimos," says Granda. "It's shifting marmalade to Ulstermen that'll get us out of this hole."

◆◆

Granda finds a motor for Granny in *The Autotrader*. An absolute gem of a car. Ten years old. In decent nick. Two previous owners. Cash in hand. He takes the bus over to Lisburn to pick it up.

There is a man in the backseat of the car. Ruth spots him as soon as Granda pulls into the yard. He's a largish fella of farmer build. He wears reading glasses and a funeral suit. What remains of his hair is gray and swept across a gummy bald spot. It forms a kind of hairy flap. Ruth assumes her granda's given the man a lift, though it's odd that he's sitting in the backseat. It looks like he's being chauffeured around.

She waits for the stranger to emerge. He doesn't move. Granda hops out, leaving him there.

"Get in, Marlene," he says. "Take her a wee run round the yard. She's a nice-looking motor, isn't she? Only thirty thousand on the clock."

Granny squeezes her substantial thighs in beneath the wheel. She doesn't acknowledge the man in the back. She places her hands at ten and two, turns the key, and revs the engine cautiously.

"Aye, she'll do rightly," Granny announces. She pauses then and sniffs the air. "It fairly stinks in here." She glances over her shoulder, straight at the man, who's lighting his next cigarette off the last. She looks right through him like he isn't there. "The last owner must've been a smoker. With secondhand motors you should always ask. You cannae shift the smell of fags."

Granda has asked no such thing. Nor has he checked for the presence of a spare tire or if the electric windows actually work. (There isn't one, and they don't.) *The Autotrader*'s also failed to mention that this 1982 Sierra in Polaris Gray comes complete with the original owner, now deceased. This extra information would hardly have deterred Granda. The same man cannot pass a bargain by. He once returned from Nutts Corner market with three hundred dishwasher tablets bought for two quid. They hadn't owned a dishwasher, nor planned to acquire one, but he'd been pleased with his purchase—"proud as punch"—because dishwasher tablets were "dear enough."

The new car does fifty-five miles to the gallon. This is almost miraculous. What's more, Granda's managed to negotiate twenty quid off the asking price. It's a bargain, in his book. If Granny ever thought to complain about taxiing a dead fella around, he'd simply dismiss her concerns: *You're under no pressure to make friends with him, Marlene. Just you concentrate on the driving. Leave your man to get on with being dead.* Granny's not for complaining, though. Ruth's the only one who can see the Backseat Man. They say weans are more receptive to things unseen, and Ruth's a particularly dreamy kind of wean.

It is mid-July when the car arrives. School is out for another six weeks. Granny won't hear tell of leaving Ruth alone. And Granda spends his days in the shed. He has to keep an eye on the jam as it boils and bubbles inside the huge vats. It cannot be allowed to burn. Money's that tight, a single lost batch could be the straw that breaks the camel's back. Granda hasn't time to mind a child. Ruth offers several alternative options. She could go to Lyndsey's across the field. Lyndsey has six wee brothers and sisters. Her mother won't notice another child. Or there's cousins with a caravan up in Portrush. They're always offering to take Ruth for a couple of weeks. Or the Holiday Bible Club in the Presbyterian. Ruth's not that interested in getting saved, but she could fake it rightly for a week or two.

"No," says Granny, "you're coming in the car with me." And that's her final word on the matter. There's no point trying to negotiate.

Ruth wonders if Granny's always been this strict. It's likely just since Mummy died. A thing like that would make you clingy. You'd be feared of losing anyone else. Ruth was only three when it happened. She has forgotten the time before. She remembers Mummy from photographs. Granny and Granda don't talk about her. Ruth could hardly tell you a thing about her.

The pair of them leave the farm before eight every morning. To speed things up, Granny makes their sandwiches the night before. Ruth prefers cheese or ham. If it's tomato, the bread'll be mush long before lunchtime. If it's tuna, it's even worse. The Backseat Man is always waiting for them. He dozes across the length of the seat, his big knees triangled up in the air. When he hears Granny fumbling with her keys, he springs up into a sitting position, occupying the space behind the driver's seat. Ruth only needs to turn her head slightly to see him. They're barely down the lane before he's lighting his first cigarette.

The Backseat Man smokes like a chimney. Ruth sometimes wonders if it was the smoking that killed him. She'd ask, but she doesn't want to annoy him further. When she catches his eye in the rearview mirror, he's always glaring. At her. At Granny. At the telegraph poles, the dry-stone walls and straggly hedges which go swimming past the windscreen. He looks like Granda when the postman delivers another bank letter. Like he's taken a mouthful of vinegar. Ruth can't get a name out of him. Nor where he's from. Nor how he wound up here, in the backseat of her granny's car. He's not what you'd call a chatty man.

The first day she fairly batters him with questions. They're up Ballymena direction, flitting through the surrounding villages: Ahoghill, Cullybackey, Kells, Broughshane. Granny says the people in Broughshane have an awful notion of themselves. They've plastered the place in fancy flowers. She parks the car outside a shop. Every available ledge and container is spewing primary-colored begonias. You can't even see the sign to tell whether it's a SPAR or VG. Granny leaves the radio on. "I'll not be more than twenty minutes," she says. "Whatever you do, don't leave the car." Ruth gets out her library book. She watches Granny disappear through a curtain of cerise begonias, clutching her samples and a Tupperware full of precut wheaten squares; she doesn't want to seem uncouth, offering potential customers luxury jam off a teaspoon.

Alone at last with the Backseat Man, Ruth sets the library book aside and begins her interrogation. *What's your name? Where do you come from? What's it like being dead? Have you been to heaven? Was it nice up there? Could you have a wee look about for my mummy? She got killed in a bomb a few years back. Angela Kelly is her name.* All credit to him, his face softens a little, hearing this. But does he answer Ruth's questions? He does not. He holds his silence like a riot shield, smoking one curt cigarette after the other while Ruth continues to pitch questions at him. It is only when she asks if the Sierra used to be his car that the Backseat Man finally opens his mouth. "Jesus Christ, you've some nerve, wee lassie," he says, "it's still my bloody car." Ruth notes the language—*bad*—and the accent—*Newry*—and understands they've been landed with the *other sort* of ghost.

Later that week, in Rasharkin, her suspicions are confirmed. Granny pulls in to let a combine pass and, noticing they're outside a chapel, the Backseat Man crosses himself. *Spectacles, testicles, wallet, and watch.* Ruth's heard this off the wee lads in school. This is the first time she's seen anybody do it for real. There are no Catholics in her world. She's not a baby. She knows they exist. It was the Catholics who blew up her mummy, not for any particular reason save being in the wrong place at the wrong time. Ruth knows the difference between their lot and hers. They fly a green, white, and orange flag and paint your man with Jesus hair on their walls. *Bobby what's-his-name that died.* They have crosses on their church roofs and Mary in a box by the gate. Ruth's lot fly the Union Jack and have the Queen or curly King Billy on their walls. They paint their curbs red, white, and blue; a fresh lick of paint every year for the Twelfth.

Ruth keeps track of the differences as they drive around, labeling the places in her head. Dunloy is Catholic. Comber, Protestant. Fintona's Catholic. Holywood's too posh to tell. Ruth worries about Granny going into certain shops. Wrong time, wrong place, and anything could happen. Surely Granny must know this more than most. When Ruth asks if it's sensible, selling jam to Catholics, Granny tries to laugh it off.

"Jam's jam," she says. "I'll be grand, my love. Nobody can tell which foot I kick with. A name like Kelly goes either way."

There are other things that go both ways. Not football, obviously. If somebody's in a Celtic top, you can tell straight away they're not like you. The same goes for schools and where you live. Also where you buy your groceries. Granny says Stewarts is a Protestant outfit—even the carrier bags are loyal orange. Crazy Prices is for the other lot. "You can tell from the look of it," she says, "the food's just flung at the shelves."

Jam is not sectarian. It's equally popular with both sides, like dogs and tracksuits and that woman from here who won the Olympics and always gets asked to open things. Ruth is beginning to wonder if country music might be the same. Country and western's all they listen to at home. They make the switch to country gospel on Sundays because Sunday is Jesus's day. Granny's a great one for John Denver. She's also partial to Tammy Wynette. She keeps an old shoebox of cassettes tucked beneath the passenger seat. It's Ruth's job to flip them over when the side runs out. Ruth's also expected to harmonize when Granny's in the mood for singing along.

The Backseat Man is a country fan too. He nods along to "Rhinestone Cowboy." He taps his finger on the back of the headrest while Tammy's whining her way through "D-I-V-O-R-C-E." Ruth feels the vibrations, like Morse code twitching at the back of her head. The next time Granny leaves them alone, the Backseat Man asks if there's any Kris Kristofferson under the seat. It's the first time he's tried to start a chat. Even though Ruth's never heard of this Kristoff man and is certain sure he's not in the shoebox, she tries to keep the conversation going.

"Do you like country music?" she asks.

"Aye," the Backseat Man replies.

"So does Granny."

"Aye, I can see that," says the man.

She's about to elaborate when Granny returns with an orange ice pop for Ruth and a tin of Lilt for herself. Ruth is dying to ask the Backseat Man what he was doing listening to country and western. On the telly, Catholics only ever listen to twiddly-diddly music, fiddles and whistles and wee flat drums, the sort of music folks danced to in the olden days. Ruth's always assumed country's just for Protestants. She wonders if the Backseat Man got himself killed for listening to it. Stranger things have happened here. Like this lad she knows from Young Farmers': he got beat up for walking past a Catholic pub in an orange T-shirt. Sometimes when Granda's watching the news, he'll mumble in a sad, sort of weary voice, "Boys a boys, they're killing each other over nothing these days."

Granda worries. Especially when Granny's out in the car. He'll start to panic if they're even a few minutes late home. He keeps the tenpence coins from his change and presents them to Granny every Monday morning. She stores them in a Flora tub inside the glove compartment. Every hour or so she'll pull up at a phone box and hand one to Ruth. It's her job to call home.

*Banbridge 43157.*

"We're in Annahilt," she'll say, or "Strabane," or "Comber," depending on where they're at. "We're fine. We'll be home at the usual time."

"Grand so," Granda will say.

Ruth can always hear the relief in his voice: a slow exhalation, like the morning mist rising, as he hangs up the phone and returns to his jam.

If there's more than two hours between calls, Granny starts to get twitchety. Granda'll be going up the walls. "Keep a wee eye out for a phone box, love," she'll say. Ruth's the best at spotting them. She likes to feel that she's helping Granny. She likes having a job to do. It's why she always volunteers to do the dishes. And takes out the bin on Tuesday mornings. And cleans her own room without being asked. Nobody's ever said anything, but Ruth knows she owes her grandparents a lot. In films when your mummy dies and your da's not around, you get sent to a children's home. Though it's an odd sort of setup—living with a pair of old ones—Ruth feels lucky to have a family.

She wonders about the Backseat Man. *Does he have a family? Maybe a wee lassie of his own? Are there folks out there missing him since he died?* She observes his face in the rearview mirror. He doesn't look like a family man. There's no softness to him. His mouth has forgotten how to smile. She can't imagine him talking to children or puckering up those thin pink lips to plant a bedtime kiss on some wee girl's cheek. Still, she asks him. Thursday morning, in a layby somewhere on the edge of Larne. Granny's gone off to spend a penny, leaving the two of them alone. Ruth lowers her voice to imply concern. She doesn't anticipate hysterics—he doesn't seem like an emotional man—but you never know how folks are feeling deep inside. Granny's not a weepy woman, but Ruth has twice caught her sobbing over Mummy's school photograph.

"So," Ruth says, turning round in her seat to meet his eye, "do you . . . I mean, did you have a family yourself?"

The Backseat Man takes a long draw on his cigarette and exhales slowly. The smoke catches at the back of Ruth's throat. She struggles not to cough.

"Everybody has a family," he says.

"Yeah, but were you close to yours?" she asks.

"I wouldn't say close," says the Backseat Man. "But I wasn't bad to them." He pauses then, tapping his cigarette on the open window to dispense a dollop of ash. "I wouldn't be bad to anyone."

This proves to be the longest conversation of their mutual acquaintance. Ruth understands the significance of what's been said. It has the feel of a confession, though she's only ever seen them done on TV. The Backseat Man would not be bad to *anyone*. There's a whole world of wideness in that one wee word.

It is still hanging in the clammy air when Granny returns to the car, cleaning her hands with a fresh wet wipe. Ruth wants to ask the Backseat Man what he means. *Does your anyone extend to me? What about the rest of my lot? If you weren't bad to anyone, did this eventually make you good?* Ruth chances another look in the rearview mirror. The Backseat Man has leaned his forehead against the window. His eyes are trained on the hard shoulder as it goes screeching by. In profile he looks furious. Like somebody you'd see guldering from a platform on the news. It is hard to imagine much good in him.

Granny's fairly trucking today. She insists upon eating their ham sandwiches in transit. Ruth fills the tea mug from the big Thermos. They pass it back and forth over the gearstick, trying to contain the manic slurp as the car jolts over potholes and muddy ruts. It's mostly back roads this afternoon. One-car-at-a-time numbers with hedges so high, no part of the road lies outside the shadow. They're visiting all the wee villages around

Newry—Warrenpoint, Rathfriland, Camlough—flirting with the snaked line of the border, never daring to cross.

Ruth peers into the distance, imagining it will look different in the South. It appears to be exactly the same. Green fields. Bungalows. Scraggly patches of forest trees. This surprises her. Granny describes it differently. She has a horror of the Free State. A friend's sister once holidayed in Sligo, northern plates on full display. All four of her tires were slashed as she slept in a caravan just ten feet from the car. The implication being, she should count herself lucky she wasn't killed. Or worse. Granny likes to tell this story and other similar stories of hapless Northerners punished for naively assuming the South to be safe.

Twice Ruth glimpses the border at the end of a road. Twice Granny curses and stalls the car as she turns. She's normally a very capable driver. Ruth's never been over the border before, but she recognizes it from the TV news: the breeze-block towers and barriers like dropped arms scraping the asphalt, the young soldiers lying in ditches with guns, all the ordinary cars, engines idling as they worm their way south. This is bandit country, or so Granda says. It's a place where people disappear. Ruth knows not to say anything till they're a good mile away, heading in the right direction again.

An anxious silence has crept into the car. She feels the pressure of it pinching her forehead like a too-tight hat. Granny hunched over the steering wheel. The Backseat Man glaring at the back of her head. Ruth turns the stereo on, not really caring what music comes out, only wanting noise to ease the silence. It's Glen Campbell: "Wichita Lineman." Everyone likes Glen Campbell, even the Backseat Man. But Granny barely lets Glen get a half sentence out before flicking the stereo off. "Not today," she says. "I can't be doing with any distractions."

They are somewhere between Mullaghbawn and Crossmaglen when the Backseat Man leans over and taps Ruth on the shoulder. In the strained silence, she's almost forgotten he's behind her. All her nerves rush to the point where his hand has made contact with her shoulder. His touch is cold and then hot, like freezer burn. It seeps through the fabric of Ruth's polo shirt. She shivers, though it's stifling behind the glass.

"Don't go down the next road," the Backseat Man says.

"What's that?" asks Ruth. The words are out before she can stop them.

"I didn't say anything," Granny replies.

"Sorry, I thought I heard something outside." Ruth catches his eye in the rearview mirror. She tries to frame a question with her face.

"Make her stop," the man says.

Ruth can tell he really means it. "Stop the car," she says.

"I'm not stopping out here, in the middle of nowhere."

"Please, Granny, you need to stop."

"Why?"

"I'm going to boke," says Ruth. She clamps a hand across her mouth, bugging her pale blue eyes out dramatically.

"For goodness' sake, child. You pick your moments."

Granny pulls off the road, running two wheels up the side of the verge so they come to rest at a skew-whiff angle. Ruth leaps from the passenger side. She clambers up the verge and leans out over the prickly green hedge. She tries to look like she's being sick. She glances back to make sure Granny's buying this charade. Granny is fixing her lipstick in the mirror: drawing the wide O of her lips into a tight pucker, then dragging the edges out into a thin red gash. Even from this distance Ruth can see the red lipstick is too bright for a woman of Granny's age. The Backseat Man catches Ruth staring. He gestures with his cigarette hand, making tight firelit loops, as if to say, *Keep it up a bit longer.*

Ruth thrusts her head over the hedge. She makes a series of exaggerated puking noises. Two black-and-white cows dander over. They stand in front of her, staring, damp-eyed. In the distance a tractor makes slow, chugging progress across the horizon. Ruth hasn't a baldy notion where she is. This could be any field in Ulster. It's the same view she sees every morning when she opens the curtains in her bedroom. Her teacher claims Ireland has forty shades of green. In the North the palette's limited. Half a dozen shades of pine and myrtle form the spectrum of her world. This is all Ruth has ever known: hedges, peat moss, farmers' fields, and twice a year—if she's lucky—a run up to Newcastle just to check the sea's still there. She went to Belfast once on a nursery school trip to the panto. That was before her mummy died. There's no way Granda would let her go up to the city after. In the city there are always bombs.

Ruth counts to sixty. Then counts to sixty once again. It's a trick for marking a minute, *One thousand, two thousand, three thousand*, and so on. It's almost three minutes since she left the car. She's just about to turn and walk back to the passenger seat when, in the distance, very close, a noise rises up like drums and guns. Ruth feels the sick thud of it in her belly. Her bones understand what it is.

Up comes the bile and the vomit. This time for real. She misses the field, misses the hedge, watches helpless as it splatters over her shoes and socks. In the field a hundred thousand previously hidden birds rise from the grass and bordering hedges like raindrops returning to the clouds. When Ruth turns back to the car, Granny is already out and scrambling up the verge to grab her, vomity socks and all. Her lipstick has slid in the blast, leaving a long red gash across her cheeks.

She is crying and laughing and falling over.

She is saying, "Oh my God. Oh my God. Oh my God." And it doesn't sound like a curse so much as a thing you'd hear in church, sung by a choir.

Afterward the Backseat Man is gone.

They don't even bother to look for a phone box, they just find the nearest respectable-looking house and ask to use the telephone. When Granda comes on the phone, Granny says, "We're fine, love. We're both fine. But if Ruth hadn't . . ." and then she can't get any words out. So Ruth takes the phone out of her hand and says, "We're fine, Granda. We're on our way home now. See you later." She waits for Granda to say, "Grand so," but there's nothing except silence on the end of the line. Even though she's pure sobbing and probably isn't fit to drive, Granny still remembers to give the lady twenty pence for using the phone.

Once they're on the other side of Newry, on the dual carriageway heading home, Ruth asks if they can listen to Johnny Cash. Granny says, "Anything you want, wee pet," and turns the radio on. Their voices are like water trembling, but they still manage to sing a bit of "Ring of Fire."

Ruth sings loud, so loud there isn't any room to think.

The man in the backseat never returns.

# FAIR PLAY

There's a queue to get into Bouncy Bob's.

Andrew shepherds his boys to the back. He carries Angus. At home, they call Angus "Usain Bolt." Since the second he started walking—ludicrously early, at ten months—the child's been constantly on the move. He's at it now, wriggling and twisting in Andrew's arms. "Down, Papa. Down. Gus want down now." Shauna would've known to bring the buggy. She uses the buggy as a restraining device. The buggy's not here and neither is Shauna. She's at the hairdresser's with her mum. It is, as she informed Andrew earlier, his "bloody turn to occupy the weans."

Shauna's sounding more and more like her mother these days. Andrew's working up to saying something; waiting till she's in a decent mood. The words grate on him. "Weans," for kids. "Grand," which is now her answer to everything. "Wee," for little. "Wee," for something extra to say. "Wee" this. "Wee" that. When Shauna says "wee love," "wee shoes," "wee cup of tea," it makes Andrew want to scream.

She'd talked like this when they met in uni. Andrew had found it charming at first. Then he'd heard how it sounded in company. He was embarrassed for her and, later, for himself. An accent like that did not reflect well. He'd felt a bastard for fixating on such a tiny thing but was mortified—or skundered, as Shauna might say—every time she pluralized "you." It was a relief when London wore the Northerner out of her. Sharp consonants emerged from her mid-Ulster drawl. Then due respect for proper grammar. After a decade or so in exile, you could tell where she came from only when her mother was on the phone.

The boys have taken after him. They speak London with a side of Oxford plum. If pressed upon by his granny, Conor can still reel out a passable version of "I'll tell me ma." He has the Belfast accent down to a T but, even at six, knows this sort of speaking's just a party piece. It's funny enough within context; certainly not fit for everyday use.

There are three groups ahead of them in the queue. A harassed-looking woman with two small girls, a grandparent setup, and—*dear God, no*—what looks to be a birthday party: a dozen or more eight-year-old boys all dressed up as superheroes, clutching gift-wrapped presents in plastic bags.

Conor spots them immediately. He tugs at Andrew's belt. "Papa," he says, "you said I couldn't wear my Spidey suit because of Covid."

These last few months, Andrew's been using Covid as his go-to excuse for avoiding things he doesn't want to do ("I'm sorry, boys, the park's closed today. McDonald's is all out of Happy Meals. Don't blame me. It's a Covid thing"). So far Conor hasn't questioned the logic; he'll pout a little, then acquiesce. The child's not too sure what Covid is. In his head, it's sinister and a bit snakish, like a character lifted from his *Gruffalo* book. He knows that Covid got Great-Gran. She went to hospital. Then she died.

Covid shut his school and closed the swings in the big green park. If his dad says he can't do something because of Covid, Conor's not going to argue with it.

This morning's different. Conor's six, but he isn't stupid. He can see there's another Spider-Man heading into Bouncy Bob's. Also Batman, and Darth Vader, which would've been his second choice for dressing up.

"'S'not fair," he says. "I really, really wanted to be Spider-Man."

Angus picks up on the theme. "'S'not fair," he whines, "'s'not fair, Papa."

Caught out in his lie, Andrew scrambles around for an alternative means of shutting them down and, under pressure, can't think of anything. He once again offers the party line, shrugging as he says, "Don't blame me, son. It's a Covid thing." This makes no sense, no sense at all. He hopes the boys will hear the stern tone he's taken and back down. Conor's becoming more skeptical. Since he started school, he's been questioning everything. Andrew's going to need better excuses if he wants to maintain his authority. He wonders for a second if this is how Boris Johnson feels.

He shifts Angus from left to right hip so he can look his older son in the eye. Conor's already frowning. The next word is going to be "why." Once "why" is unleashed, it's anyone's guess where it'll end. Andrew glances around, desperate for a distraction and—*thank the Lord*—spots a man progressing slowly down the line, dressed in a scabby-looking tiger costume: head squashed into a ghoulish grin, tail flaccid and dragging along the ground.

"Look," he cries, twisting round so Angus can see, "Bouncy Bob is coming over to say hello."

He is and he isn't. The creature that's bearing down on them, dispensing high fives and hand sanitizer, is not the smiling tiger on the Bouncy Bob sign but, rather, an ancient version of Tigger the—equally jumpy—tiger from Disney's *Winnie the Pooh*. It is neither the time nor the place for raising issues of copyright. It can't be easy to source a tiger in a pandemic. *Fair play to them,* thinks Andrew, *Bouncy Bob's has done their best.*

As soon as he lays eyes on the tiger, Conor forgets all about Spider-Man. Angus is similarly distracted: Bob's female assistant has given him a green balloon, and he's already infatuated. It doesn't take much to charm a two-year-old.

"D'ye wanna selfie with Bouncy Bob?" asks the girl.

She can't be much older than fourteen. Her skin's a particularly virulent shade of orange. It complements her Bouncy Bob polo, which is standard-issue luminous green. She is addressing the ground at Andrew's feet. From this angle he has an uninterrupted view of her forehead. He is hypnotized by her eyebrows: two thick black rectangles like Hitler mustaches, dominating the area above her eyes. Andrew's so distracted that the boys get in before he can answer.

"Yes," says Conor.

"Yep," says Angus, who can be relied upon to parrot whatever his older brother says.

"No," says Andrew, snapping back into consciousness. The last thing he wants is his boys cuddling up to a mangy tiger. God only knows where it's been. "Sorry," he says, "it's a Covid thing, social distancing and all that . . ."

Angus lets up a howl of dismay. He extends his arms toward the tiger, making it abundantly clear he now prefers Bouncy Bob to his own dad. "No, Angus," says Andrew. Angus, like any self-respecting two-year-old, takes exception to this word. He throws his head back and screams. Unfortunately, the word he's chosen to scream is "shite." Andrew is certain he's learned it from Shauna or her dad. When Andrew says "shit," it rhymes with "pit," and he is more careful around the boys. The other adults in the line turn around and glare. The old lady gives him a particularly vicious look. You have to watch the old ones here. It's not as cosmopolitan as London. Most old people are born-agains.

Though everyone's spaced out at socially distant intervals, Andrew can feel their judgment boring into him. Every other kid has had a photo taken with Bouncy Bob. They've hugged and smiled and snuggled up to his padded belly. You'd hardly know there was a global pandemic on. Some of the adults have also asked for selfies, grinning shyly as they produce their phones. None of them are wearing face masks, not even the grandparents, though they're pushing eighty and quite overweight. Of course, you're not obligated to wear a mask when standing outside. But Andrew likes to go above and beyond.

Andrew wears his mask religiously. He doesn't take it off when he's filling the car or walking the two hundred yards between the butcher and organic grocer where he insists upon buying all their fruit and veg. He keeps a small bottle of sanitizer clipped to his belt loop with a carabiner. It reassures him to feel it there, brushing insistently against his thigh. Andrew prefers it when there are rules. Shauna is the opposite. She routinely enters through exit doors and steals small items from hotel rooms. She has been known to swim in places where the signage expressly forbids swimming. Once in a fountain. Another time in a reservoir.

Each time she pulls one of these moves, Andrew is both attracted and repulsed. He admires the wild, wanton streak in his wife yet knows he's not capable of such deviancy. He can't get over the tight, unyielding thing his parents have passed down to him. Multiple visits home with Shauna have convinced him that she is typical of her race. The North is overrun with rule breakers. The worst are out-and-out deviants: people who chuck their rubbish out of car windows, let their dogs shit liberally, and, fully aware of what they're doing, drive the wrong way down one-way streets. Even double yellows aren't sacrosanct. Here, rules are rules only if you feel inclined to follow them. It must be something to do with the Troubles. Here, everything's related to the Troubles. Andrew can't get used to it. Since the second he clapped eyes on Shauna, the ground hasn't felt firm beneath his feet.

"Gwan," says the girl in the green polo shirt, "it's safe, so it is. Bouncy Bob's double-vaxxed."

"Gwan," says the solitary man in charge of all the birthday boys, "it's only a photey, your weans'll not catch anything."

As he once again declines, Andrew's acutely aware of his English accent. He can hear himself speaking, and his voice is uncomfortably close to Stephen Fry's. He's wearing his pale pink button-down shirt—prawn cocktail–colored, according to Shauna—and oatmeal chinos. There are brown suede deck shoes on his feet. Expensive ones. From Italy. No one else in the line is wearing deck shoes or chinos or anything much except branded sportswear: Adidas lines are trumping Nike ticks two to one. He is reminded of the first time he accompanied Shauna to a Northern wedding. He, in his second-best blazer and open-necked shirt, had felt like a right gallumph surrounded by all the men in their funeral suits and women dressed for Royal Ascot, satellite dishes clamped to their heads. Occasionally underdressed, frequently too dapper, Andrew has been coming here for almost a decade and still doesn't know what you're meant to wear.

He looks down at his eldest son and, for the benefit of everyone listening, speaks in a louder than usual voice: "Sorry, bud," he says, "your silly dad's left his phone at home. We'll have to come back another day if we want a photo with Bouncy Bob."

Even as he's speaking, Andrew knows he's tempting fate. Sure enough, the words are barely out of his mouth when the phone in his back pocket chirrups loudly, heralding an incoming text. Green-polo girl raises an eyebrow. This is something of an achievement, given the sheer weight of the eyebrows. Though it'd be hard to make out what anyone was saying through a wad of foam and synthetic fur, Andrew's pretty sure that Bouncy Bob has just called him a wanker. All along the line, people shake their heads and tut. Prior to this morning, Andrew didn't think tutting was something people actually did.

He doesn't dare reach for his phone, though it rings a further four times before they make it inside. Eventually—just as Angus is tottering on the edge of a meltdown—they're ushered through the electric doors, past the sanitizing station and the counter where Andrew is forced to leave his nice shoes on a shelf, into the cavernous bowels of Bouncy Bob's. The noise is deafening, almost orchestral. Andrew feels a migraine coming on.

He finds a grubby-looking table between the mini trampolines and the zip line. He gets out his Dettol wipes and gives the table a thorough seeing-to. The boys are itching to be off.

"Don't go too far," says Andrew, "I'll stay here where I can keep an eye on you. Conor, look after your brother. Don't let him go on anything too high."

They're off before he can even finish. Like rockets. Like bullets just fired from a gun. Like a pair of small boys suddenly released after twenty-five minutes standing in line. Andrew watches them dash across the lino. They are magnificent in flight. His sons. His boys. His little men. Sometimes he can't quite believe they belong to him.

He sits back in his pinchy plastic chair and allows himself to relax. *Maybe this won't be too bad after all.* The boys can entertain themselves, and he has the *Guardian* on his phone. If he can get his head round Bouncy Bob's violent green cups, he might treat himself to a double espresso. He'll take the boys through the drive-through on the way home. *Job done,* he'll say when Shauna greets him at the door. *They're fed. They're wiped out. They had a great time. Did you enjoy yourself? Hair's looking gorgeous, by the way.* And his wife will look at him with something approximating respect, perhaps even a bit of lust, for Andrew has recently discovered there's nothing that turns his wife on so much as him pulling his weight around the house. Emptying the dishwasher. Engaging in unsolicited hoovering. Getting the boys into bed before eight. *Job done,* he'll announce, and upon saying this, he'll feel like a king.

Andrew extricates his mobile phone. He's about to check his texts when a polo-shirted staff member descends upon him with intent.

"No photos," he shouts. "There's signs, so there is."

He gestures wildly at the walls. Andrew looks around. There are indeed signs, printed on standard-issue green paper in blocky type. "No photos. No running. No shoes. No smoking. No shouting. No alcohol. No animals. No fighting. Please remove your child from the play area if they vomit, soil themselves, or incur an open wound."

*Jesus Christ,* he thinks, *what sort of place is this?* He must take a photo of the signs for Shauna. She'll think it's funny. At least he hopes she will. He'll have to make it clear that he isn't mocking the Northernness of it so much as the way it's generally grim. Shauna says soft play areas are designed to put women off having more kids.

The Bouncy Bob man leans across Andrew's table. He is uncomfortably close. Andrew can smell his bitter coffee breath, though both have face masks on. He leans back instinctively. The man repeats his mantra: "No photos, mister. Can you not read the signs?" Andrew explains he has no intention of taking photos. The last thing he wants is a permanent memory of this place. He's just checking his messages. He holds his mobile up as proof. There are several unread texts on the screen.

The first of the four is from Staffo. "Pints later mate?" followed by a beer emoji and what's meant to be an inebriated face. Andrew hasn't seen Staffo since the first lockdown lifted. He's lost track of all the lads. Before Andrew and Shauna left London, they'd sometimes meet Niall in the park with his wife. His kids are roughly the same age as theirs. The others haven't settled down yet. Mel's in Hong Kong with his start-up. Stevie's loved up with some girl off Tinder, and last time Andrew heard from Staffo, he was going for a job in Manchester.

Staffo mustn't have heard that they've moved. There was no scope for the kids in London. No green space. When Shauna suggested moving across the water for a while, Andrew couldn't argue with her logic. Yes, their money would go much further in Belfast. And yes, they'd have family to help out. And he could easily work remotely. She wouldn't have to work at all. And it went without saying, there'd be so much more space for the boys. The mountain, ten minutes away in one direction. The sea, fifteen the other way. But it would still be crap. By this, Andrew meant, it wouldn't be London: the argument to end them all.

He'd tried to explain what London represented. To him. To them. To the way he wanted their life to be. It sounded petty when he did. "Grow up, Andrew," Shauna had said. Two months later, they were on the ferry to Belfast. Now they live in a bungalow on his father-in-law's land. It's beautiful up in the Craigantlet Hills. "Peaceful," is what Shauna says, as if peaceful's a thing you should aspire to when you haven't even turned thirty yet. Yes, there's so much scope for the boys. They've got green space coming out of their ears. And having the family close to hand has been a godsend. And working remotely is going well. Andrew relishes the extra hour in bed. But it isn't London. It is Belfast. Shitty Belfast. He has no love for this place.

"Are you by yourself, mister?" asks the man in the green polo.

Andrew notes his accusatory tone. "No," he says, "why would I come here by myself?"

"You could be a pedo. Soft plays are like Disney for pedos, all them wee ones in the one place."

"I'd hardly tell you if I was a pedophile," says Andrew and, noting the man's confused expression, immediately changes tack. "Do I look like a pedophile?"

The man in the polo takes him in from head to toe: prawn-cocktail shirt, oatmeal chinos, floppy lockdown Hugh Grant hair, and the last clean socks in the house, recently liberated from the laundry basket. In the cold light of Bouncy Bob's, Andrew can see they're actually Shauna's: pale blue with a daisy print.

The man—God bless him—exercises some degree of diplomacy. "Nice socks," he says, and does not answer Andrew's question, though the answer hangs there unspoken. Yes, dressed like that, Andrew could well be a pedophile. "There's other single fellas who come here," he continues. "These two lads from the gym across the way are in most afternoons. They come for the milkshakes. We do the best milkshakes in Belfast. Sure, there's nothing dodgy in liking a milkshake. Are you in for the milkshakes yourself?"

"No," says Andrew. "I'm here with my sons." He holds Conor's hoodie up as an alibi. "They were just here a second ago." He looks around. He can't see either of them anywhere. Bouncy Bob's is a blur of primary colors and sweaty noise. "They were just here," he repeats. He's not yet panicking, but there's a tightness in his throat.

"They'll be grand," says the man, "sure, there's no way out, unless somebody's lifted them . . ." He lets this thought hang in the air until it feels uncomfortable. "It's good for weans to run about and let off steam. I'd have loved a place like this when I was wee."

Andrew nods. He's not going to tell this man his son's only two. Two is far too little to be running about unsupervised. Angus should be curtailed in the Baby Bob's section with its safe foamy walls, minuscule slides, and anxious mothers hovering around like sniffy fruit flies. He lets his eye sweep across this corner of the room. Angus is not in Baby Bob's. *God knows where the child actually is.* He hasn't the sense to understand he's little. He'll follow his brother wherever he goes. Andrew has a brief but disturbing image of Angus falling from a roof-mounted cargo net, landing headfirst, his soft parts splattering across the concrete floor. This scenario's not even possible. Bouncy Bob's has a padded, spring-loaded floor. Nevertheless, Andrew's bowels churn.

"Excuse me," he says, "I'd better go check on my boys."

"No worries," says the man. "And here, if you're having a milkshake later, the salted caramel one's the business, so it is."

Andrew does his best not to look harried. He walks slowly, sedately, across the floor. He is practically sauntering in his daisy-print socks. He is not a perturbed man. He is just an ordinary father, casually checking in on his sons.

Son Number One is in the ball pit, being consoled by a teenage employee. His eyes are vampire-red from crying. The snot is streaming out of his nose. When he spots Andrew, his volume level cranks up a notch. He half wades, half swims through the balls to meet his father by the exit hatch.

"Papa," he howls, "the big boys took my socks. And *she,*" he hisses, pointing at the teenager in the luminous green shirt, "says I have to get out if I don't have socks on."

The teenager shrugs, her shoulders making temporary contact with the enormous gold hoops that hang from her ears. "No bare feet in the ball pit," she states bluntly. "He might have a foot fungus or something. You can buy socks over there." She raises a finger and points to a vending machine standing guard between the toilet doors. Andrew notes without surprise that her fingernails are talon-like and painted a vicious shade of neon green.

Andrew wishes to leap to Conor's defense. His son's feet are pristine and recently bathed. He wants to punch the wee bastards who stole his socks. He doesn't care how young they are. He wants to march up to reception and ask what sort of scam they're running here. Is Bouncy Bob recruiting kids to steal the socks of younger children so their hapless parents are forced to cough up for further socks? Andrew knows without checking that the socks for sale in the vending machine will be green and extortionately priced.

This sort of thing wouldn't happen in London. In London there are lovely places to take your children at the weekend. Mostly parks, and also museums, like the British Museum and the Museum of Childhood, and the Natural History Museum with the big dinosaurs, which both boys adored. The children who frequent those places are well behaved and astute. They certainly wouldn't steal socks off another child. A montage of images runs through Andrew's mind: flaxen-haired children chasing pigeons in Trafalgar Square, a family sat together on the top deck of a London bus, a little boy in a Prince George getup posing next to the big teddy bear at Hamleys' door. He's aware that this is not reality so much as a London tourist ad, but it's nice to feel bitter for a moment. To relish the injustice of it all. Andrew could cry for everything he's lost.

He'd like to yell at someone in a Bouncy Bob's shirt, but the absence of Angus is more pressing. He can't return to Shauna minus a son. He scoops Conor up and tries to shoosh him. He promises snacks, sugary ones, and a new pair of socks. Conor can even do the machine himself. They just have to find his brother first.

"Where's Angus?" he asks.

"My socks," howls Conor.

"Never mind your socks. We need to find Angus." Andrew's not quite shouting, but he's not speaking normally either, and the harsh voice he has slipped into only serves to make the child cry harder. People are staring. Possibly tutting. Andrew knows they're causing a scene.

He sets Conor down and, holding him firmly by the hand, begins to drag him around the various sections of Bouncy Bob's. Trampoline Zone. Jungle Land. Dinosaur Valley. Under the Sea. Sparkly Kingdom, which is full of small girls in princess dresses and a single boy dressed as Buzz Lightyear. This child is picking his nose as he stares at the princesses with a mixture of jealousy and undisguised rage. Angus is not in Baby Bob's. Angus is not in Trampoline Zone, Dinosaur Valley, or Under the Sea. Andrew knows his son would not set foot in Sparkly Kingdom, but he checks thoroughly nonetheless. Angus isn't in the queue for Bob's Café or the toilets. Andrew checks the gents' personally and asks a woman in a cat jumper if she wouldn't mind looking around the ladies'. She wouldn't mind at all and emerges ninety seconds later, shaking her head desolately. Angus is definitely not in the loos.

Angus is, in fact, standing at the mouth of the giant tube slide. Andrew has not thought to look this high. There are at least fifty steps to the top of the slide. He hadn't thought Angus capable. But three different strangers have now approached him, all saying roughly the same thing: "Here, mister. Are you looking for a wee fella in a yellow T-shirt? He's up the top of the big slide."

And yes, there is Angus, approximately sixty feet off the ground, happy as Larry in his sock soles. He spots Andrew and shouts down, "Papa, look. Gus go slide." He waves a little manically. "Papa, watch Gus go." Andrew stares at the platform where Angus is standing. Surely there must be an adult up there, someone fulfilling a supervisory role. He scans slowly along the roofline, desperate for a flash of luminous green. He can't see anyone but other small children. And his youngest son, who's barely a dot from this distance, a cheery pink and yellow smudge, peeking over the safety rails.

"Don't move, Angus," he shouts, "stay where you are."

But before he can even make a start on the steps, Angus hollers,

"Three, two, one, blastoff." Arms extended, Superman-style, he launches himself into the slide's plastic mouth.

"Jesus," says a man standing next to Andrew, "yon wee lad's fearless."

Andrew stands frozen to the spot, staring at the tail end of the slide. Any second now the tube will belch his son out onto a padded mat. Andrew imagines there will be friction burns, bruises and cuts, perhaps even a dislocated shoulder. He's wondering how he'll explain this to Shauna. She'll never let him out again unsupervised.

He stares and stares and silently follows his son's descent. The slide is shaped like a piece of fusilli, or twirly pasta, as it's called in their house. There are six coils, then a viciously straight drop at the end. In his head, Andrew pictures Angus negotiating each turn before progressing to the final descent. Thirty seconds come and go. Then forty. Fifty. A full minute. There is no sight or sound of Angus. He is trapped within the guts of the slide. He's possibly turned head over heels. Very probably lodged himself lengthways. Because Angus is little, far too little for such a big slide. He's only as tall as the tube is wide.

Andrew's mind races. *What to do when your child becomes lodged inside a slide?* They didn't cover this shit in parenting classes. It was all breastfeeding and sleep cycles, stuff you could easily find on the Internet. He turns to the nearest teenager in a Bouncy Bob's shirt.

"My son," he cries, automatically adjusting his voice when it comes out as a frantic squeak, "my little boy is stuck in the tube slide. You need to get him out."

"Don't worry," says the girl, "this happens a lot."

She removes a walkie-talkie from the pocket of her tracksuit bottoms and speaks into it. "Code Crocodile. I repeat, Code Crocodile." Then, turning to Andrew, she explains, "All our emergency codes are animals, so the wee ones won't panic if they hear. Code Elephant's a bomb scare."

Andrew is just taking in this information when the man next to him pokes him viciously in the ribs. "Here," he says, "your other wee lad's away up now." Andrew looks upward, and sure enough, there's Conor standing at the top of the slide.

"Don't worry, Papa," he shouts down, "I'll rescue Gus."

Andrew opens his mouth to yell *no*. No sound comes out. He lifts a hand and waves frantically at Conor. This wave is meant to say, *Stop! Don't even think about going down that slide*, but the child misinterprets the gesture. He raises two thumbs to the crowd below, grasps the slide's mouth in both hands, and launches himself down the tube, bare feet first.

To Andrew's left, the Bouncy Bob's girl raises her walkie-talkie to her lips and calls in a Double Code Crocodile. She no longer sounds so self-assured.

Thirty seconds pass. Then forty. Fifty. A minute. More. No children emerge from the slide. The man standing next to Andrew offers a running commentary, stating the bloody obvious. "They're not out yet. They should be out by this stage. Looks like the pair of them's stuck now." An announcement comes over Bouncy Bob's Tannoy system: "First-aid responder to Adventure World. Double Code Crocodile." Andrew's chest tightens. He automatically reaches for the inhaler he always keeps in his pocket. He raises it to his mouth and only then realizes he's still wearing his mask.

A crowd has gathered around the bottom of the slide.

Andrew catches the tail end of one conversation, whispered behind a pair of raised hands: ". . . broken neck . . . dear love him . . . never walked again." It's like tuning in to a radio station, then instantly losing the signal. A couple of people have their mobiles trained on the end of the slide. They're waiting to capture the boys emerging.

A woman appears to be filming Andrew. As soon as he notices her watching, he's suddenly aware of himself. There's an expectation. He is the father of these children. It's up to him to save his boys. He can't wait for Bouncy Bob's to intervene. His feet unstick themselves from the lino. His voice comes thundering back up his throat. "Hold on, boys. Papa's coming." He doesn't care how poncy he sounds. Or how many people are thinking ugly thoughts about him. He's off, at speed, slipping about as his daisy-print socks struggle to find purchase on the lino floor. He takes the steps two at a time, shouting, screaming, "I'm nearly there. Hold on, boys!"

As soon as he's launched himself into the slide, Andrew knows he's made a mistake. The slide is small. He is big; bigger than he's ever been. He hasn't exercised since lockdown started, and Shauna's mother—God bless the woman—is always baking delicious buns, and they've ended up drinking almost every evening, and sure, even the TV experts keep saying you should do whatever it takes to get through. No guilt. No judgment. Everyone's living through difficult times. But Andrew is pushing 210 pounds now. Will the tube slide be able to contain his bulk? It's tight enough. He isn't stuck, but neither is he sliding. He feels like toothpaste squeezing slowly out of a tube. He braces himself against the dusty plastic and begins to edge his way down an inch at a time. His shirt comes untucked and rides up to his armpits, exposing his flab. His chinos gather uncomfortably between his legs.

Andrew plows on, shouting as he descends, "Papa's coming, boys. Just hold on." He has not yet begun to question the logic of approaching feetfirst. There's barely any room to maneuver inside the tube. Hands first would've been the more sensible option. This way he'll be untangling the boys with his toes, incapable of lifting his head more than a few inches to assess the situation in front of him. Andrew can't afford to let himself panic. He must take it one foot at a time, focus on the bend ahead. He scooches onward, confident he's getting closer to Angus and Conor. Any second now his feet will make contact with a solid lump of squirming boy flesh. It is only after several minutes of frantic wriggling that Andrew notices how quiet it is. When he pauses to catch his breath, he can't hear anything but his own lungs rasping, his heart going mental inside his ears.

As he approaches the final descent, gravity grabs Andrew by the heels. His weight begins to work in his favor. The last few yards fly past at a dizzying speed, and before he can brace himself, the tube has unceremoniously spat him out. For a second, he lies on the landing mat, discombobulated and puffing, waiting to catch up with himself.

People approach. Tentatively at first. Then, all of a sudden, there are dozens of them gathered around the edge of the mat. Perspective renders them out of proportion, freakish, even: their feet enormous, their heads minuscule. They look like a circle of bowling pins.

"Are you all right?" they ask. "Are you okay? Should we call an ambulance?"

The girl in the Bouncy Bob's polo might be crying, or it could just be sweat. It's hellishly hot and hard to tell anything from the floor. She's talking to the lady in the cat jumper. "I mean, it's only my second shift," she says.

Andrew staggers to his feet. The crowd widens to give him room. "My boys?" he says. "Where are my boys?"

The Bouncy Bob's girl looks at the floor. She raises her shoulders lethargically, as if she is incapable of mustering enough energy for a proper shrug.

"Were they not in the slide?" asks stating-the-obvious man. "You'd think you'd have seen them if they were."

"Did they not come out?" asks Andrew.

"Naw," says the crowd. "Nope. Sorry, mate. Nobody came out since you went in."

"Well, where are they, then? Children don't just disappear."

As a unit, the crowd turns to stare at the tube slide. There's a question hanging in the air.

"They're definitely not in there," says Andrew.

"Well, where else could they be?" says obvious man.

Bouncy Bob's begins to swim. The lights. The tinny pop music. The unmasked faces pressing in. "My boys," Andrew repeats. "You have to help me. I've lost my boys. Please, can someone call the police?"

"Give it a wee minute or two," says the woman in the cat jumper. "You never know, they might still appear." She glances expectantly toward the slide. "I'll say a wee prayer to Saint Anthony. He's your man when things get lost."

The other fella's off again, echoing what they already know. "If the pair of them went into the slide and they're not out yet, then they must still be in there. You'd think they'd still be in there, wouldn't you?"

The girl in the Bouncy Bob's polo is saying she'll have to fill out an incident report. This will require a supervisor because she's not done all her training yet.

Andrew's no longer listening. He's kneeling at the mouth of the slide, peering up into its big, raw throat. He's calling out to his sons. Pleading. Begging. Making a holy show of himself. "Angus, Conor, where are you? Papa loves you. Please come down." He knows they're already lost to him.

This place has eaten them alive. It's always been anxious to have his boys. Andrew's known it since the second he laid eyes on them. Even back then he could see the thranness; the bold, bold way they stared back at him. They were always going to take after their mother and her kind. Andrew is able to admit this now. It was always only a matter of time. They'd have lost their accents, their roots, their reason. They would have drifted further and further away. This place is hungrier than other places. It sinks the teeth in early on. It clings. It cleaves. It will never let go of its own. Now it has taken his boys from him.

Andrew knows he's failed his sons. Andrew suspects he's failed himself. He shouldn't have let Shauna talk him round. He should have kept his boys on the Mainland, where they'd have had a fighting chance.

# TINGED

She makes tea and carries it out to the cowshed. As she crosses the yard, the security light comes screeching on, and though the same light's been there longer than she has, Ellen starts a little, sloshing hot sugary tea over her wrists. It's not nearly warm enough to do damage, but for a brief second every inch of her skin shrieks. She wants to drop the mugs. She does not drop the mugs. By the time she arrives at the cowshed door, her hands are shaking with the effort of not letting go.

"Tea," she shouts, and slides the corrugated metal door open with her hip. "I've made youse a cup of tea."

They can't hear her over the din. The sick cow's making a real racket, bellowing and honking like a stuck goose. Maybe that's a good sign. Ellen knows that dying things don't make half as much noise as the living.

She pulls the door behind her. Force of habit. She likes a closed door; something to do with being a farm child. She picks her way down the cowshed, sloshing through the damp straw. Her own wellies no longer fit, so she's wearing her mum's, with balled-up socks stuffed into the toes. She doesn't like using Mum's left-behind stuff. Her boots. Her umbrella. Her special shampoo. It's too soon. It doesn't feel right. But when she'd asked for new wellies, Dad had said, "There's your mum's good ones sitting there, going to waste. Stuff the toes till you grow into them." And Ellen hadn't known how to say, *Don't make me put my feet where her feet have only just been.* She knew her dad wouldn't understand.

So here she is, slopping about in her dead mother's Wellingtons, skin smelling of fancy peach-blossom shower gel. The pair of them are still working their way through the toiletries Dad brought back from the hospital in Mum's soap bag. Her dad is too practical to get rid of anything useful. Sentimental things are different. There's not a photo of Mum left in the house, not so much as a holiday snap pinned to the fridge. The living room wall's covered in squares and rectangles now, bright interruptions in the faded wallpaper where the family photographs used to hang. Sometimes at night, when she's pretending to watch TV and not really watching at all, Ellen tries to remember which photo hung in which lemony-yellow slot. Mum and Dad on their wedding day. The three of them leaning over her fifth-birthday cake, cheeks puffed out like a chipmunk's. Mum and Grandmum, squinting into the sun on Portstewart Strand. She wonders where the photos are now. Hopefully in the roof space with the Christmas tree and the suitcases. She can't bear to think of them shoved into the wheelie bin, greasing, splintering, churning around with the kitchen scraps. The thought of this seems meaner and more pressing than the thought of Mum never coming back.

It's only been six weeks—all of June and a slither of July—but the sense of her has already left the house. The air has lost its soft, feathery smell, and there's dust gathering on the slatted lengths of the blinds. For dinner, there's never anything but dry meat and potatoes. Dad sometimes doesn't even bother with gravy. Ellen does not cry. The missing of her mum is no longer as sharp. Now that school is over, she rarely sees other people. It is easier to forget what's missing when they aren't always there, prodding at her loss. She doesn't have to bear their snaking arms or the wet lilt of their voices, coaxing the tears up and out. "Uch, pet. I was so sorry to hear about your mum. You must be in bits."

Now she feels more tired than sad. Mornings are worst. And evenings. Though sometimes in the afternoons, she finds herself climbing back into bed just for a lie-down. She tents the duvet over her head so Dad won't find her when he's upstairs at the loo. He caught her once, about a week ago, and raised his voice like a hard slap: "It's nice for some, lying in their pit all afternoon, doing nothing." Afterward he didn't apologize, but there was Arctic roll for pudding, so he must've felt bad.

The cowshed is dark and gloopy. A single lightbulb on a cord is suspended over the sick cow. When Ellen comes upon her dad and Mr. O'Neill, they are all lit up, like the Nativity scene on a Christmas card. She lingers for a moment, resting the tea mugs on a stack of hay bales as she watches the two men going at the cow. Her dad is holding its head, one hand clamped on either side of its big, gloomy eyes. He's speaking to it gently, like you'd speak to a feared child. "There now, girl. Just you calm yourself." Ellen remembers him using this same voice on her, years ago. She recalls grazed knees. A broken kite. A series of terrible nightmares around about the age of four, the shock of them driving her out of her small bed and into her parents' big one, always to the left side, where her dad slept. She hasn't heard him talk like this in years.

Mr. O'Neill is hunkered down in the straw, rubbing at the cow's belly. He should know better. Dad's drummed it into her: "Never put yourself in the way of a beast's legs. Not if you don't want a kick in the teeth." Mr. O'Neill has his face bent right into the cow's belly. He's muttering something too, louder than her dad, and faster. He's not talking in real words. Ellen can tell this from the sound of his voice, which is like a river rising and falling quickly. *It's probably a spell,* she thinks, for Mr. O'Neill has the gift. The gift is a kind of magic. Not the sort of magic Paul Daniels does on the telly; the other kind, practiced by witches in fairy tales. Then again, it might not be a spell he's doing, because Mr. O'Neill's also a Catholic and Ellen knows, from playing netball against other schools, that their sort speaks a second language: a slippery, tingling kind of talk which doesn't write the way it sounds. Maybe it's both: Catholic talking *and* a spell. This would be the smells-and-bells nonsense Granda says they do in Mass.

Ellen would like to know what Mr. O'Neill's saying to their cow. If Mum was still around, she'd ask her. Mum would tell you anything and always give an honest answer. She spoke to Ellen like they were two grown-ups having a chat and, when Dad wasn't about, let her have the odd cup of coffee out of a Sunday mug. Ellen can't ask Dad. He's already told her not to be telling anyone Mr. O'Neill's seeing to their cow. She's not sure why this should be such a great secret. Perhaps the other farmers don't approve of cures. Or maybe it's the Catholic thing. She knows not to push him on the issue.

These days there's a look off her dad like a fraying rope. He hardly ever speaks. Just basic talk about the house and groceries, things she's to do around the farm. The chickens. The dogs. The wee vegetable patch beyond the kitchen window which has always been Ellen's responsibility. In a way, it's good to be kept busy. It wears the howl out of her. She wonders if it is the same for Dad. By the day's end, there's no talk left in either of them. They sit silently in front of the telly, watching whatever's on and, when there's nothing on, rising and heading up to bed early, though the light's still seeping through their drawn curtains.

The cow's belly is swollen, taut as a birthday balloon. It's not normal fat, nor the milk-thick heaviness that descends upon the heifers just before milking. No, this is the sort of tightness that comes from eating too much fresh grass and bloating on it. Round here they say the beast is tinged. If you catch it early enough, you can stick a knife in its side and let the gas come hissing out. *Phsssss,* like a kettle losing steam. Left too long and there's nothing to be done with knives or paid-for medicine. Eventually, you'll have to put the poor creature out of its misery, which is a waste, and Ellen's dad hates waste of any kind. This cow's gone beyond the pricking stage, but he's still sent for Mr. O'Neill; got him out of his bed at this time of night to see if there might be some sort of cure worth trying.

"Yes," Mr. O'Neill had said, "I've a few things I could try," and driven right over in his battered Land Rover. He's been firm from the outset that he won't be accepting any form of payment—not even a side of beef for the deep freeze—though he'd not say no to a wee cup of tea, strong, with five sugars stirred in. Which makes Ellen think the heifer's a hopeless case and Mr. O'Neill's only here because he feels sorry for the pair of them, what with the cow dying on top of everything else. Still, she's made his tea and stirred in five heaped spoonfuls of caster sugar, and she is, in some unspeakable part of herself, grateful to him for only mentioning the cow.

For weeks now, a steady stream of old men has appeared on their doorstep: some with wives, some awkwardly alone. They do not come in. They stand on the step twisting their caps like dishrags, staring at their boot toes as they mumble, "Powerful sorry for your loss, Mr. Fowler," like they've played some personal part in her mum's death. Most have brought a casserole with them, or a pie of some sort. Ellen finds their drooping mouths unbearable, their slow talk, their hung heads. These old men are just another thing to carry, and she hasn't got the strength.

Mr. O'Neill has been the first to arrive and not mention her mum. "I'm here about the cow," he announced when Ellen opened the door. "My dad's out in the cowshed with her," she replied, and showed him the way herself. They walked together across the backyard, he in his navy blue boiler suit; she wearing her Garfield pajamas stuffed inside the too-big wellies. Only once did he break the silence to say, "I'll do my best for the cow. It might be too late, but I'll still try."

Ellen couldn't care less about the cow. The cow is stupid. It has eaten too much grass and bloated on its greed. There are dozens of other stupid cows in the front field and, in the other, smaller field, even more half-wit sheep. All the animals are replaceable, unremarkable, indistinct. Only the bull and a couple of the dogs have even been given the dignity of a name. If this cow dies, Dad will go up to the market next week and buy another similar cow. The same goes for sheep and pigs and pretty much every creature except the cats, which seem to multiply unaided in the hedgerows. And yet when she led Mr. O'Neill into the cowshed, the look on her dad's face was rawly apparent. Desperation. Relief. Something shaped a bit like hope. You'd have thought him down to his very last cow.

"I know it's a bit of a last resort," he said, shaking Mr. O'Neill's hand in both of his own, "but I'm desperate to hold on to this one. I'll try anything."

It made no sense to Ellen. He, with a hundred head of cattle grazing in the front field, looking like he might hang his head and weep over this one daft cow. She could not bear to see her dad so greatly reduced. "I'll make the tea," she said, turning away before the mumbling began.

All the time it takes to plod across the yard, to fill the kettle, and boil the kettle, and carry the mugs carefully back, Ellen has been thinking about her dad's desperate face. She has been remembering another evening similar to this. The Thursday evening in late May when she'd opened the door to a man in a dark suit and a woman wearing a Sunday frock with a sad dollop of a hat plonked flatly on her head. Ellen had known she should know them, but in the moment, she could not place either of their grave, unsmiling faces.

Then the man had said, "It's Ellen, isn't it?" And she'd nodded yes, not saying anything out loud, for they'd lately taken to silence round the house, so as not to disturb Mum, who was, by this stage, mostly sleeping. "You're in the year above our daughter, Hannah," the woman said. Ellen could see the likeness round the eyes but hadn't said this, only held the door open so they could enter and follow her down the hall, through the stale vomit-stunk air, to the living room, where they'd sat next to each other on the sofa. "What a nice room," they'd said, and she'd replied ever so quietly, "Thank you. Would you like a cup of tea?" and had been just about to rise and put the kettle on when her dad came into the room and said, a little louder than usual, "What can I do for you?"

The man in the suit had risen quickly from the sofa to shake Dad's hand. He'd said his name and his wife's name. Mr. and Mrs. Adger. No first names had been offered, though they were not nearly old enough to have reduced themselves in this way.

"We heard about your wife," Mr. Adger had said. "We've come to see if we can help. Mrs. Adger has the gift of healing. She'd like to pray for your wife; lay hands on her, if you'll allow it." The woman had risen then to stand next to her husband, smiling and also not smiling at Ellen's dad, like you would with a distraught child.

"I had a word," Mrs. Adger had said. Her voice was thin and wavering, as if unused to hearing itself out loud in such a quiet place, "a prophetic word. The Lord wants to heal your wife. He's going to drive the cancer out of her body. Please, Mr. Fowler, will you let me pray for her?"

The whole room had drawn breath and leaned into this question. You could feel the suck of it: the thinning air. No one moved. No one spoke. Even the summer breeze seemed to settle against the windowpanes and, for a moment, held itself entirely still.

Ellen hovered in the doorway that linked the living room to the kitchen beyond. She stood there watching. She pinched the loose skin between her thumb and first finger to keep from crying out. She watched her father's face clench and tighten. His hands became fists, his whole face a brick wall. And yet there remained a softness in his eyes, the same damp desperation with which he would later regard the sick cow.

Ellen had understood she was watching a man dividing in two.

Her dad wanted something that could be achieved only by going against himself. This was a cruel kind of ask: his wife or his God. She knew it would seem to him there was no way of holding on to both. She could see the screws turning inside his guts. It was like watching a story from the Bible playing out for real: Abraham holding his knife to Isaac's throat; Jesus in the desert, Devil-tempted. The whole pathetic book of Job. And this had made Ellen seething mad. Why was God always making folk wrestle and squirm? Why could He not be kind for a change, kind and good like He was in choruses? Why was He always putting His people to the test?

She'd known her dad would see this as a test and try not to fail. But right up until the very second when he'd said, "I'm sorry. We're Presbyterians, Free Presbyterians. We don't believe in that kind of stuff," Ellen had hoped—no, actually believed—that desperation might turn him. She'd wanted to say what he could not bring himself to say: *Lay hands, speak in tongues, do whatever you see fit. We're desperate here. We'll try anything.* She'd wanted to whisper Satan-like in his ear, *Sure, we don't have to tell the ones in church. They'll never know.* But she'd been small in herself back then, worn down by so many hospital visits and the sight of Mum, like a newborn bird, with all her hair fallen out.

The rage hadn't risen up in her yet. The rage would come later, after the sadness and the long weariness of summer. By Christmas she'd be spit and fury, flinching every time some well-meaning sister said they were praying for her or her poor father. By Easter she'd have a wall running right down the middle of her, a solid thing which seemed to slide up and stick every time the minister began to speak. She could not see past the things he said, though she knew God was out there somewhere, stuck behind the bigmouthed eejits who were always speaking on His behalf. The Charismatics, for that's what Dad said they were, had left without tea or any further petition. Strong as their convictions were, they would not run to causing a scene.

"We'll continue to remember you in our prayers," the man had said. Her dad had nodded gravely at this, the same deliberate tucking of chin into neck he performed every time he drove past a neighbor in the road. At the door the wife had hesitated and, turning toward them, asked, "Why?" and her dad had barely missed a beat, just fired back the same thing the minister said every time he came to visit and would not pray for Ellen's mum to be made better, only for God's will to be done.

"It's not for us to question why." Then he'd closed the door gently so as not to wake his own wife, who was sleeping slowly away, upstairs on the right-hand side of their marriage bed.

As she approaches the sick cow's pen with a mug in each hand, Ellen is still thinking about the night her mother nearly got healed.

"Here's a cup of tea for you," she says, loud enough to be heard over the cow, who is snorting and howling like a laboring woman. The men quit their mumbling and look up as she enters the stall.

"Good woman, yourself," says Mr. O'Neill. He raises himself up from the ground to reach for his tea. There's a tiny scrap of cloth clutched in his hand. It is the pale brown color of wheaten bread. "Here," he says, "take yourself up to the top of the field and bury that for me and, when you're done, put a stone on top of it."

Ellen hands Mr. O'Neill his tea and takes the scrap of cloth. It's rough and scratchy, filthy with bits of cow dung and straw clinging to it. She pinches it between her finger and thumb. She doesn't want it anywhere near her.

"Why?" she asks.

"Ah," says Mr. O'Neill, smiling, "we've a skeptic on our hands here."

"What's burying this got to do with the cow?"

"Do as you're told, Ellen," says her dad. "It's part of the cure. Nobody understands why it works. But sometimes it does."

"It's not for us to question why," says Mr. O'Neill, and winks at her as he takes a long slurp of his tea. "Away off now, pet. Bury that wee scrap of cloth, and fingers crossed the beast'll make it through."

Ellen looks at her dad. He's turned back to the cow. He's roughing its ears in a familiar kind of way, trying to talk the calm back into its eyes. She leaves his tea on the ground by the door of the pen and picks her way back through the cowshed. Outside the sun is beginning to pale across the top field. There's a watery orange line running the length of the horizon. The cows are lumbering their way up the hill in anticipation of milking. She goes over to the wheelie bin and opens the lid. She drops the scrap of material in and shoves yesterday's newspaper on top of it.

As she closes the bin lid and heels her wellies off at the door, she tells herself that she doesn't believe in all this miraculous stuff: healing prayer and cures and silly bits of magic cloth. Sure, it's all just the same thing dressed up different. And it doesn't work. At least not for the likes of them. She goes upstairs and climbs back into bed. And it isn't the worry that keeps Ellen from getting back to sleep, it's the hard knot that's in her now, like a stone. Like a heavy, heavy stone.

# QUICKLY, WHILE THEY STILL HAVE HORSES

Paola would not come home to meet his parents.

"I am not good with mothers," she said, and left the table suddenly so the conversation could go no further.

Paola would not come home for Christmas.

"I don't like Christmas," she said. "It gives me sadness behind my eyes."

She pointed out the exact spots where the sadness would swell to form bad memories and migraine headaches. "Here, and here."

He went home without Paola, leaving her to Christmas alone in their Camden flat, which was above a launderette and smelled like summer should smell, even in December. Before leaving, he bought perfume and tucked it inside the fridge door so she'd find it and know he hadn't abandoned her entirely. It was expensive perfume, the sort displayed behind the counter in Boots, the name of it written in sloping French. When he returned, just in time for New Year, the perfume was still in the fridge, still gift-wrapped and wedged between the margarine and a jar of own-brand marmalade.

"I suppose I didn't see it," Paola said. "There are so many other things to see when I'm in the fridge: for example, cheese and tomatoes and the light which is always turning on when the door opens."

He didn't entirely believe her. Nor did he doubt her ability to see only those things she wished to see. She opened the perfume to please him and wore it out on New Year's Eve. The smell of it was not strong enough to overpower the soap-soft smell of laundered air. He wished he'd spent his money on good wine instead.

Paola would not come home for his sister's wedding, or his other sister's baby, or the possibility of seeing firsthand all his growing-up places. Vicky Park, where he'd learned to ride a bike, weaving his way through the swans and vicious greylag geese. The sweetie shop in Ballyhack. The bus shelter at the Holywood Arches where he'd had his first dry kiss and the alley opposite where, later that night, the same girl had let him slip the tongue in. Paola was not tempted by the scenery even when he showed her pictures on the Internet. Together, they watched television programs that had been filmed at home on account of the tax breaks and the lovely scenery.

"Look at it," he said, "isn't it gorgeous?"

Paola looked hard at the hills and the windswept beaches. Eventually, she said, "It's okay, I guess. There are better beaches in Spain. It's not raining on those beaches."

Paola would not come home for a dirty weekend at the Port, or half-term in the mountains, or even the Twelfth, which he tried to sell as a genuine cultural experience. He knew this was something of a long shot but could no longer anticipate what weird shit would catch her interest. The previous week she'd expressed a desire to learn quilting. This week it'd been calligraphy. He had never seen Paola as the sort of person who'd practice craft of any kind. She was never still.

She was something like a hovercraft, buzzing with nervous energy.

No matter what he said or implied—love, duty, some kind of unspoken *I'll owe you big-time*—Paola would not come home with him. This didn't seem fair. They'd been together for almost two years, two and a half if you counted the months of trying to talk themselves out of each other. Granted, he hadn't been to Spain, or met any of her family, but she'd never asked. She found her parents deplorable, and Spain was much farther away. In his outside head he told himself, *Never mind, you only want her home so everyone can see you have an exotic Continental girlfriend now; so all the lads will be jealous, embarrassed by their own doughy women.* In his inside head, he knew he was softer than this. He understood, without admitting, the desire to have everything he loved together in one place.

"Would you not come home for *me,* Paola?" he kept on asking. "Just because you love me." But she always said, "No. No. No chance, buster," each individual "no" wrapped up in its own neat excuse like a filling buried so deep inside a back tooth you couldn't see the problem with it.

Paola would not come home for anything he said or did until one day he heard from his mother, on the telephone, that they still had horses in Belfast.

"They've two or three of them left," she said. "There's one in Ormeau Park and another in Botanic. You can get tickets from City Hall. It's free, but you've to wait your turn. Your auntie Liz says the line's all the way down to Primark now." This was before Primark burned down.

When he told Paola about the horses, she wanted to leave immediately.

"We must go to your home," she said, "quickly, while they still have horses."

"I never knew you were into horses," he said, all the time wondering what else he didn't know about her: birthmarks, allergies, previous marriages to much older men.

"Oh, I'm not that specially interested in horses," she said. "They're okay, I guess. I am much more into fish. But I don't like the idea that they're here and then, the next day, gone—*poof*—like David Bowie or that other singer who is also dead. I don't have a just-for-myself memory of Bowie. It was too expensive to see him live in concert. Now I can't. I do not want to have such regrets with horses. Horses will not be like David Bowie to me. We must take a picture of us standing with this last horse, smiling. Later, we will show the photograph to our grandchildren and say, 'Look at us, so young in this picture. They actually still had horses then.'"

He thought Paola was a little mad, or perhaps just Continental, but the idea that they might last long enough to produce grandchildren was reassuring. He wondered if they would one day own a house together or, if a house was out of the question, a small apartment or mobile home like the one his grandparents kept at Portrush.

He put the flights on his credit card and texted his mother: "Me and Paola are coming home. Can we stay with you?" His mother texted straight back. (She always did. Even during church.) "That will be lovely. Is Paula a vegetarian?" *Paola* was not a vegetarian, but his mother assumed all Continentals were anti-meat. "I could do a nice salad for lunch," she added in a second text, "with olives." He didn't bother replying. He knew it was going to be a long weekend.

Paola didn't sleep that night. She sat up in their bed googling images of horses on his work laptop.

"Look at this one, running," she said. "Look at this one, up on its back legs like a statue of itself."

He'd always been a feeble sleeper, so instead of trying to sleep through her talk, he sat up beside her, faking an interest in shire horses, piebald ponies, and previous Grand National winners, all the time thinking, *Tomorrow she is coming home with me*. There was a tune that accompanied this thought. It was something like the chorus of a good Smiths song, which is to say hooked and chirpy, a little like a playground taunt. *Tomorrow, tomorrow Paola is coming home with me.*

Finally, Paola closed the laptop and set it aside. He thought she might be ready to sleep then, or that she'd want to have sex (as she often did on a Thursday). He touched her lightly on the spot where her neck became a shoulder. This was his usual way of asking. She didn't say no. Instead, she turned her back to him and asked, "Do *you* like horses?"

He did *not* like horses. Once, when he was a child, his grandfather had given him Polo mints to feed the horse which spent most days shuffling round the field next to his grandparents' bungalow. Polo mints, his grandfather said, were treats for horses, like ice cream was for children, while hay was just like everyday vegetables.

His grandfather hadn't shown him how to hold the Polo mint, like a little bird balanced in the flat of his palm, so he'd pinched the sweet between finger and thumb, stretching his arm over the fence to let the horse get a good, long whiff of it. Suddenly, before he could withdraw, the horse's teeth had clamped around his fingers. His face became damp with hot horse breath. All the blood ran to his fingers and he began to shriek. Panic set in. He couldn't get away. The pain was dull and prolonged, like a heavy weight pressing into a bruise.

"OH SHITE!" his grandfather had shouted, the first time he'd ever heard a bad word on the old man's tongue. He'd pulled hard at his grandson's trapped arm, tugging and sharply tugging, digging his boot heels into the sloped verge which ran beneath the fence, grunting with effort as his feet slipped around on the damp grass until, finally, the horse opened its mouth and let go. They hadn't toppled backward, like in a film, and there was no blood, but he'd known straight away that the fingers would bruise. Later, when he thought about this incident, he'd picture his grandfather pulling him by the waist, bracing his feet against the ground, and leaning away from the weight of him, like the old man and the turnip in his fairy-tale book, with his wife dragging at his waist, the neighbors and farmyard animals all strung out behind.

The horse left teeth marks in his fingers. He could still see the pale pink ghost of them when he was hot and sweating from sport, or outside in the sun. Paola had never noticed. She didn't pay particular attention to his fingers. He could have held them under her nose and said, "Look at this here mark," and told her the story of the Polo-mint horse. But he didn't. He couldn't risk anything that might put her off coming home.

"I love horses," he lied. "If I get the chance, I'd really like a wee ride on that last one. So I can tell the grandchildren."

He wanted to see if the mention of grandchildren would make Paola smile, but when he leaned over her shoulder to look, her mouth had slipped into the loose shape it always made when sleeping. It was no closer to a smile than a frown.

The next morning, they flew home. Paola was insistent that they go straight to the horses, so they took a taxi from the airport to City Hall.

Paola did not like Belfast. First it was too rainy. Then it was not as rainy as she'd expected. The people were watery-looking, or maybe they looked like potatoes round the face, all pasty-skinned and lumpy.

"I do not find anyone attractive here," she said, "not even the young girls." He wondered if she included him in this judgment but hadn't the gall to ask. "And the houses," she said, "don't get me started on the houses," and rolled her eyes toward the taxi's roof. She said the houses were all stuck together like they couldn't breathe. Those that weren't were mostly bungalows, and Paola had no time for single-story buildings. She said the hills were ugly, hardly worth a photograph. She wondered what they'd done with the coastline, why they'd hidden it behind all those shipping cranes as if beaches weren't the very best way to frame an ocean. She said the accent was "freaking impossible"; that the people talked much too fast, through their noses. Whiny. Whine. Whine. Like stretched rubber.

"Sure, you must be used to it by now," he said. "Haven't I the very same accent?"

"Exactly," she said, and all afternoon he was overly conscious of the way his mouth moved when he spoke.

When they arrived at City Hall, they dragged their pull-on suitcases up the cobbled path, round the statue of Queen Victoria looking like she'd absolutely no interest in the city, and past the impressively pillared entrance. *Chu-choonk. Chu-choonk. Chu-choonk,* went the suitcase wheels. The line was out the door and round the War Memorial twice. Most people looked defeated, like they'd been standing in line for years, neither experiencing nor expecting any significant progress. Everyone turned to stare at them. It was raining, absolutely pissing down, and they hadn't brought an umbrella.

"We'll be here all afternoon," he said.

"I don't do lines," Paola replied.

Before he could stop her, she was striding up the steps and through the marbled foyer to the front of the queue. She was telling the desk lady that he was dying of "the cancer"—"belly cancer," to be specific—and wasn't able to stand for hours in the rain. Quite conveniently, the desk lady had a neighbor, recently dead, of "belly cancer." She understood it was the sorest cancer of them all. Back Paola came with a wheelchair and a big black umbrella to keep the rain off his poorly head.

"Look sick," she said. "Hold your belly like it is full of painful tumors."

"What did you tell them?" he asked.

"Only that you are dying. That you want to see a horse before it's too late."

"Jesus," he said, "you can't be making up stuff like that. There's probably folks in this queue actually dying." But he got into the wheelchair anyway, letting her manhandle him past the line, over the juddery cobbles, and up the ramp into City Hall.

Paola parked him in the corner of the foyer by the stained-glass window commemorating Votes for Women. She arranged their luggage in a little tower beside his wheelchair, so he looked like a pilgrim waiting on the bus to Lourdes. He felt, as always, less than her and dependent.

"Don't move," she said. Her tone was matronly, but her body language was far from it. She leaned heavily on his lap, kissing him softly on the cheek. Up close, he could smell the fancy perfume on her.

"I love you," he said.

She smiled. The light streaming through the stained-glass window was red, blue, and cut-grass green. It fell across her face, marbling her olive skin. He thought, as he often thought, *There's something not quite right about this woman.* This was half the pull of her.

Leaving him with their luggage, Paola approached the counter and asked to speak to the nice desk lady in the white blouse. He could hear her overenunciating all the way across the rotunda. She was using the voice she kept for small children.

"We need two tickets to the horse," she said.

"We'll get you sorted out, pet," said the desk lady. She printed out two tickets and slid them across the counter. Paola was always encountering this kind of preferential treatment.

"Why do you still have horses here?" Paola asked, and he wondered why she'd not asked him; what other questions she'd taken to strangers.

The lady paused and glanced up at Paola. She smiled. He recognized this smile. It was a smile the people here kept for visitors. He'd often used it himself on American relations. If this smile had been a sentence, it would have read, *Ah now, it's a local thing. How would you be expected to know when you're not from here?*

"We're losing our horses too, sweetheart," said the desk lady. "They're a drain on the economy, so say the politicians, anyway. The horses on the Mainland are all gone now, either culled or shipped to places where they still use horses for pulling carts, or where they'll eat anything. It's a shame, so it is. Horses are lovely creatures to look at, even if they are no use. If you ask me, they'll be after the cats next. It's not like there's any point to a cat."

"I know all that," Paola said, interrupting the desk lady mid-flow, "I watch the news. I was just asking why you still have horses here when the rest of Britain has already lost theirs."

The lady smiled the same slow smile. "Well, the Mainland's already adopted the new legislation. You can't keep a horse over there because horses don't do anything of any real use . . . and we get everything six months after the Mainland, so . . ." Then she leaned away from the counter as if she'd just delivered the punch line to a great old joke. Across the foyer, he also smiled. He couldn't help himself.

When Paola returned, she was not smiling. She looked tired.

"I do not like this place," she said. He knew she was actually trying to say, *I do not understand this place.* This place that was all the way through him like blood or bone. Still, he wished to sit her down on a chair and say, *Hold it all loosely, girl. Give it time. Try to see the funny side. There's good stuff here too. You just have to wait on it.*

"Let's go to the horse," she said, "before I change my mind."

"Where is the horse?" he asked.

"Botanic Gardens," she replied. "There is no room for horses at City Hall."

Paola did not question the sense of selling tickets to an attraction almost fifteen minutes away, though she did seem somewhat weary. Perhaps she was beginning to understand the perverse logic of the North.

She wheeled him out to the gates of City Hall, where he made a seemingly miraculous recovery, rising from his wheelchair to hail a black taxi. He bundled her into the backseat. Up the Dublin Road they flew, past the place where the big cinema used to be and all the grotty student bars, past Queen's University and the stout gates of Methodist College, to Botanic Gardens, where there was a horse waiting for them.

"It's the last one, mate," said the taxi driver, "the very last horse in Britain."

"But there's one in Ormeau Park," he said. "And another one somewhere round Enniskillen."

"Them ones died," said the taxi driver. "Loneliness, I'd say. Horses are wild social. Same goes for penguins." Here, his wisdom ran dry.

Paola tipped the taxi man two pounds because she liked penguins. He tried to tell her you didn't do that here, that the driver would think them flash or, worse still, tourists, and Paola said, "But we are tourists," and he wondered if this was true. It was five years since he'd lived here for more than a fortnight. Just thinking about this made him feel like he was wearing a jumper one size too small.

Botanic Gardens was hiving with people. The rain had morphed into a sad drizzle. The people lined along the path waited listlessly in damp waterproof jackets, their bowed heads hooded and glistening so they looked like uprooted plants waiting to be rehomed. There was a special enclosure for the horse in the middle of the Gardens. A sign read, "LAST HORSE IN BRITAIN this way," with an arrow so you couldn't mistake it for the Tropical Ravine. The gardeners had constructed a sort of paddock, running a ten-foot fence round the green so you couldn't see anything worth seeing without paying for the privilege. There was another line. They took their place at the end of it. It was mostly children in front of them and adults who might've been using their children as an excuse. Paola tried to skip the queue using the cancer card again, but the man two in front said, "Sorry for your trouble, girl, but I've a wife with Alzheimer's here, and I'm not giving up our spot."

So they waited for an hour and a half, edging their pull-on luggage forward one foot at a time. They ate dry-roasted peanuts from Paola's handbag to stave off the hunger and, for shelter, ducked their damp heads under the canopy of tree branches tickling the edges of the green. By three, they were inside the paddock; by three thirty, surrendering their tickets to a young lad in a fluorescent vest.

"No flash photography," he said. "No videos. Will you be wanting a ride on the horse or do youse just want to get your picture with it?"

"A ride would be great," he said. The teeth marks on his finger began to sing in anticipation.

"I am fine with just the photograph," said Paola. "Both of us together with the horse."

He could not have been easier in his own skin or happier with a money fortune. Up came the jangly Smithsonian refrain, *Paola's coming home with me* . . . Up came the memory of horses and her and growing up in this fine place. It was all muddled together like a Saturday-evening stew. Grandparents were in there and hometown God, his parents and the lads he used to kick football with, big school, wee school, sheet rain and street preachers howling, Portstewart Strand for the holidays, the gut-twist relief of belonging somewhere specific. He was glad that Paola was here with him, seeing the horse. She would understand now what it meant to be from this place.

"In you go, mate," said the young lad, opening the Tensabarrier and ushering them into the inner enclosure. "There's the wee horse there. He goes by Buttons. Youse are welcome to take as many photos as you want."

Buttons was not a horse so much as a pony. A dog-sized pony.

He looked up at them from under an enormous fringe, his eyes sunken raisins, blinking back the flies. He was the color of damp sand.

"I thought it would be different," he said. By different, he meant bigger. He could feel Paola standing behind him, saying nothing, probably thinking about Spanish horses thundering across Spanish beaches.

"That's the last horse left, mate. They kept Buttons till the end 'cause he's so good with the wee ones. Like a kitten he is, round children and ones with special needs."

"I understand," he said, though really, he didn't. "Sure, we'll just get our picture with him and be off. Paola, give the man your camera."

"But I thought you wanted a ride on the last horse," she said. "You said you did."

He looked at Paola. Her hair was plastered across her forehead. Her leopard-print suitcase leaned against her ankles. She was less poised than usual but still in control of the situation. He tried to say with his eyes, *Have some mercy* or *This could be the end of us*. He wanted to ask her, *Do you not think I've suffered enough?* But he could see she was a brick wall now. "Get on the horse," she said, "and I will take your picture for our grandchildren."

He did what he was told. He was well practiced at this.

He climbed the fence. He straddled the horse, holding its reins loosely in one hand. There was a good half foot of air between his crotch and the saddle, but he couldn't bear the humiliation of squatting bowlegged in front of her. So he stood over the very last horse, smiling a different kind of smile, equally hard-learned.

"Got it," Paola said, and put her camera back into its holder.

He knew she wouldn't agree to a photograph now, so he didn't bother asking. He could see she was already looking for the exit. She was halfway back to Camden in her head.

*What about our grandchildren?* he wanted to ask. *What about our little apartment or mobile home?* He felt small in her eyes, small and faintly ludicrous. He struggled to imagine them recovering from the horse.

*Maybe,* he thought, *there might still be a chance*. Compromises would need to be made, and he knew he'd be the one to make them. He could, with effort, picture the pair of them together at forty, in London, or Spain, or perhaps the States. But not here, suffocating, in this damp excuse of a place.

# VICTOR SODA

Nobody knew how old Victor Soda was. He could've been anything between thirty and fifty-five. If pushed, I'd have said he was just shy of fifty, which would've put him on a par with my ma. Victor was wearing it better. He'd all his hair, though it might well have been thinning; you rarely saw him without a hat. No doubt he took it off for church, but his pew was three rows behind ours, so I never got a good look at him.

I could usually tell a man's age from his clothes. My brother and the lads he ran with were wearing their trousers wide that year. Our da, who was pushing sixty, wore his straight around the ankle. He was always taking the mick out of Jamesy. "You better pin them boyos down. If the wind gets up, you'll be blown away." Though the trend was edging toward boiler suits, Da was an old-fashioned kind of farmer. He still wore heavy trousers and a knit jumper out to the fields. He looked like he belonged to a different time.

Victor didn't dress like an auld boy. He wasn't particularly fashionable either. I couldn't have told you what was going on around his ankles, for he kept his trousers nipped in with bicycle clips. His style set him apart from the other men. Patterned suits with matching waistcoats. Shiny lace-up shoes. Hats like detectives wore in films. A hankie, tightly triangled and tucked into the pocket beneath his chin. Bow ties. *Bow ties, indeed!* Nobody in our village wore a bow tie. Not even Martin Murray, though he and the wife were big into their ballroom dancing. The dancing took them up to Belfast almost every weekend. I asked our Francey if there was a name for Victor Soda's style. Francey knew all about style. She was married by then and living in the city. "Dapper," she said. "I'd say Victor Soda was a dapper wee man."

There were other things Francey could've told me about Victor Soda. I'd have appreciated the heads-up. But I was only fifteen that summer. I expect she thought I'd have no need of Victor for another few years. Aye, well, Francey didn't see what was coming. I didn't see it coming either, and I was only up the lane.

His name was Keith Hannah. He was three years older, a big lump of a fella with flaming-red hair. He came up our lane one Tuesday morning looking for the lend of a trailer. I swear I'd never noticed him before, though the Hannahs lived on the next farm over. You could see their house from our bathroom window. I suppose they could probably see ours too. Every year we helped them get their potatoes in. They always returned the favor. It varied from one year to the next whose spuds went first. We took it time about.

There was a whole rake of Hannahs, at least nine the summer I fell for Keith. There was only the three of us Brownleys: Francey, Jamesy, and me. I was the youngest. We palled around with the appropriate Hannah, whichever was closest in gender and age. The other ones faded into the background. We knew they existed, just not by name. Mine was called Sharon. Francey's was

Catherine. I'd a vague notion the rest were mostly boys. My da used to glare at our Jamesy, plonked in front of the telly. "There's William Hannah, across the field, with all them big strapping fellas helping him out, and I'm stuck with a feckless hippie who spends half the day in his pit." This sort of talk never bothered our Jamesy. It was water off a duck's back to him.

I wasn't as thick-skinned as my brother. I'd always been a daddy's girl. I was forever licking up to him. "Yes, Daddy. No, Daddy. Do you want me to go and put the kettle on?" He called me his wee Buttercup. I got up before him every morning, even in the holidays. I'd the breakfast sitting on the table exactly the way he liked it when he came down the stairs: three fried eggs with runny yolks, two bits of bacon, bread fried in the pan. I did not do the same for my ma. Da said I was a powerful good wee girl. He said not to tell the others I'd always been his favorite one. He had big hopes for me.

He wasn't talking about a good job or even getting decent exams. Da hoped I'd marry local—ideally, somebody with a bit of land—then settle down and have a load of weans. Francey had married a furniture salesman. This was considered grand for her. She'd always been highly strung. Da said it came from her mother's side. She'd never have settled on a farm. And Jamesy? Well, Jamesy was almost worse, because Jamesy was not a stupid lad. Jamesy was the very top of his class. With marks like his, he could have got into Greenmount College, studied farming, and done it right. But Jamesy was not one bit interested in the farm. At the end of the summer, he was heading up to Queen's to do a degree in philosophy. What use was philosophy to a farmer? Sure, you couldn't analyze a cow. Every time somebody mentioned our Jamesy, my da would roll his eyes toward the ceiling. "I despair of that boy," he'd say.

I was different. I was settled. I was the one who wouldn't leave. Like the big monkey puzzle in the front yard, my roots went deep down into the farm. I was grand with this. I liked the farming, and I liked our village. I'd been up to Belfast a couple of times. Once to get outfits for Francey's wedding. Another time when Da took me to Balmoral Show. The city didn't sit with me. It was far too loud. All those cars and buses screeching. All them people rushing about. The poky wee streets. The grayness of it. I wondered how city folks managed without trees. I preferred the fields and the deep green quiet. I would get on my bike—an old hand-me-down of Francey's—and go flying around the country lanes, watching the birds rise from the hedges when they caught the whoosh of me zipping past.

I'd be fine with staying put. Though I preferred my own company, I would even be grand with marrying a farmer. Anything to please my da. I hadn't given the matter much thought. I was fifteen. Marriage was years away. It was only when Keith Hannah appeared in our yard with his tanned arms out and the boiler suit rolled down to his waist that I began to think otherwise. Here was a fella of marriageable age, and wouldn't you know, he was also a farmer. More to the point, my eyes seemed to like him. That afternoon, as Keith dragged our trailer down the lane, then slowly dragged it back, my eyes were fairly glued to him.

Something happened to me that summer. It was not easy to put in words. I was the same wee girl I'd been the previous summer, but now my skin felt that bit thinner. Everything left a mark on me. Like reading a book could make me weepy if there was somebody in it sad or hurt. Or walking across the fields at sunset would make me feel sort of glowy inside. Once I caught myself crying in church. We were singing that hymn "Abide with

Me." My ma leaned over and whispered behind her hymn book, "Catch a grip of yourself, Louise." I wanted to whisper back, *Are you not listening to them words, Ma? Do you not think they're powerful sad?* I didn't say anything. I knew she wouldn't understand.

As for Keith Hannah? Well, I was butter. I melted every time he crossed my path. And the same boy crossed my path a lot that summer. Down the bottom of the big field. Behind the milking parlor every afternoon. Most Fridays at some dance or social, where he'd spin me chastely round the room, then take me outside to get some air and kiss me up against a wall. I let him. I did not stop him. I liked the way he made my insides run. I was not myself around Keith Hannah. Or maybe I was finally myself. The same wee girl I'd been last summer. Also somebody entirely new. I would have talked to Francey about it, but Francey was busy having a baby. She was in the always boking stage, too tired to come down and visit us.

Nobody noticed I was different. At least nobody said anything. That summer was just like other summers. I did not know it would be an end. Da got the hay in with help from the Hannahs. Then we went over and got theirs in. Ma done her jams early and a dose of pickles too. I helped her. It took the guts of two weeks. My hands turned red: first from raspberries, then from beetroot chutney. I tried to fade them in a bucket of bleach. The week after the Twelfth, my cousin Andrea got married. The wedding was over in Randalstown, then afterward to the Country House. I was not a bridesmaid, though Andrea said I definitely would've been if her fella hadn't had so many sisters. What kind of people produced eight daughters? My ma said it wasn't Protestant. I was glad not to be in the wedding. I didn't like folks looking at me, and my hands were still a desperate shade of pink.

In August, Jamesy went up the North Coast with a bunch of fellas who'd a caravan in Castlerock. Before he left, Da gave him a tenner and told him not to be getting drunk. Jamesy said, "Aye-aye, Captain," and turned to show me his hands tucked behind his back. Both sets of fingers were firmly crossed. I waited till Da had left the room, then I said, "I despair of you, James Brownley," in the same voice Da kept for telling us off. Jamesy thought this was hilarious. "What's got into you, Louie?" he said. I wanted to say Keith Hannah, but me and him were still a secret. We hadn't told a living soul. We thought we were getting away with it, till Victor Soda waded in.

It was bad luck. If things had been different, him and my da never would have crossed paths. My ma was the one who got our messages, and she always went in the afternoon. But Ma was down with a tummy bug, and somebody had to go down to Thompson's for the basics: milk, bread, cooked ham, and a *Telegraph*. I was for going myself. I'd the bike out and all when the rain came on. Ma said, "You can't send the child out in that." Da did a fair amount of huffing and puffing. He asked could it not wait till the afternoon. But there wasn't a drop of milk for the tea, and neither of them could take it black. Eventually, Da got the Land Rover out and went down to Thompson's himself. He was in and out in a matter of minutes, for he didn't want to be seen buying groceries. Groceries were a woman's concern.

Da was coming out the door as Victor Soda was going in. I could picture the scene quite clearly because Da came home and gave us a blow-by-blow. The pair of them stood for a moment on the doormat, making small talk about the weather. Victor was drenched from the cycle in. Da offered to run him home; he could easily throw the bike in the back of the Land Rover.

Victor said thank you but no. He was grand himself. The rain was almost passed, and he didn't want to take up Da's time. Da already had enough on his hands without driving him halfway round the country. Da said he was no more occupied than usual. It was always busy on a farm. Victor Soda looked straight at my da and said, "Oh, I'm not talking about the farm, Davie. I meant that wee lassie of yours. You'll be wanting to keep her on a tight leash, now she's taken up with that Hannah lad."

This was the first my da had heard of it. He was mortified. Did I hear him? Absolutely mortified! I nodded as he told me. I kept going over it in my head. It was desperate bad luck, no matter what way I looked at it. If it weren't for Victor sticking his oar in, me and Keith could've kept going the way we were: meeting up for a kiss and cuddle, sneaking about behind the barn. Everything was ruined now. We were no longer our own secret thing. If only my ma hadn't caught that tummy bug. If the rain had held off for another half-hour. If my da had stopped to check on the sheep. If Victor Soda had not been such a sly old bastard. If he hadn't had his eye on me.

People couldn't see the bad in Victor. But he was more calculating than he let on. He was a planner, a meticulous planner. He never deviated from his routine. Every morning he cycled into the village. He got his messages from Thompson's, then done ten circuits of the Main Street. Folks said this was his way of keeping the flab off. Victor Soda was very trim. On Sundays he attended morning service but didn't return for the evening meeting. It was more of a casual affair and not to his liking. He didn't approve of acoustic guitars. Mondays and Fridays, Victor called in to the village post office. The Royal Mail handled all his correspondence. Parcels. Letters. The occasional telegram. He did not own a telephone. This was unusual, even for a village like ours. No one knew if the lack of phone was a choice on Victor's part. Most likely, it was a consequence of his living situation. Victor Soda lived in a static caravan at the bottom of his brothers' field.

There'd been some sort of falling-out between the brothers. No one could recall the ins and outs. Something about a bit of money left by an uncle in Canada. There hadn't been a word passed between the two parties since the spring of 1963. Victor wasn't like his brothers. They were ordinary enough: three bachelor farmers living in the house their parents had been buried out of. They survived on champ and packet biscuits, appearing once a week on Sundays to infect their corner of the church with their fuggish old-man smell. This was not unusual in our village. There were several similar setups: the Farleys, the McIlhinneys, the Mitchell boys. Victor Soda's brothers—known locally as the Dairy Bennetts, to distinguish them from the Bennetts who kept sheep—were nowhere near as unusual as Victor. He was what you'd call a character.

It was said that Victor was educated. He'd a degree of some sort and had lived abroad, in Oxford or London, for the three years necessary to acquire it. Dear only knows if this was true. If it was, it begged the question, why had Victor ever returned? There was nothing in our village for a man like him. Nobody to talk to. Nothing to do. Nobody who looked or dressed like him. You'd think he'd have been better off in a city. A place like Belfast would've suited him. What did Victor Soda do for money? This was a mystery to us all. Something to do with stamps, folks thought. He was definitely a collector. Joan at the post office verified this. Would this be enough to keep him? Surely the overheads would be low on a static, and his diet was clearly frugal.

There wasn't a pick on Victor Soda. We speculated about a small inheritance from the dead parents or perhaps an aunt. Though never directly spoken of, there was also the money he got from teaching girls.

Nobody told me about Victor Soda's girls, yet something in me must have known. When he cycled past or came striding up the path to church, my whole body would clench and shrug, like it was trying to get away from him. Francey could have warned me. She'd been one of Victor's girls. Nearly every woman of a certain age had had a wee visit to his caravan. Afterward, I'd watch the way they were around him. I could tell which ones had been his. There was something in the way their mouths set; a sort of flinch about the eyes.

If circumstances had been different, I'd like to think Francey would've taken me aside. After she moved to Belfast, she must have realized this kind of carry-on wasn't normal. Not every village had a Victor Soda, or if they did, they weren't so accommodating of him. In most places—right-thinking places—men like Victor were considered a shame. But Francey wasn't around that summer, and all my pals were my age or younger; none of them married or even courting. They didn't know about Victor Soda. We were young for our age, and isolated. We didn't talk about such things.

I suppose the blame lay mostly with Ma. It's a mother's job to take you aside and tell you the things you need to know. My mother never talked to me. I mean, she talked away about the weather and jobs needing doing around the house. She just never talked about women's things. The very mention of anything to do with "down there" had her blushing furiously. When my monthlies started, Ma never explained or sympathized, just pointed to the hot press and said, "There's things in there, tucked behind the bath towels. Don't be leaving them lying about." She was the same when it came to bras. Pants could be hung on the washing line or draped over the radiators to dry. Both men and women were in need of pants. Bras were relegated to the hot press, as if my brother or Da might stumble upon one and realize we had breasts and they did not.

In our house, modesty was everything. No nighties or pajamas outside the bedroom unless concealed beneath a voluminous dressing gown. No discussion of bodily functions; even the sound of a stifled fart was enough to turn Ma puce with shame. The telly got flicked to a cleaner channel at the merest hint of anything racy. We were just as stiff with each other. We rarely touched. Polite cheek kisses for special occasions. I don't remember a single hug. Bodies were not to be trusted. They were to be hidden and always restrained. It was dirty to talk about your body. A body was a private thing. Dear only knows how my parents managed to conceive the three of us. Once might have been excused as accidental. Three children suggested something akin to prior knowledge. I imagine my ma was mortified.

This sort of prudishness wasn't common. Neither was it without precedent. Ours was a tight-lipped sort of village: Presbyterian and terribly staunch. I can't imagine many of my friends had frank discussions with their mothers about the ins and outs of intercourse. It was not uncommon for a girl like me, married young in a rural spot, to find herself clueless on her wedding night. There were books, of course—but my ma wouldn't have had such filth in the house—and rumors which spread round the school corridors of what a man might try to do to you. Later, long after I was married and settled, there'd be classes taught in all the schools. My own weans would benefit from these, but there was nobody around to teach me. Nobody but Victor Soda. He'd been offering his services for the better part of a decade. What he did had become acceptable; just another village custom no different from Harvest Supper or the parade on the Twelfth of July. If your daughter was getting married, you packed her off to see Victor Soda. You didn't broadcast what you were doing. Neither did you see the harm in it. You never asked what happened inside that static. It was enough to know Victor sorted things out. Your wee girl would learn everything she needed to know, and you'd avoid an embarrassing chat.

I turned sixteen on August 10. By this stage Da had come round to the idea of Keith Hannah. He was no longer opposed to us courting. He was actively encouraging it. Keith was a decent Protestant fella, a hard worker, and, as the oldest of the Hannah boys, likely to come into a fair whack of land when his father passed. Once the shock had settled, Da went from naught to sixty in less than a fortnight. Maybe he shouldn't run the lad off with a shotgun. Keith might be the very thing he'd been waiting for. If the two of us were to marry, it'd be one less thing for him to sort out. There was no point in hanging around. The lad might go off me. There were other, prettier girls in the village. Dear knows why Keith had taken to me. There was no sense in continuing with my schooling either. I was to be a farmer's wife. Everything I needed to know could be learned in the kitchen or a field.

The pair of us were quickly engaged. This was as much our fathers' doing as a decision we made ourselves. I wore his great-granny's engagement ring. It slopped round my finger like a Hula-Hoop. I was heart-feared of losing it down the drain. I tied it around my neck with a length of baling twine and enjoyed the feel of it scratching gently at the hollow cleft between my breasts. I was told we'd marry before the year was out, somewhere between Harvest and getting the last of the spuds in. It would be a smallish affair: his oldest sister for a bridesmaid—wearing a dress she'd worn before—and Francey as matron of honor, if she wasn't a complete house side by then. I was a wee fool that summer. I couldn't see past the fancy towels, the tablecloths, and the baking bowls Ma was putting aside for my bottom drawer. I spent hours in my bedroom with an old school jotter, practicing my new signature. "Mrs. Keith Hannah. Mrs. K. Hannah." I could not wait to surrender my name.

I was going to be a married woman before any of the other ones in my class. This would give me the edge on them. I ran quick on their jealousy. I was such a lucky girl. I thought Keith would be the same forever. Sweet and shy and full of little pinchy compliments. "Your hair's the exact same color as straw. When you kiss me, it tastes like jam. You've good strong arms for a girl, Lou." Nobody told me that husbands were not the same as boyfriends. A husband would be a much heavier thing. Permanent. Every day. Dragging. Like another version of myself. Nobody told me what I was losing, that I wouldn't have my young years back. Jamesy tried. God bless Jamesy. He was never really one of us. He could see the shame in it. He took me aside and said, "You're so young, Louie. Are you sure this is what you really want?" But I was. Back then I was absolutely certain. And Jamesy wasn't going to argue with me. He was never the sort to cause a scene. Two weeks later, he left for uni. It was different for him. He was a boy.

The date was set for December 7. We would be married and moved in by Christmas. For some reason it was vital to be in by Christmas. Everybody told us so. Round our way there was always a panic to get things redd up by the twenty-third. You wouldn't want to be decorating your living room over Christmas, or trying to get an extension finished, or waiting on your father to pass. Babies were also encouraged to make an appearance before December so they could be in and conveniently settled before the tree went up. As for babies, so for young couples. The open end of us could not be allowed to drag on and on. Christmas would come down like a guillotine, severing this year from the next. It would find us already launched into married life.

Now, I could've understood this logic if we'd been moving into our own wee house. I could've seen how we wouldn't want to be eating Christmas dinner off our knees. But we'd no notion of a house. We were sixteen and eighteen that year. We'd hardly a penny saved between us. Keith's job was working for his da. We could not afford privacy. We'd begin our stint as man and wife in my old bedroom. I'd shoved the two single beds together to make a double—Francey would hardly be looking for hers back—taken down all my magazine posters, and donated my teddies to a younger cousin. It took the babyish look off the place, but everything was very pink. The curtains. The carpet. The fussy wallpaper. The duvet cover, which was daisy-printed in six different shades of violent cerise. I couldn't imagine Keith in this room. It was not a space that could take a man. Nor was I brave enough to ask my folks to redecorate. I hoped somebody would take pity on us and give us bed linen as a wedding present or maybe a set of bedside lamps. There was talk of a site on Keith's da's land. We could, if we saved up, build a bungalow. That would be many years away.

Looking back now, I'm amazed by how little say we had. It was our wedding. It felt as if it belonged to our parents. The date was set. The dress was picked. Arrangements were made for where we'd live. I don't remember making any of these decisions or even being asked for preferences. I clearly recall one specific incident, about six weeks before the wedding. Me, my ma, and Auntie Jean were sat around the kitchen table going over the food. There was no money for a hotel do. The reception would be a buffet in the Orange Hall. Cold meats. Vol-au-vents. Cocktail sausages and mini sausage rolls. A platter or two of egg mayonnaise. Nothing that required serious cooking. There were limited facilities in the Orange Hall.

"And what about a cake?" asked Auntie Jean. "You'd need to get the wedding cake sorted soon."

"I thought I'd go for a Madeira," I said, and before I'd even had the chance to say, *I don't like sultanas and neither does Keith,* Ma was in there like a bullet.

"Don't be silly, Louise," she said. "You don't do Madeira for a wedding. You'll have a fruitcake like everybody else. Your auntie Maureen'll make it for you. She can bake an extra one when she's doing her Christmas cakes."

Just like that, it was decided. We were going to have a wedding cake that neither me nor my future husband would actually want to eat.

It was just the same when it came to bridesmaids, picking hymns for the service, and deciding upon a honeymoon. Keith and I thought we might get the ferry over to Ayr and spend a long weekend in a guesthouse there. But an uncle of Keith's had offered two nights at a B&B in Cushendall. It was only down the road. We could be back for church on Sunday. Keith could still help his da with the cows. We agreed. We professed our thanks in a handwritten letter, painstakingly written on my ma's best

Basildon Bond. Cushendall was no place for a winter honeymoon. We were not given any choice. We were not trusted to decide for ourselves. We did not think to put up a fight.

It was in this same passive spirit that I found myself four days before the wedding, standing on Victor Soda's doorstep, shivering in my Sunday dress. I was clutching a carrier bag containing a wheaten loaf, a dozen eggs, three jars of my ma's freezer jam, and two twenty-pound notes folded up inside a brown envelope. I'd no idea why I'd been brought here. Around an hour before, Da had risen from the dinner table and announced, "You've to go over and see Victor Soda now." No further information was forthcoming, and I wasn't bold enough to ask. Ma had told me to put a good frock on, to wash my face and brush my teeth. Then Da had driven me over in the Land Rover, with a towel on the passenger seat so as not to get dog hair on my dress. "Behave yourself," he'd said when he dropped me off, "and listen to whatever Victor says. Don't be letting your ma and me down." Then he'd passed the carrier bag out through the driver's window and said he'd be back in about an hour. I'd hung back, practically clinging to the car. "Go on now, Louise," he'd said, and nodded toward the static caravan, raising one finger off the wheel like he sometimes did with passing cars.

I, like the silly girl I was, did exactly as I was told. I went down the field, picking my way through the crusty cowpats, trying to keep my Sunday shoes nice. I climbed the steps to Victor's caravan and knocked shyly on his door. The carrier bag was biting into the soft flesh of one hand. I'd the nails dug deep into the other. The pain was the only thing keeping me anchored. I'd have bolted if I'd had any place to run to.

When Victor Soda opened the door, he was all dolled up in one of his suits: green velvet with a polka-dot hankie and black patent shoes, so slick and shiny they did not look right on the feet of a man. He reminded me of this china-faced boy doll my granny used to have in her good room. She kept it in one of those glass-fronted cabinets, displayed next to a green velvet girl doll and a whole rake of other ornaments. She called them her Irish dolls and, every year on St. Patrick's, brought them out to sit for a day or two, legs dangling over the mantelpiece. I never liked that boy doll. Its face was an unnatural shade of white. Its stuck-on eyes were black and beady. They reminded me of the eyes of crows.

"Hello, my dear, it's good to see you," said Victor Soda. He was not wearing his hat. I'd never seen him inside before. He was thinning a bit on top but wore the hair combed over his bald spot like a flat cap. I couldn't take my eyes off it. I was wondering what it would look like peeled back and flopping round his ear.

"Come in, come in," he said, "you're letting all the hot air out." He held the caravan door open so I could squeeze past.

The static was much like every other caravan I'd ever been inside. It had that plasticky, mildewed smell you often get in a caravan. Also another peculiar aroma, a kind of cinnamon and burnt-Christmas smell, which I'd later realize came from the clove cigarettes Victor Soda smoked. There was a tiny kitchen running the length of the closest wall and a bay window covered in yellowing lace curtains. The walls were paneled in dark wood and decorated with framed pictures. The Queen and Prince Philip on their wedding day. A Bible text of the Twenty-third Psalm. A watercolor of Ballintoy Harbour. Two old ones photographed in black-and-white times. The living room was sparsely decorated with a Superser heater, a U-shaped sofa, and a coffee table with a book sat on it—*Great Expectations*—the spine bent back upon itself, as if I'd interrupted Victor in the middle of his reading. I wondered if he was expecting me.

"This is for you," I said, and held up the bulging carrier bag. I didn't know what else to say.

Victor peered inside it, poked around a bit, and made a kind of grumbly noise. "I got more for your sister," he mumbled. "Then again, she was a handful. I don't suppose there'll be much work in you." He set the bag on the kitchen counter and began opening cupboards, lifting down glasses and packets of biscuits, arranging the items on a tray. I did not know what to do with myself. I felt too large for this tiny space. There was a loud noise trying to climb up my throat.

"Sit down, sit down," he said, turning to glance at me over his shoulder. "We only have an hour or so."

I looked around for a place to sit. I could go over to the sofa, but even in a caravan, this would've felt like leaving the kitchen and venturing into another room. My manners would not allow it; I couldn't bring myself to go wandering uninvited round somebody else's house. I glanced behind me, looking for the table. Maybe I could sit on a kitchen stool. But the table was no longer a table. It had been dismantled and rebuilt in the form of a bed. It was already made up with a candlewick bedspread of palest hospital green and two doughy pillows which had not been white for quite some time. I didn't want to sit on this bed. I wanted to distance myself from it. I leaned my weight against the wall and tried to keep my panic still. I kept both eyes on the clock. I watched the progress of its little fidgety hands. Fifty-five minutes till Da came back. Fifty-five minutes till I could leave.

Once Victor had finished his preparations, he lifted the tray and carried it into the living room, indicating with his head that

I should follow. I sat on one side of the U-shaped sofa. He sat opposite. He placed the tray between us, nudging Dickens out of the way.

"Now," he said, "what about a wee glass of cream soda?"

I shook my head. I managed to squeak out a polite "No, thanks." Even terrified, I was mindful of my manners. My ma had trained me reasonably well.

"Uch, come on, now, Louise. Everybody loves cream soda. I'm mad for the stuff myself. It's the only thing I drink. I'd nearly take it on my cornflakes if I could get away with it." He smiled then, as if taken with his own wit. "I've put a wee something in your glass. Just to relax you. You won't even taste it over the sugar. Don't be taking thran with me. Have a wee sup of your cream soda. It'll help you loosen up."

"No, thank you," I repeated, "I don't like cream soda. It makes me boke." This was actually true. I glanced down at my hands. My fingers were dug so far into my knees that the knuckles had turned a toothy white.

"Suit yourself," said Victor Soda, and poured a generous measure out of the mineral bottle. He lifted the glass to his lips and knocked the whole thing back. In the course of the next hour, I'd watch him drink the entire bottle of cream soda. I understood then where he got his name from, and why his teeth were nicotine yellow, peppered with filthy clumps of black.

Once he'd drunk the tumbler dry, he set it on the coffee table and helped himself to a custard cream. He peeled one biscuit from the other and licked the cream out with his tongue. I always ate sandwich biscuits the same way: gypsy creams, bourbons, custard creams, anything you could peel apart. Yet watching Victor Soda eat his biscuit made my stomach turn. He was like a snake or some slimy creature, going at it with his tongue. Once he'd finished the custard creams, he leaned back in his seat and looked me up and down, taking the whole whack of me in with his mean crow eyes.

"You know why you're here, don't you, Louise?"

I nodded. I didn't. But I knew enough to know I didn't want to know. I could see there were only fifty minutes left on the clock. If I played my cards right, maybe I could put off the knowing until Da came back and rescued me.

"You're getting married soon," Victor said.

I nodded.

"Nice lad?"

I nodded again.

"And you're a nice wee girl?"

This was clearly a question, not a statement. I nodded until it felt like my head was about to come off. My hands, not knowing what to do with themselves, were tugging the hem of my dress down, desperately trying to cover my knees.

"Good, good. I'm glad to hear that. I thought you'd be a nice wee girl. Your folks have clearly brought you up right. Biscuit, Louise?"

He held the saucer of biscuits out toward me: the last of the bourbons, ginger nuts, and two lone pink wafers, extending wobbly over the plate's raised lip. I lifted a hand to politely decline.

"Well, your parents have asked me to have a wee word with you. It's nothing to be frightened about. It's just that a nice wee girl like you probably doesn't know what to expect when it comes to marital practice between a man and his wife. Do you know what I'm talking about, Louise?"

I stared at Victor Soda. It felt like a brick was sitting on my throat. I couldn't get even the smallest word squeezed past it.

I nodded. Why on earth was I nodding? I wanted to scream. I wanted to kick him in his horrible teeth. More than anything, I wanted to get up and run away. Out of the caravan. Across the field. Anywhere that wasn't here. Instead, I nodded. I nodded like an idiot. Victor settled himself back on the sofa, stretched his arms out, and smiled at me in a wolfish way. I understood then that I would not be able to make this stop. There were forty-five minutes left till Da came back. Each minute would be an eternity.

"It could be a bit of a shock for you," said Victor, "that first night when you go to bed with your new husband and he wants to do things with you; dirty sorts of things. Your mother and father don't want you getting upset, so they've asked me to step in and make sure you know what to expect."

He sat up straighter then and began to fiddle with his belt buckle. "Now, Louise," he said, "I'm going to show you something you won't have seen before. I don't want you to be alarmed."

Something in the way he said this—forceful but also kindly, as if speaking to a very young child—reminded me of my da, who was always talking down to me, telling me what I needed to do. Not just my da, also the minister from our church, who would not let girls do the Bible readings or even lift the offering. And Mr. Gibson, who taught me English and said that Shakespeare was a bit beyond me and was really more for the fellas. Even Keith—though, God, I loved him—Keith was always bossing me around. ("Wear the red skirt tonight, Lou. Don't be ruining your face with makeup. Make sure and agree with what my da says.") All these men talking down to me, telling me what I had to do, like I wasn't capable of deciding myself. Something inside me snapped when Victor Soda started to unzip his fly. I was innocent as the birds back then, but I'd a notion from growing up on the farm what I was about to be presented with. I did not like it. And I did not want it. More to the point, I did not want to be told what I wanted, what was supposedly good for me.

I did the first thing that came into my head. I opened my mouth and lied through my teeth.

"Oh, I know all about that stuff, Mr. Bennett," I said. "I don't need any help from you."

Victor Soda was not expecting this. "You what?" he said.

"I've seen loads of them things before."

I might as well have punched him. He sat bolt upright in his seat. He'd the belt buckle back in place before I could even catch my breath.

"What?" he repeated, and his voice was like a woman's voice, all high and scratchy and stuck in his nose as if he was on the verge of tears.

"Sorry," I said. Though I knew I hadn't done anything wrong, I could not stop myself. Apologizing came naturally to me.

"Sorry! Sorry's all you've got to say for yourself! I cannot believe what I've just heard. *You've seen loads of them things before!* Does Davie Brownley know what sort of wee girl he's raised? A bold girl. A dirty girl. A filthy hoor. Tell me that, Louise, does your daddy know he's raised a hoor?"

I shook my head. I was all a muddle. I couldn't seem to get the moment straight. Victor Soda was so furious that wee bits of spit were coming out of his mouth and landing like drizzle on my face. I could feel the heat rising in my cheeks, the first pinching sting of tears beginning to gather behind my nose. I looked at the clock with desperation. The hands seemed to have stopped moving. Everything in the room felt drunk.

"Well, if you think I'll be teaching you now, young lassie, you can go and take a running jump. I've no interest in helping a dirty girl."

It wasn't shame that made me cry. I knew I hadn't done anything to be ashamed of. Still, it was hard to sit beneath such ugly words. After a few minutes, I started to feel as if they were taking root. I was evil. I was ugly. Though I couldn't have told you the definition, I even wondered if I might be a hoor. I couldn't keep myself from crying and, once started, could not seem to stop. I cried because a man was shouting at me. I cried because my da had left me here with this man. I cried because of what had happened. This made me think of what might have happened, and then I cried with sheer relief. I sat on the U-shaped sofa and cried for forty-three more minutes, watching the clock's hand tick out the hour while Victor Soda sat at the opposite end. In between mouthfuls of cream soda, he called me all the names of the day. Hoor. Slut. Bitch. Cow. Hoor again. There were only so many ways to shame me, and Victor Soda was not an imaginative man. He didn't ask me to leave the static. I made no attempt to get up and leave. We were both trapped inside this awful charade. We knew it would be easier to last the hour out than explain ourselves to anyone else.

At seven my father rang the Land Rover horn: two short blasts, then a longer one. I rose from the U-shaped sofa, wiped my eyes on my cardigan sleeve, and left the caravan. I did not acknowledge Victor Soda. I did not slam the door behind me. I wanted to, but I didn't have the strength. It took me about three minutes to walk up the field, through the mud and the cow shit and the long damp grass. I did not look back. I did not need to. I could feel Victor Soda's eyes drilling into me.

When I got to the top of the field, Da shoved the Land Rover's door open from inside. I climbed into the passenger seat. I did not turn to look at my da. I kept my back to him and stared out the side window for the whole drive home. The dark made a mirror of the window. I could see Da's face reflected in it. His face was angry and also sad.

As we were pulling into the yard, he asked, "Well, how'd you get on with Victor Soda?"

"Grand," I said. I was watching my mouth moving in the wing mirror. My face was pale as milk. My eyes were red. It was obvious I'd been crying. "Grand," I repeated. "Victor said to say thanks for the jam and stuff."

Da patted me twice on my right knee. This was high affection in his book. "Good girl," he said.

He wasn't looking at me when he said it. He was staring at his hands on the steering wheel. The right one was rolled up in a fist.

"Louise," he started, and turned toward me.

I did not want to hear what my da had to say.

I opened the door.

I got out of the Land Rover.

I closed the door and went inside.

# PILLARS

Elaine is forty-seven when her pillar arrives. She has not ordered one. She doesn't have the sort of money required to maintain a subscription. Even a moderately sized short-loan number would be beyond her means, and yet this is a deluxe model, almost three feet tall and equipped with both day and night functionality. She doesn't know where the pillar has come from or how to make it go away.

On Monday she wakes to find the pillar floating at the end of her bed. It is still dark. The pillar is in night mode: a child-sized block of flames, hovering just below the ceiling. It hasn't scorched the roof. It isn't even real fire, though the similarity to flame is uncanny. Elaine doesn't know how long it's been there. Minutes. Hours. Days. These days she's not the most observant. Important things slip past her: friends' birthdays and dental appointments, gas bills, tax returns and parent-teacher interviews. People are quick to make an exception for her. "You're not yourself at the minute," they say, trying not to look perturbed when she arrives two hours late for dinner. Elaine is a muddle since Martin left. She can't seem to get the line of herself straight.

She tries to remember Sunday night clearly. Was there a pillar of fire hanging over her bed or not? She recalls the evening as a series of snapshots only vaguely linked, like cells sandwiched together in a comic strip. She remembers a third glass of wine and a voicemail from Martin. "Please do not call here again. Goodbye." Another glass of wine. Then a valiant attempt to mark Year 9's *Animal Farm* essays. Tears in front of the television. Rising to mute the volume because the remote couldn't be found and the sound of canned laughter was making her feel anxious. Falling over the coffee table. Spilling the wine. Crying some more, then losing the energy for it, because what was the point in sobbing when there wasn't anyone around to sympathize? Finally, crawling into an unmade bed. Not sleeping. Sleeping. Not sleeping again. No sign of a flaming pillar. No sign of anything untoward. But had she looked up? Had she, hell.

Elaine has not looked up in over a month.

When she wakes, the whole room is flaming around her: curtains flicker, tongued shadows dance against the wallpaper, the wardrobe mirror pitches each warm lick back at her and shimmers. At first she wonders what this fiery thing is and why the smoke alarm hasn't gone off. It takes her a moment to realize it's a pillar. She's never been this close to one before. It looks different from the pictures she's seen on the Internet. Taller. Brighter. Less threatening. There's something captivating about the way it is neither moving nor standing completely still. A line of Yeats comes to mind, *nobleness made simple as a fire,* quickly followed by the shudder of remembering what it feels like to teach this poem to Year 11, rows of faces curdling with boredom. There is no heat off the pillar. No noise either. But it is beautiful. Elaine cannot take her eyes off it. Consequently, she is late for work.

Later that evening, emboldened, she will run her hand through the pillar's flaming core and find it is not even warm to the touch. The sensation will be similar to holding a hand beneath a garden sprinkler: soothing, liquid, vaguely reassuring. It will tickle.

By the time she finally leaves for school, it is light out and the pillar has transitioned into daytime mode. Now it is a three-foot block of soft, vaporous cloud. Like a long winter breath streaming in front of her. It precedes her journey, guiding her out the front door, into the car, and all the way along the dual carriageway. It hangs just above the end of the Fiesta's bonnet, high enough to ensure it doesn't form an obstruction, low enough to remain visible. At school she doesn't mention the pillar, though it's painfully apparent, the only one in the staff room. Her colleagues are too well mannered to say anything. They look round the side of the pillar—which is easier to do when it's in cloud mode—and ask if she's had a nice weekend.

It's been misery from start to finish.

"Lovely, thanks," says Elaine.

In class, the children stare. Some of them have their own pillars: smaller models, decorated with baubles and bright stickers. Every term, another handful of students acquire a pillar of their own. The head has called it an epidemic and proposed a series of special assemblies on more traditional solutions. He favors medication, therapy, and extra rounds of detention. In response, the deputy head has said that "epidemic" is a very reactionary word. These children aren't troubled, she's said. They are suffering from mental health issues and should be treated with all due care. And isn't it wonderful, she's added, that there's help out there for young people nowadays, even if it is a little unorthodox?

The deputy head listens to a lot of Radio 4. She is very popular with those students who are struggling to cope. Sometimes they follow their pillars to her office at lunchtime and eat their Müller fruit corners sitting around her desk. The deputy head has even helped some students receive pillar referrals from their GPs. She has not yet encountered a colleague with a pillar. In the staff room at break time, she makes a point of looking directly at Elaine and smiling, as if to say, *I see you there, with your pillar. What a brave woman you are. What a role model for us all.* Elaine smiles back. She doesn't want to join the lunchtime picnic in the deputy head's office. She feels it would be unprofessional. Still, if her pillar thinks it's for the best, then she won't have much choice in the matter.

The pillar, Elaine realizes, constantly preempts her next move. "Don't eat the chocolate," it suggests, and sleeks across the kitchen ceiling, drawing attention to the fruit bowl sitting on the bench. "Don't phone Martin again tonight," it whispers, and coerces her away from the telephone, out into the back garden, where she finds herself weeding flower beds. Don't do this potentially disastrous thing. Do this sensible thing instead. It isn't rocket science. Anyone with a functional thought-life could make these sorts of decisions for themselves. But Elaine is not functional at the minute.

She begins to rely upon the pillar. The pillar is one step ahead of her, guiding her eye to the student who requires a little extra attention, pointing out the shortest checkout line at Tesco, dragging her off the road to the petrol station when she's just about to run out and hasn't noticed yet. It doesn't take Elaine long to accept that the pillar knows better than she does. She is happier and more efficient when she isn't making decisions by herself.

She loses weight. She joins a walking club. She manages to mark all of Year 9's *Jane Eyre* essays without resorting to wine or sarcastic scribbles in the margins. After a few weeks, she even builds a profile on a dating website. She includes an upbeat blurb, likes and dislikes, and a flattering photo taken in Alicante last summer: early-evening sunshine, tanned shoulders, Martin cropped out so you can barely see the ghost of his arm creeping into the shot. She hasn't let her profile go live yet. But she knows she will. Very soon.

Elaine wonders how she ever managed without a pillar.

The pillar brings its own problem. Everyone who sees it knows Elaine needs help. She might as well write "NOT COPING" across her forehead in permanent marker. It's that obvious. She frequently clocks people trying not to stare, which only makes their staring more pronounced. She hears the things they're not saying. *Look at the sketch of that one. Can't even catch the bus without a bloody cloud to guide her.*

Elaine's sisters are the kind of people who mock pillar owners. They'd never say anything to a person's face, but in private, on the phone, after a drink or two, they can be absolute bitches. Elaine isn't naive. She knows that she's exactly the sort of person they'd be laying into if she weren't their sister. Her clothes don't sit right. Her lipstick gets on her teeth. She talks over other people in conversation. "A disaster waiting to happen," her late father would say. So far, she's managed to avoid her sisters, but there is a niece's birthday party at the weekend and, shortly afterward, Christmas. She can't hide the pillar from them forever.

She tries telling her mother on the phone. "Mum," she says, "what do you think about pillars?" Her mother starts into a long story about Jean next door who has a son, who has a girlfriend, who got a pillar last November, just to help her through Christmas. How at first it helped, and later didn't, so she wound up trying to kill herself by drinking toilet cleaner and managed to get the dosage wrong and in the end didn't die but ruined her speaking voice altogether. Afterward, they wouldn't give her a refund on the pillar. This seems to be the main point of the story.

"Oh," says Elaine when her mother finally pauses for breath. She isn't sure how to segue into discussing her own pillar. She asks her mother about the garden instead.

Her mother is never any help. Elaine calls hoping for sympathy or at the very least a listening ear. She wants someone to say, "Yes, it is shit that Martin left you for a girl who is twenty-five years younger and still able to get away with pigtails. But you are brave and you are strong. You will get through this terrible time. Cry. Drink wine in moderation. Don't be so hard on yourself." Instead, her mother is resolutely chipper. "Look on the bright side, Lainey," she says, "at least there's no children involved. Divorce is wild hard on children."

Elaine thinks that she would have liked a child. It might have helped to stave the loneliness off. It's too late for children now. There are so many parts of her life that feel like they are suddenly over. She can make herself cry just thinking about the things that will probably never happen to her: children, grandchildren, wearing a bikini, changing careers, going to Thailand or Vietnam on the sort of holiday that isn't a package deal. She tries not to admit any of this to herself. Instead, she sticks motivational quotes to the fridge with magnets. "Be your best self." "Yes, you can!" "You are fearfully and wonderfully made." This is a bit from the Bible that one of the classroom assistants once wrote down after finding Elaine crying in the book cupboard. It was nice at the time, and she'd wondered about the possibility of becoming friends with this woman, whose name was Melanie. Later, Melanie had tried to coerce Elaine into joining an Alpha group at her church, and all the niceness evaporated out of the situation. She'd felt then like one of those people targeted by double-glazing salesmen on the phone and immediately stopped bringing extra Kit Kats to share with Melanie during coffee break.

Still, she's kept the Post-it. She relishes the idea of being fearful and wonderful. It makes her feel like Kate Bush, and also a little unhinged. Sometimes she dances round the kitchen singing "Wuthering Heights" in her dressing gown, making the sleeves flap like wings. Before the pillar, this was a large part of her coping mechanism. Also, reading the sort of books that would attempt to take her messed-up life and turn it sideways so she wasn't lonely, she was actually free.

At first she borrowed these books from the library. Then she began to suspect the librarians were mocking her reading habits. So she tried to mix it up, slipping a few romance novels into the pile, dabbling in the travel section. Eventually, she ran out of energy for subterfuge and began ordering her self-help books off Amazon. Now she has the pillar, Elaine can't possibly go back to the library. She doesn't want the librarians to see they were right about her all along. She cannot bear the soft way they'll look at her as they pass her books across the counter. She is accumulating fines. She doesn't even care.

Elaine is determined to be shot of her pillar before the end of term. She looks the process up online. There are only two ways to "terminate your relationship" with a pillar. You can cancel your subscription or you can become functional enough to negate the need for a "bespoke life guide." It is impossible to cancel a subscription you haven't set up, so she decides to focus instead upon becoming functional.

She files for divorce. This is hard, and requires some wine, but she gets through it, phoning Miranda—who teaches history and is currently on her third (or is it fourth?) husband—for advice when the paperwork starts to overwhelm her. She feels significantly better once the divorce is in progress. She cleans out the garage, donating Martin's ski gear to Barnardo's. Then, she purges the mantelpiece of photographs and knickknacks, until there is nothing left of her ex-husband, not a single mug or sports sock. The pillar hangs over all her good work: cloud by day, fire by night. Sometimes Elaine thinks it is twinkling with pleasure. But this could well be a trick of the light.

Her colleagues have become accustomed to the pillar. She notices them not noticing it. Occasionally, they pass right through its cloudy edges en route to the toaster or microwave. They don't even flinch. She is reasonably popular these days, more than she's been in years. People can see her newfound confidence. They compliment her outfits. They include her in discussions about films and politics, assuming she'll have something insightful to contribute. They draw her aside by the photocopier to ask her advice on unruly students, new haircuts, and where to go for half-term break. Elaine carries herself differently when walking. Head high. Shoulders back. Belly sucked and tucked, like a much younger woman.

She changes her dating profile from dormant to active. The pillar doesn't exactly tell her to do this, but it does hang over her laptop throughout. Three men contact her within a matter of hours. One lives in Alaska. This is hardly practical. One sends her a picture of his penis. He is only twenty-one. It is not a bad-looking penis. She doesn't reply but keeps the picture just in case she might require cheering up at some point. The third man is called Nigel.

He seems reasonably normal. He has an approachable look, like a kindly greengrocer. His interests are reading, conversation, and his pet tortoise. Because her eye is now drawn to such things, Elaine notices the shadow of a pillar clouding just behind his ear. In some strange way, this reassures her. She writes back: "What's your favorite book?" "What's your tortoise called?" "Do you fancy getting a coffee sometime?" Her own pillar undulates above the laptop, rising and falling gently as if it is breathing. This is the closest it's ever come to exhibiting emotion.

Elaine goes on three dates with Nigel: coffee, dinner, cinema. They don't talk about pillars or the circumstances which have led them to acquire one. On the first date, Elaine says, "Sorry, I didn't mention it before. I hope it's okay . . ." Nigel says, "I have one too . . ." and shrugs. Then they both glance up and smile. They don't say the word out loud. Not yet. Not before they've even got started. After the third date, they kiss clumsily up against Elaine's Fiesta, which is parked behind the shopping center. While they are embracing, their pillars combine to make an enormous flaming beacon. It flares up into the night sky, eight feet above their heads. Elaine hadn't expected this. It is quite romantic. Thankfully, it's late at night and she's parked on a quiet street. Neither of them is the sort of person who appreciates an audience.

For the fourth date, Elaine invites Nigel round for dinner. She makes risotto and shaves her legs. She hopes he will stay over, then wonders if this is a dreadfully bold thing to hope for. She asks Miranda if sex is considered appropriate on a fourth date, at her age, with the divorce not even properly through. Miranda says, "If it was me, I wouldn't even have made it to the second." She makes a mental note not to ask Miranda for relationship advice again.

Nigel arrives five minutes early with a bunch of chrysanthemums. He has made the effort to dress up. He is wearing a freshly pressed pair of slacks and a burgundy pullover which perfectly complements his pillar. Elaine leaves him in the living room with a glass of wine while she goes to find a vase. They call back and forth to each other across the hall. "How was your day?" "Is the traffic bad out there?" The normalcy of this is tremendously reassuring. She can imagine the two of them years from now, in the same room or someplace similar, having the same conversation. The pillar does its deep-breathing thing. She thinks it must be happy and wonders if this means she is happy too.

She is trimming the flowers' stems at a diagonal angle—because this means you'll get a few days' extra bloom out of them—when the office phone rings. "Excuse me," Elaine calls out, "I'll just get that." She leaves the flowers sprawled across the kitchen table. It will be her mother. No one else calls at this time of the night, no one but her mother and Nigel, and he is already here, making himself comfortable on the sofa. It isn't her mother. It is a person in a call center somewhere in England. She thinks it is a huskily voiced woman, but it could just as easily be a man.

"Mrs. McCall?" asks the voice.

"Yes," Elaine says. "I'm in the middle of something. It's not convenient to talk."

"This will only take a minute."

"I don't have a minute."

"I think you'll want to hear this. There's been a mix-up. I'm calling from Pillars.com. You own one of our bespoke life guides, don't you? A deluxe model with day-and-night functionality?"

Elaine doesn't speak.

"Mrs. McCall?"

"A pillar?" Elaine manages. "Yes. Although I never ordered one."

"Exactly. As I said, there's been a mix-up. The pillar wasn't intended for you. It was ordered by a Mr. Martin McCall."

"My ex-husband," Elaine says, very quietly, for it's like being punched, just hearing his name out loud.

"Ah," says the voice, "that makes sense. There was a mix-up with the addresses. His credit card's listed to this house, but I'm guessing he doesn't live here anymore."

"No," says Elaine, "he doesn't bloody well live here anymore."

She puts the phone down quickly, before the voice can say her pillar is going. She looks up into its dark, flickering eye and stares. She doesn't know how to function without it now. How to stand, and walk into the living room, and lead Nigel by the hand, up the stairs, into her bedroom. How to talk, and sit, and seem like a normal person in his presence. She doesn't even know how to get the risotto from pot to plate without burning the arse out of it. Even the smallest action suddenly seems impossible without a pillar to guide her.

She keeps staring, eyeballing the pillar, until the memory of it is implanted on her retinas. She thinks about Martin, with his high-flying job and his pigtailed lover. Martin sitting in front of his computer, ordering a pillar to lead him through the mess of his own sadness. She pictures him crying. This is easy enough to imagine, for he's the sort of man who weeps at the drop of a hat, and it's been a particularly emotional year. It is a mean little comfort to realize that Martin is weak too, weak and struggling. *Maybe,* thinks Elaine, *we're all just holding it together for show.* What a strangely liberating thought.

When the light goes out of her pillar—the snuff of it lingering as a thin twist of birthday-candle smoke—Elaine doesn't feel hopeless. Neither does she feel lost. For there's only one door out of this room, and it opens into the room where Nigel is sitting on her sofa, nursing a lukewarm glass of merlot. She will walk into the room and join him. This much is obvious to her. She has no idea how the rest of the evening will play out. Perhaps she'll know, without being told, how to move easily and confidently from one moment to the next. Perhaps she'll require leading. But isn't this how it is for most people, almost every living day?

# JELLYFISH

I am pruning the roses when I find the first one.

As I reach through the stems, secateurs in hand, my skin makes contact with something gelatinous. It is slick and slightly cold, like a peeled grape or how an eyeball might feel if accidentally touched. It is probably a slug. It hasn't been a good year for slugs. Earlier in the summer, they wreaked havoc on the vegetable bed, leaving my lettuces in shreds. Now they're making nightly advances on our front door, their snot trails silvering up the gravel path. They have yet to come after my roses, but there is in gardening—as in life itself—a first time for everything.

I push the rosebush aside to investigate. I lean in for a closer look. There's no need. The jellyfish is immediately apparent. It sits on top of the soil, slick and glutinous as an uncooked egg. It looks up at me with its enormous marbled eye and doesn't move. Though I know it's definitely a jellyfish, it doesn't resemble any variety I've seen before. Further investigation confirms it is dead.

Most of Malcolm's jellyfish will be dead by the time I find them. Once removed from the beach, jellyfish don't last long. They stiffen and set, losing their sting. In death, their transparent parts turn slightly opaque, like cheap Perspex scuffed from overuse. I can see this jellyfish is no longer alive, yet I can't bring myself to touch it with my bare hands. Instead, I slip the edge of my spade underneath, scooping up an inch or two of soil as I ease it free of the flower bed. Small granules of humus are stuck to its skin. They look like chocolate cake crumbs. This thought disgusts me. There's something placenta-like about a jellyfish; something crude and internal which should not be associated with food.

When Rob was born, I asked to see the placenta. I was muddled from the birth and unsure which pronoun to use. *Should the placenta be referred to as mine or the baby's?* Perhaps the most accurate term was ours, seeing as we'd both been attached to it. In the end, I simply pointed at the kidney dish they'd put it in and said, "Can I see it?" The midwife brought the dish over. A blue paper towel was draped over the contents. I peeled it off and held the dish for several minutes, staring at the sleek red thing it contained. The cardboard felt warm in my hands. I understood that this heat had come from inside me. It would not last long in such a well-aired room. I raised the placenta to my face and breathed in. It smelled strongly menstrual, like stale greenhouse air. How like a jellyfish it was. How odd and globular. I prodded it gently with my finger and wondered if this was the closest I'd ever get to touching my own insides. Some blood came off on my finger. I considered licking it, and probably would have if the midwife hadn't been watching me. I felt no desire to protect the placenta. I simply wanted to see it: this thing my son had trailed into the world behind him; this suddenly useless part of me.

There was a real craze for placentas back then. It was the end of the seventies. The Body Shop had just opened. Everybody was going natural. In other, more modern places, people were having placenta ceremonies, blessing them and burying them under trees. I'd even read an article in a women's magazine about how you could make pâté out of your placenta and serve it up to friends and family. No special accoutrements were required for this recipe. All you needed was an ordinary kitchen blender and a fridge. The placenta pâté could be seasoned for taste.

I showed this article to Malcolm. "Look what they're at on the Mainland," I said. We laughed together. It was not a cruel kind of laughter. We were often amused by the things which passed for progress in other parts of the world. We were quite content to remain backward if backward meant not eating bits of afterbirth slathered on Ritz crackers. Malcolm said eating placenta sounded suspiciously like cannibalism. I agreed, though a little bit of me understood the logic. After Rob, I'd felt hollow inside. This emptiness persisted for almost six months. Some solid part of me went missing. There were days when I'd like to have shoved everything back inside me: the baby, the afterbirth, the heaving sense of hope I'd had in the weeks leading up to the birth. A baby was meant to be a gift. And Rob was. He was such a gift. But in gaining him, I'd lost something too. The baby made a kingdom of Malcolm and me: a tight little unit, smug and self-sufficient. For a time, we were so close we could not see past ourselves. Now I wonder if we should have been different with each other. If we didn't hold the baby too tightly.

I carry the jellyfish carefully up the garden. It shudders gently on the surface of the spade. I am not yet used to Malcolm's jellyfish and treat this first specimen with a kind of reverence. This will not last beyond jellyfish number three. After the third jellyfish, I will be blasé. I will treat them like common garden refuse. I open the wheelie bin one-handed and let the jellyfish slime its way off the spade. It lands on top of the previous night's ashes. I use the spade to push the contents of the bin aside, so the jellyfish slips beneath the rest of the rubbish. I don't want to forget it's in there, then come across it unexpectedly when I'm out with the dinner scraps. I don't want Malcolm finding it either. I don't want him knowing I know what he's done. Over the years I've come to realize that much of marriage is based on not knowing things you know full well. In the last year Malcolm and I have grown particularly good at not knowing. This often involves not seeing and not hearing, both of which are acquired skills. How do I know my husband is responsible for this jellyfish? Wifely instinct. Intuition. The logical elimination of all other suspects. If I haven't put the jellyfish in the flower bed, then Malcolm must have. Since Rob, there's been no one else here.

Since Rob, Malcolm's been obsessed with the ocean. I'm not surprised to discover he's lifting jellyfish now. Sometimes when I'm sorting the laundry, I find handfuls of sand in his trouser pockets, seashells and crispy strands of dried-out dulse. He is bringing the beach home one handful at a time. Once I discovered a tiny crab skeleton, sun-bleached and hollow. Its legs were still jointed and malleable, though they'd separated from the shell. I buried it under a stone in the rockery. I couldn't bring myself to throw it in the bin. Though it was in bits, it had retained the look of a living thing. I've never said anything about my findings. I wouldn't know how to begin that conversation. On the wrong day, in the wrong tone, my words might be taken for criticism, and the last thing I want to do is criticize Malcolm. He is losing the look of a living thing.

I haven't gone searching for his hoards. It wouldn't be right. I try not to notice what he's bringing home. This is easier than you'd think. The bungalow is large and spacious. We bought it for the space. We'd hoped to have guests: Rob obviously, his wife and children. We have not had as many guests as expected. I try not to hold on to the disappointment of this.

We have our private spaces, Malcolm and I. He has the office bureau, which he keeps locked. I have Rob's old room. It is just a spare room now, bland and sterile. It is waiting to host all the overnight guests who will probably never come. There's nothing of Rob left in his room, but I go there to think about him and read his letter. Malcolm allows me to be lonely. Being lonely is different from being alone. Both are necessary during this period. Loneliness is the only thing we can give each other right now.

I'd never invade Malcolm's private space. I understand that he is keeping his pain in there and, every so often, poking at it. When I hoover the carpet around the bureau's feet, I can hear the sand shivering up the plastic nozzle. When the central heating's on, a briny smell rises off it like seaweed shriveling in the sun. There are things in there that have no place being in an office bureau: sad, dead things which are beginning to rot. I can't work out why Malcolm's holding on to them. *Is he collecting the ocean piece by piece or trying to erase it altogether?*

I don't say anything about the first jellyfish. We eat and sleep and, the next morning, rise to eat again, and I do not ask my husband why he's hidden a jellyfish under my rosebush. I wait, hoping this is just another stage. Maybe it will be a shortish one. Before the ocean, there was silence and, prior to this, insomnia which lasted for weeks but was easier to understand. (I'd been struggling to sleep myself.) When I find the fifth jellyfish, I know that I will have to say something. It has only been two days since the rosebush, but I've discovered other jellyfish in the compost heap, hidden beneath the petunias in my hanging basket, and slopping about in a mop bucket, shoved under the kitchen sink.

The fifth jellyfish is the final straw. I find it floating in the bleached water of the utility room toilet. I happen to glance into the bowl before sitting down. It takes a second to register what I'm looking at. At first I assume it's something anatomical: an organ or discharge of some sort. For a brief second I hope for a clot. A medical issue would give us something concrete to rail against. It doesn't take me long to realize it's just another jellyfish. I pull the toilet lid down and flush, then check to see if it's gone. It isn't. I flush again. Jellyfish do not flush easily. It takes four attempts and an encouraging prod with the toilet brush to be sure it's made it round the U-bend. I'm livid by the time I leave the utility room, nauseated too. Little bits of jellyfish flesh have come off on the toilet brush bristles. I have to pick them out with balled-up wads of toilet paper.

I know I must talk to Malcolm straight away, while the rage is still on me, but he isn't here. He's down on the beach, as he often is in the dragging hours between lunch and the quiz shows we watch before dinner. I put on my coat and welly boots and go out to meet him. I am loud with anger. I barely notice the cold. As I pick my way down the path, I spot an unfamiliar mound in the corner of the lawn. The grass has been peeled back, then replaced inexpertly to disguise something large and lumpy. It could be the corpse of a small dog—a Jack Russell or Scottie—but I know it isn't. I place my toe on the peak of the mound and apply pressure. The surface slips beneath my boot. The lawn ruptures. A clear jellied substance comes oozing out. I should stop pressing, but I don't. I lean my whole weight on the mound. There must be two dozen jellyfish down there. I want to pulverize them all. I need to have my smooth lawn back. When the corner of the lawn is once more flattish, I quit stomping. I wipe the jellyfish guts off my boots and head down to the beach.

Malcolm spends as much time as he can on the beach. Three or four times a day he'll clear his throat and shuffle forward in his chair. He'll claim that the dog needs walking. The dog has no interest in walking. The dog turned fourteen last April. It is slow and lardy and would be quite happy to remain indefinitely in its usual position, curled up next to the radiator. The dog is just an excuse to go to the beach. Or maybe it is an excuse to get away from me. Most likely it is a combination of both. One thing repels. The other attracts. It's hard for my husband to be around me. It's not just my face, which is Rob's face but older; it's all the things he doesn't want me to say.

Distance helps, and the television is a great distraction, but nights pitch us together, and we have not yet learned how to negotiate such close silence. In bed, we share the same thin space. Then the quiet bears down on us. Then we lie there, suffocating in all the things we cannot say. Neither party is willing to offer respite, though respite could be easily achieved. I could say, *Shall I sleep in the guest room tonight?* I could claim to have a cold coming on. Malcolm could easily fall asleep on the living room couch while watching the rugby or the golf. He doesn't. I don't. Neither party can offer respite. The bed is the only place we touch now, and though it's always accidental, we both understand that abandoning touch would be the end.

We rarely talk. Instead, we watch each other watching each other as we tiptoe round our loneliness. I often watch Malcolm when he's down at the beach. It puts the afternoon in. I use the Fisher-Price binoculars we bought for Rob when he was small. I don't know where the proper binoculars have got to. I can hardly ask Malcolm. He'd want to know what I was using them for. The rubber eye pads have grown brittle with age. They pinch the soft skin around the bridge of my nose. I press against them hard. The pain keeps me sharp. I spin the little plastic wheel to focus the lenses. The horizon comes swimming in and out. I hold my husband in the center of each eye. He is a smudged black blur, an elderly man in a green waxed jacket, then a smudge once more. I sweep my gaze along the horizon. The beach becomes a thick oil painting and Malcolm a fleck of paint slurred against the sky. He has his back to me. He is barely there. I am watching him. He is watching the ocean. He is always watching the ocean. There is something out there he's trying to learn. I've offered to walk with him, but he doesn't want company. He says it's cold outside and likely to rain. He says this firmly, as if we have different standards for the weather and I am not as hardy as he is.

Malcolm has forgotten how it was before. I say forgotten, though I suspect he's chosen not to remember. I used to swim every morning in the same pinching sea. Before Rob, the ocean was my space. My separate time. When we first retired and bought the bungalow, we were spending every minute together. We went straight from weekends and evenings to twenty-four/seven, and this proved too much for me. I loved Malcolm, but it was harder to love him when he was always there, hovering. The sea became my excuse. Each morning the cold waves swallowed me up. They cleared my head and emptied me out, then spat me back onto the beach sharp and steady-minded, ready for the day ahead. I learned how to lean on the sea. I became evangelistic about it. I told anyone who'd listen how much it helped. "It's not just good for you physically," I said. "It's great for your mental health too." I actually used the words "mental health." I'd been reading all sorts of articles. I knew the lingo.

I told Rob. I told him so many times I wore him down. He was already coming apart. It didn't take much to wear him down. By this stage he'd moved back in with us. Work had given him extended leave. He'd put the flat up for rent. I had not seen him this fragile since the divorce, but Malcolm said it was a good sign. He was asking for help. This meant he wanted to get better. I chose to believe Malcolm, though sometimes, when I stood at the window watching our son pace round the garden in long, anxious loops, I felt like I was looking at the situation through the wrong end of the binoculars. I was very much afraid. I wanted to help Rob. No, that's not quite right. I wanted to fix him. But this was not a thing I could fix, as I'd once set to fixing his grazed knees with kisses and waterproof Band-Aids.

"Come swimming," I said, over and over again, till he finally agreed. He was a good swimmer; not fast, but strong. He took to the ocean. He said the cold shock of it made him feel alive again. He said it was helping. I needed to believe him when he said this.

We swam separately. Sea swimming was an act like prayer, best practiced alone. I never once asked Malcolm if he wanted to come swimming. Back then he was the one preaching caution. It was always too cold or too windy for the beach. There was rain forecast or the possibility of a storm sweeping across the channel from Scotland. I was to be careful and cautious and sensible. He would prefer it if I did not go. I almost always went anyway. Reassuring Malcolm became part of my routine, no less familiar than squeezing into my Marks & Spencer one-piece or, afterward, rinsing the salt water out of my hair. "I'll be grand," I'd say. Every morning, regular as high tide, Malcolm would reply, "But what if you're not?" Then I'd place both hands on his shoulders, going up on the balls of my feet, flip-flops gaping, as I kissed him squarely on the forehead and repeated, "I'll be grand," slower the second time, and with more confidence.

He'd see me to the bottom of the garden, stopping every so often to twist the dead heads off flowers, so it looked as if he'd come out for the plants' sake. Forty-five minutes later he'd be waiting with a mug of tea when I came shivering back through the front door. We had a signal for the tea. The signal was me putting on my red toweling bathrobe. Malcolm couldn't pick me out with any clarity. The coastline was a quarter mile away, and he was increasingly shortsighted. Still, he'd stand at the living room window waiting for the red blur of my bathrobe to begin moving up the beach, at which point he'd put the kettle on. Once we were sat in our customary positions in front of the fire, he'd always say the same thing: "So, the sea didn't get the better of you, then?" and I'd always reply, "Not today, my love." Then he'd say, "Sure, there's always tomorrow." We'd hold off on our first sips of tea till we had this ritual by us.

After Rob, it was no longer possible to talk about the sea lightly or with humor. In fairness, we could not talk flippantly about anything else either. After Rob, I lost the sea. I let Malcolm have it. I did not want it anymore.

◆◆

I see Malcolm before he notices me. He is picking his way slowly through the sand dunes. He's hunched over himself like a much older man. The dog slouches behind him. If this were a scene from a television ad, the pair of them would be advertising chronic pain relief or antidepressants. The voice-over would ask, "Do you feel like you just can't go on?"

The sun shifts behind the clouds, and there is a moment—a tiny heart-blip of a beat—when my eyes deceive me and it isn't Malcolm I see coming over the dunes. It's our son returning from his morning swim. If Rob got his face from me, then he inherited Malcolm's walk. It was in the child's bones. The first time he hauled himself up on the sofa's edge and tottered forward, I saw it. He already looked defeated. That weariness never left him. It was there in his school photos and the way he sat at a dinner table, noticeably slumped. When he finally managed to graduate, he hauled it with him across the stage. It was impossible to tell if he was happy in this moment or simply resigned. Like his father, Rob was never content in himself. It took him years to admit this, but I knew. I always knew. It did not make me love him less. I'd been with Malcolm for such a very long time. I was used to loving defeated men.

I thought the swimming would help. If the water couldn't cure him, perhaps it might wear down the hurt in him like a shell reduced to shingle. For a few weeks last year, when Rob's mood seemed lighter and he was inclined to linger in the kitchen chatting while I prepared dinner, I believed the sea was helping him. This was not the case. My son was sick in a way that could not be fixed with water. Though he told his father the ocean relaxed him and added a second early-evening swim to his regular morning dip, though he swam farther and harder and longer each day, this was not a sign of recovery. He was not getting any better. Malcolm will tell you that Rob was getting better just before he left us. I'm not sure if he actually believes this. I know the truth. I can't unknow it. I've read Rob's letter. "Dear Mum and Dad, I'm so sorry." The ocean did not take my boy. My boy gave himself to the water; a little more each day, until finally, he reached the end of himself and could not find a way back.

When Malcolm eventually spots me, he stops in his tracks. "Stay where you are," he shouts. I freeze. It's months since my husband last spoke with any authority. Malcolm's never been decisive, but these last few months, he's been fumbling his way through even the smallest decisions. I catch him standing over his sock drawer, staring at the balled-up socks like there might be serious repercussions associated with choosing the wrong pair. He is slothlike in his movements, dull and fuzzy, as if anesthetized. I'd suspect drink if the grief hadn't left me similarly lethargic. It's worst in the morning when even the slightest gesture feels gluey. In the morning, our voices struggle to gruff their way out. My husband has not raised his voice above a quiet mumble since the day after Rob's funeral. Even then his fury was misplaced.

Malcolm has always loathed a scene, so that afternoon, when I heard the loud of him thundering down the hallway, I knew something in him had come apart. I excused myself from the sympathetic mourners supping tea in our living room and stood outside the office door listening to him rant. I was waiting—just waiting—to intervene if an intervention proved necessary. It did not take me long to work out that Malcolm was on the phone with someone official: the coroner, perhaps, or the coroner's assistant. "Are you trying to tell me I don't know my own son?" he said. He was not yet screaming, but the possibility of a scream was there in the way his voice fractured on the word "son." "I don't care what your report says. Rob would never do that to us. He wouldn't put his mother through it."

I let Malcolm yell. I didn't think it would help. If he was shouting, he couldn't be listening, and he needed to listen to what this stranger was saying. Still, it was neither the time nor the place for straight talking. There were people—friends and extended family—eating buttered scones in our living room, and I didn't want them to hear. I pulled the office door to and returned to our guests. When Malcolm appeared five minutes later, he was flushed from shouting.

"Who was on the phone?" I asked.

"Nobody," he said.

He has not raised his voice since.

Malcolm is shouting now. Specifically, he is shouting at me. "I mean it," he yells, "don't come any closer."

My feet aren't listening. They're moving toward him. I am angry. I am also concerned and a little disgusted. He is stooped over, holding something in his arms. I know what he's holding, though I do not want to know. My stomach heaves. His arms are cupped round the whole slithering mess of it. He looks like he's cradling a baby; holding it uneasily in the way men unaccustomed to holding babies will carry them, low and loose, like a rugby ball.

"Put them down," I say. "Just let them go." I try to keep my voice calm but insistent. I do not want to panic him.

He turns his back to me. He's like a child hiding his guilt. This movement grates against an old memory and sticks. Rob, aged three or four, caught with a mouthful of Christmas chocolates, turning away from me so I could not see and punish him. I did not punish him. I only said, "You mustn't hide things from me, son." I never punished Rob; never raised my voice or told him off. Perhaps I should have been firmer with the boy. It might have helped. I can't be firm with Malcolm either. I'm scared of crushing him. The wind rushing across the sand dunes has flung his hair forward, exposing a white circle of baldness. He is so old;

so frail and pitiful. It is not good to pity your husband. *How can I be with a pitiful man?*

I take him by the shoulders and turn him slowly toward me. I am gentle with him. I used to touch my father like this at the end, when I could no longer see the man in him. I would pull my husband toward me, but the jellyfish are in the way. He's clutching them against his chest: huge, slobbering handfuls of them. They're dribbling down the front of his pullover, running in thick snottery trails through his fingers, dripping onto the ground at his feet. He stands in the middle of the mess he's made. He cannot look me in the eye.

"Oh, Malcolm," I say, "what have you done?"

He still won't raise his head, though he opens his arms and lets the last of the jellyfish go slippering down his chest and legs. They make a vile slurping noise as they settle between us. We are standing on either side of the jellyfish now, our boots toeing the edge of the pile. I do not know how we have arrived at this point. I do not know how to back away.

"Why?" I say, glancing down, then up to hold my husband's gaze.

Malcolm begins to cry. The tears on his cheeks are sleek and slimy. I wish he'd stop.

"I'm getting rid of the jellyfish," he says, "so they won't hurt anybody else."

"Right," I say. I nod like I understand. I do and I don't.

I take my husband's poor blistered hands in mine. They are red raw and swollen. I hold them tightly, though I know it must hurt. I lead him through the sand dunes and up the garden path, to our front door and the silence beyond. I do not say anything more about the jellyfish. It's not necessary. I know they'll stop now. There will be no more nasty surprises in the rosebushes. By the end of the week, Malcolm will have found something else to blame for Rob: the freak currents which circle beneath the surface of the bay, the weather, the water, the lifeguards who do not patrol this particular stretch of the beach, the last thing he ate before entering the water, the whiskey we drank the previous night. Me. It is only a matter of time before Malcolm settles upon blaming me. Perhaps I'll know what to say to him then.

# MOSTLY PEOPLE JUST THROW BRICKS

You are late for work. Not massively so. Monday mornings are always brutal. You hit snooze twice instead of once. Those seven minutes are the difference between catching the 8:08 and the 8:12. The 8:12 stops at every hole in the road. You don't have time to swing by Pret. The caffeine lag kicks in as you run upstairs. You apologize your way into the boardroom. The meeting's already in full swing. In fact, the meeting's almost over. All the decent assignments have been assigned.

Isak's bagged the Capitol riots. No surprises there. Isak's sleeping with the subeditor. Larissa's covering the landslide shot. Somewhere in Asia or East Africa, pure arse-end-of-nowhere stuff. You squint at the people in the photo. It's hard to tell what color they are. Larissa'll know. She'll have asked for the landslide specifically. She's twenty-seven and American, which is to say overeager. You've covered your fair share of natural disasters. The mud. The mosquitoes and Red Cross rations. The all-pervading stench of death. Larissa's more than welcome to it.

You had your eye on Greece. *Such a powerful image,* you were going to say, *it's the juxtaposition of the sunbathing tourists and the bodies drifting in on the tide. Those poor people deserve to have their stories told.* You don't not care about asylum seekers. This isn't the same as actually caring. You wanted Greece because Greece is sunny. It's six months since you last saw sun. But Jamal has managed to get in there before you. Some bullshit line about empathy. Jamal likes to play the foreigner card. Which is rich, considering he's a Hackney boy. You're from Leeds. In London terms, this puts you on a par with real immigrants.

With Greece off the table, Belfast is the only thing left. Belfast or the vigil for the murdered girl. They've gone with the photo of Kate Middleton laying flowers. Country-casual getup. Light makeup. No Covid mask. In your opinion, not the strongest image. But the editor's a royalist.

"I can do Belfast," you announce. At least Belfast's somewhere. Clapham Common's only down the road.

"You don't have a choice," says the editor. "Sam's got childcare issues. I can't expect her to travel to another country."

"Belfast's not another country," says Larissa.

The editor pretends she hasn't heard. Sam was on *Woman's Hour* two months ago discussing motherhood and workplace discrimination. She called herself Annie and did a funny thing with her voice, but everybody still knew it was her. Management's been on eggshells since.

"Cool," you say. "I'll cover the burning-baby shot."

You lift the Belfast photo off the table. You've seen it a hundred times before. The boys with football scarves wound round their mouths. The peace line looming in the foreground. The adults flanking either side. The baby temporarily suspended overhead. It looks like a comet or a shooting star, hot red flames trailing from its toes. You look again, resisting the urge to romanticize. It mostly looks like a petrol bomb. It's a cracking photo. Ten times more interesting than Kate Middleton.

"Now," says the editor, "you all know the drill. Two thousand words on the story behind the photograph. Get over there. Talk to the people on the street. Give me something new; an angle we haven't covered yet. You should be thanking your lucky stars. You're all working with actual humans this year."

Larissa glances at you, confused. It's her first "World Press Photo of the Year" gig. You lean over to whisper, "Last year, Simone got lumbered with the polar bear on the melting iceberg . . . You know that shot?" Larissa nods sympathetically. "Tough gig," she says.

"Okay," says the editor, dismissing the five of you with a queenly wave, "off you all go. Copy deadline's midnight on Thursday. Try not to get yourselves killed."

And off you go. First to your desk, where your emergency rucksack is stashed. You keep the essentials packed and ready: passport, toothbrush, pants and pens, packet of Tetley in case they send you overseas. You train to Gatwick, booking a flight on the easyJet app. £49.99. You do the sums. It's significantly cheaper than a train ticket home. *Why isn't everybody going to Belfast?* Why indeed? You only book one way for now. You've no idea how you'll get on with the locals. They're a grim-looking breed when they're on the telly, not unlike the Glasgow contingent, and you know firsthand it's pure torture getting Glaswegians to talk to the press. If this lot are forthcoming, you could be in and out in a single day. If not, you're looking at a budget hotel. Expenses won't stretch to a fancy place. It'll be an Ibis, a Premier Inn, or a Travelodge. It is impossible not to feel tragic waking up in a Travelodge. It's the showers that wreck you: the single wall-mounted dispenser of shampoo, conditioner, and shower gel in one. You prefer to treat your hair and genitals as separate entities. It's a basic dignity thing.

Belfast is ugly from the air. The city's a grayscape of building sites. The lough, a hungry gulping mouth. You pick out the cranes—two yolk-yellow staples—squatting on the water's edge. A green-pond park swims up to meet you. The airplane judders and, just like that, you're on the ground. The airport's provincial, to say the least. It is constructed chiefly from Portakabins and corrugated tin. Inside's rocking a nineties leisure-center aesthetic, back when primary colors were in. The walls are lined with floor-to-ceiling *Game of Thrones* stills and advertisements for those yellow crisps. Shots of Rory McIlroy swinging away. All pixelated. All dog-earing at the corners where the laminate's peeling off. It's like stepping back in time, though not far enough to be considered charming. It is simply out of date.

You show the taxi driver the photo on your mobile.

"You know it's not a real baby?" he says.

"'Course I know," you reply. "People don't set real babies on fire."

The taxi driver doesn't reply.

"Can you take me there?" you say. "To the place where the photo was taken."

"All right," he says. "I'm guessing you're press."

When you nod, he launches into a speech about growing up on the Falls Road during the Troubles. Tourists probably love this shit. It's not what you're after this afternoon. You've Wikipedia'd the Troubles on the plane. And you've watched both series of *Derry Girls*. You did your best to read the novel that won the big prize. Your official take was "groundbreaking, brave, a worthy winner." Unofficially, you couldn't make head nor tail of it. You wouldn't have given her the Booker yourself. You thought the woman couldn't write. You know more than most about Northern Ireland. Enough for a short human interest piece. You don't require a taxi driver's ten cents on the NI Protocol. You stop him midflow, placing a cautionary hand on his shoulder.

"That's so interesting," you say. "I was wondering if you knew any of the people in the photo. I'm looking to talk to them."

You pass your phone into the front. He steers one-handed while he manipulates the screen, enlarging the photo till it pixelates, scrolling slowly from one face to the next. "Aye," he says eventually, "I know Declan there. Good lad, so he is. He coaches the under-sixteens team."

"Football?"

"Aye, football," says the driver. It seems you've asked a ludicrous question, though you know there are all sorts of unconventional sports played here. There's Gaelic football and some mad thing with big flat-headed sticks.

"Do you know where I could find Declan?"

The taxi driver checks the time on his dashboard. "He'll be down the Astroturf, coaching, I'd say. My nephew trains with him three times a week. I could drop you there."

◆◆

Declan is far from enthusiastic. "You know it's not a real baby?" he says as soon as you produce the photograph.

"I know," you say. "But a burning baby's not the first thing you expect to see at a riot. Mostly people just throw bricks. It must've been a shock to see that come sailing over the wall."

Declan shrugs. "I didn't see it," he says, "I'd me eye on them pair of boyos up the front."

He points out two boys in North Face jackets, their hoods drawn up over their heads, green scarves bandaged across their mouths. One's got his fists raised like a boxer. The other's captured with his arm shot out in front of him, seconds after chucking something. The missile's already passed out of frame.

"The two of them play for us," Declan continues. "They're not bad wee fellas. They just don't know what to be at. I was down there that night trying to get them to wise up, me and a couple of the youth workers from the community center up the road. I'd me eye on them when the baby appeared."

You stare at the photo, focusing in on Declan's face. His forehead is concertina'd in deep frustration. He's yelling something. You couldn't say what.

"Look," he says, "all sorts of things came over the wall that night. Bricks, petrol bombs, bottles. At one stage, the other lot tried to ram a car through the gate. I wasn't really paying attention. I was there for the lads. It was only when the women started screaming that I noticed the baby lying on the ground. I knew straight away it was only a doll. Its face had melted. A real baby's face wouldn't've melted. And it didn't sound like a baby either. I knew right away it wasn't real."

"What do you mean it didn't sound like a baby?"

"It was making this god-awful racket, shrieking and beeping like how a fire alarm goes when the batteries run out."

You write this down: "Baby. Melty face. Fire alarm. Batteries." It's the first you've heard about a noise. No wonder the women were hysterical. It must've seemed like something possessed. You take another look at the photo. It could be an artist's impression of hell. You have other questions, but Declan's itching to get away. There are two dozen boys in football kits waiting for him down on the pitch.

"Thanks, Declan," you say. "Here, before you run off, would it be possible to talk to one of the lads in the photo? Just a quick word. No names printed or anything. Are they here?"

You can tell they are from the way his eyes dart toward the pitch. You know to press on. It's instinctual. You've been at this game for twenty-odd years. *Maintain eye contact. Pitch your voice low. Lean in like the pair of you are old pals.*

"Honestly, just five minutes, mate. It'd be good to get their perspective before I head over to the other side."

Eventually, Declan agrees. "Give me a second, I'll ask. Though I can't guarantee they'll play ball." A minute later, you're face-to-face with the two boys from the photograph. They could be anything between twelve and twenty. They're small and pasty, sharp round the eyes. Both are dressed in the same black kit, the same zip-up hoodie and Reebok trainers. They're sporting identical haircuts, short on the sides and floppy on top. One's three inches taller. Otherwise, you'd struggle to tell them apart.

"Deccy says you're asking about the burning baby," says the short one.

"Yeah," you say, "I'm a journalist. Is there anything you can tell me about that night?"

"Aye," says the short one, "we didn't chuck any babies over the peace wall. Go and talk to them bastards on the other side."

"Yeah," says the taller one, "fuck away off."

You offer them money, but they're not for talking. They only came over to make a point. They spit on the ground next to your shoes, then turn and swagger back to the Astroturf. Declan catches your eye from the side of the pitch. He shrugs as if to say *Sorry* or maybe *Told you so*. The fat lad in goal gives you the finger. You wonder if it's because you're English or because you are a journalist. They're teenage boys. They're probably the same with everyone.

It's too late to do anything else tonight. You book a room in the Ibis by the university. Unsurprisingly, it's almost empty. There are no tourists about this year. You ask for a room with a window. They give you a room on the second floor. It has a view of next door's industrial wheelie bin. It smells of bleach and hot plastic. The remote is missing. You watch the first ten minutes of *The One Show*. You can't be arsed to get up and switch to something else. You decide you will go out to eat. It's takeaway only, so you take away. You are careful to spend all twenty-five pounds of the budget allowed for a main evening meal. It's a challenge to spend twenty-five quid in a chippie, but you don't for a minute consider scrimping. Expenses should always be spent in full.

You eat outside in the drizzle, sitting on the steps of a church. You only make it through half the food. You still eat enough to make yourself sick. You look for a bin. No bin is apparent. You bag your rubbish and leave it propped against the door. After half a block, you return and move it to a more neutral spot: the ladies' hair salon, opposite. You don't want your littering misinterpreted as a hate crime. They're funny about churches here.

You walk back to the hotel and throw up in the toilet. Half-digested battered fish. Battered onions. And the battered Mars bar which proved to be the tipping point. Brown and lumpen, it bobs around in the toilet water. It's so shitlike that just looking at it provokes another tide of boke. You fall asleep on top of the sheets, lard-drunk and greasy in your clothes. You dream of burning babies. Actual babies. You wake up wondering where you are.

"Belfast." It's written in a jaunty scrawl across the wall behind reception: all loose loops and funky ink blots. The font is trying way too hard. It might work in Zagreb or Barcelona, someplace sunny and quick to smile. Belfast's got more of a Times New Roman vibe. Drizzly. Stolid. Skeptical.

"Just the one night?" the receptionist asks.

"God, yes," you confirm.

You begin on the other side of the peace line, stopping people in the street. Nobody wants to talk to you. You can hardly blame them. In their position, you'd run a mile to get away from yourself. You home in on a trio of old boys sitting on a bench. You clock their walking sticks from a distance, the arthritic Yorkie curled at their feet. They won't be able to run away.

"Excuse me, gents. Are you locals?"

All three nod. The one in the flatcap glares up from behind his bifocals. He cuts straight to the chase. "We're not giving you any money," he says.

You smile. You laugh. The laugh pooters out like a suppressed fart.

"I'm not after money," you say. "I'm a journalist. Can you tell me anything about this photo? Please."

You hold up your phone. They squint at it.

"I can't see anything on that footery wee screen," says Flatcap. "What's it of?"

"It was taken at the riots a few months back. There's a couple of young lads stood at the peace line and a burning baby flying through the air."

"It's not a real baby," says Flatcap.

"It's a doll," adds one of his mates.

You pretend that this is news to you. You take pains to write it down in your notebook. They need to see you're a journalist. "I see," you say, "and do you know anyone in the photo?"

Flatcap makes a sort of donkey noise. "Hrrrmmmpphh," he says, wet lips flapping as he lets the air come sniding out, "that's the other side of the peace line. I wouldn't know them fellas from Adam . . . or Gerry Adams, I should say." He laughs at his own wit, a dry, wheezy laugh. The other two harmonize.

"I could tell you who chucked it, though," says the one with the dog.

"Really?" you say. "That'd be great." You double-click your biro. You raise your notebook in anticipation. You are practically Lois Lane.

"Now, I don't know the lad's name, but his mother works in the SPAR and he has a sister who cuts hair in the place opposite the bookies. They're either Andersons or Allens. Actually, the name could be Agnew. It starts with an A, anyway. You'll get him over on the other side of the park where the young ones hang out. Just say you're looking for the fella that chucked the babby. Somebody'll point him out."

You approach four dozen boys before you find Corey. They soon begin to blur into one homogeneous Belfast teen. Black trackies. Black T-shirt. Black North Face jacket. E-cigarette in one hand. Mobile in the other. Can of Monster propped between their feet. They're dotted all across the park. Gathered in fours and awkward fives around a bench or bit of wall. They stand fifteen feet from a composite handful of girls. Not really talking; associated, nonetheless. You call out your mission as you approach. Tentatively. Notebook visible. Doing your best to look the part.

Half the time you get no response. Or somebody mutters, "It wasn't a real baby," and you know you won't get anything more. One lad fires an empty can at your head. He tells you what you can do with your bastarding English self. You don't understand. You were under the impression they liked the English on this side. The Queen's face beams down from every other gable wall.

It's lunchtime before one of them finally helps you out. "It's Corey you're after. He's usually hanging around the swings. He's not a pedo or nothing. His girlfriend's got a wee one, so she does." You give this lad a tenner and what's left of your cigarettes. He pockets them quickly so the others won't see.

Corey doesn't want to talk. He's trying to put the photo behind him. It hasn't gone down well with his mother. Or his big sister. Or the ones in school. "I got suspended for it," he says, "and my girlfriend nearly finished with me. She still doesn't see the funny side." He glances over at her as he's explaining. "She says it's different when you've weans yourself. Things like that aren't funny anymore." You nod knowingly, implying that you have children of your own. You watch his girlfriend pushing a chubby toddler on the swings. Neither of them looks to be having any fun.

You ask if they've been together long.

"Aye," says Corey, "two and a half months."

"Congratulations," you say. Two and a half months is a decade in teenage years. "Well, I don't want to get you in trouble or anything. I'm only after ten minutes of your time. I'd make it worth your while."

You feel like a big fat cliché saying this, but you know it's what he expects you to say. You fish in your pocket for an envelope. Fifty quid. In used fivers. Folded, so it feels like more than it actually is.

"You could take your girlfriend out," you say, "or buy something nice for her wee lad."

"It's a girl," he says. "Lily-Rose. It just looks like a boy 'cause its hair won't grow. Lisa's for getting its ears pierced so people can tell."

You hold the envelope under his nose. You keep it pinched firmly between finger and thumb until you hear him say, "All right. I'll talk, but only if you promise not to print my real name."

You nod. "No problem at all." It's common practice; half the people you interview aren't themselves.

"Can I be called something like Timothy?" he asks.

"Absolutely," you reply. "Timothy it is." You can backtrack later. He'll be Kyle or Dean when it goes to print.

You start with the basics.

*How old is he?* Fifteen, coming sixteen in July.

*Is he still in school?* Most of the time. Though this year's weird. "Teachers can't tell if you're there when it's online," he says. "They're not that bothered. It's easier on them if we don't show up."

*How did he get involved in the riots?* Corey's eye drifts toward his girlfriend. She's opening a packet of Wotsits for the child. You look at him. He's gone a bit swimmy around the eyes. You know this look. He's going to give you something profound. About having no prospects and wanting a future and dreaming of something better than this. He'll say it in his own words, of course—mostly things he's heard other people saying—but you can lick it into shape.

You repeat the question. "Why did you get involved in the riots, Corey?"

He grins. His eyes are sleepy-sharp again. He scuffs at the tarmac with the toe of his trainer. "It was something to do, wasn't it? Everybody else was at it. I didn't want to be missing out."

"What about issues with the PSNI and Bobby Storey's funeral? What about Brexit and the Protocol? Did any of those factors influence you?"

"Aye," says Corey, "all that shit. That's what we were rioting about."

"Do you think the riots achieved anything?"

"Dunno. You'd have to ask somebody else about that. We were getting somewhere. Then your man died. Prince what's-his-name. I'm sorry for the Queen and all, but I don't understand why we had to stop."

You jot this down. You're wondering how you'll get two thousand words out of it.

"What about the baby?" you ask, changing tack. "Where did you get the baby from?"

"It wasn't a—"

"I know," you say. "Still, I'm guessing you didn't bring a doll to a riot. Unless . . . is that something people do around here?" Having spent twenty-four hours in Belfast, nothing surprises you anymore.

"Naw," says Corey. "I just brung myself and a scarf for my face. And a couple of empty bottles I lifted from the recycling bin. They said on Facebook to bring any bottles you had lying around."

"For petrol bombs."

"No, mate, they were for teaching us how to make lemonade . . ."

You smile. You force yourself to laugh. You had not thought

him capable of wit. "The baby," you say, "tell me a bit more about it?"

"What sort of stuff do you want to know?"

"Anything. Everything. Where did it come from? Who did it belong to? How did you end up throwing it?"

"Well, it wasn't mine, obviously. There were all these wee girls just standing around, taking videos on their mobiles. I knew some of them from school. Sasha McKeown and a couple of her mates. One of them—Chloe—had the baby. I could tell it wasn't real from the way she was carting it about. She had its head clamped under her arm. I thought it was a bit weird, because Chloe's my wee sister's age. She's far too old to be playing with dolls. Then the doll started gurning, and it wasn't a normal baby noise. It was like a machine or something. Everybody was telling her to shut it up. Chloe wasn't bothered. Not one bit. She just laughed. 'You know what weans are like,' she says, 'you just have to let them cry it out.'

"Some of the older ones were getting really pissed. There were all these newspeople filming stuff. The stupid doll was taking their attention away. Somebody must've got the baby off Chloe and pitched it down the road. I looked down and there it was, lying at my feet. I didn't think. When you're rioting, you just chuck whatever comes to hand. I picked it up, and once I was holding it, it just seemed right to put my lighter to it. It went up like a firebomb. *Whoosh.* I wasn't expecting that. I was feared of setting my trackies on fire. I just wanted to chuck that thing as far away as I could."

This is better. Much better. You press on. "Did you consider how it would look on the other side: a burning baby flying over the wall?"

"No," says Corey, "like I said, I wasn't thinking."

You look at his face. You focus in on his mouth. It's twitching slightly at the corners. He's only giving you half the truth.

"And afterward, did you feel bad?"

"No," says Corey. "Not one bit. Don't be putting this in your article—my girlfriend'll have the balls off me—but I'm glad I done it. That photo's cracking, so it is. The look on their faces. They're pissing themselves. You can tell they actually thought it was real."

This is golden. You scribble it down, knowing full well you'll run it verbatim. Corey's fifteen. He won't lodge a complaint. You are basically home and dry.

"Do you know the girl's second name? Chloe what?"

"Chloe Millar. She lives two streets over from us."

"Do you think she'd talk to me?"

"Chloe'll talk to anybody. Especially if you're flashing the cash."

Corey doesn't have Chloe's number, but another tenner coerces his girlfriend into texting her. The reply comes back almost instantly. Chloe's happy enough to chat—three thumbs-up emojis in a row. But she's not about this evening—sad face, crying face, sad face again. She does Sunday to Wednesday at her dad's in Carryduff. She'll be back tomorrow, after school. She'll meet you next to McDonald's. There is no specific emoji for this, so you get a burger, an ice cream, and another thumbs-up. You phone the Ibis immediately and secure a room for a second night. It's fifteen quid more than yesterday. Apparently, there's a late-booking fee.

"Do you want the same room as before?" the receptionist asks.

You feel strangely loyal to the shitty room on the second floor. "Okay," you say. Another night without a remote. Another night of the hot-plastic smell, which may well be general throughout the hotel.

It is still raining. There are limited indoor eating options. You can dine in your room or perch inside a plastic bus shelter. You go for the room. It offers a certain degree of privacy and doesn't smell of yesterday's piss. You buy a Tesco meal deal for dinner and spend the remainder of your expenses on household basics for your larder at home—instant coffee, packets of soup, chocolate Hobnobs, and a large bag of basmati rice—stuffing it all inside your rucksack. You feel smug each time you look at your bag, bloated and bulging in the corner. You've saved half your grocery bill for the week.

You eat in bed with the telly on. It is stuck on BBC NI. Some sort of politics-themed chat show. Two men are shouting at two other men while a fifth man attempts to maintain order. He isn't shouting and therefore is not being heard. Three of the five men are extremely red in the face, like alcoholics or sunburned farmers. Four are significantly overweight. All are sporting jaunty socks. You rise and mute the television. You try to work out what they're saying without the sound. The show is significantly more entertaining when viewed this way. You fall asleep with the telly on and dream about politicians with baby faces and tiny babies with politician faces. All their faces are on fire.

You wake to a text message from Jamal. He's sent a photo. A beach in Greece. His hairy legs plunged shin-deep into blue water. The sand is bleached white from too much sun. The accompanying message reads: "Taking it for the team." You scooch the curtains open and snap a picture of next door's wheelie bin in the rain. "Another day in paradise."

You have almost a whole day to waste in Belfast. This would be difficult at the best of times. With everything closed and the rain unceasing, it's an eternity you're looking at. You spend an hour in Boots, another in Lidl. You loiter on a petrol station forecourt until someone comes out and tells you to piss off. You walk up and down the aisles in Tesco, considering what everything costs. Things are cheaper here than they are in London, but there's not the same variety. Just after two, you walk up the hill, out of the city. You're half an hour early for Chloe, but you've run out of ways to distract yourself.

Chloe is in her school uniform, a gloriously ugly mud-brown getup. She's accessorized it with big gold hoops. They spiral viciously from her ears.

"All right?" she says, and plonks down beside you. "Twenty quid and I'll tell you whatever you want to know."

You have fifty ready to give her. It's in an envelope in your inner pocket. You're not about to tell her this. You get your wallet out and remove two tenners.

"Cheers," she says, "what d'you want to know?"

"Tell me about the baby," you say. "Where did it come from?"

Chloe laughs. She takes out her phone and pulls up a picture of herself cradling a doll in a pale pink babygro. "There she is, wee Lizzie. That's what we called her, anyway. She's one of them dolls they used to give girls to put them off getting pregnant. My ma found her up in the roof space a few months back. My ma used to teach HE in the Tech."

"And your mum gave Lizzie to you?"

Chloe nods.

"Was she worried about you getting pregnant?"

Chloe picks at the polish on her fingernails. It's a particularly arresting shade of yellow: fluorescent, like a highlighter pen. It matches the green streaks in her hair.

"Did your mum have you when she was young, Chloe? Is that why she gave you the dolly?"

Chloe looks up at you with her big doll eyes, inexpertly rimmed in kohl. "My ma was fourteen when she had our Tanya. It was awful for her, so it was. By the time she was twenty, there were four of us. All our dads had buggered off. She worked her ass off, so she did. Two jobs and night college on top of work just so she could get her teaching degree. She practically starved herself to put food on the table. All credit to her, we never went hungry, and she always made sure we were clean. She didn't want nobody looking down on us. She made us girls promise not to make the same mistakes as her. Not that Tanya paid any attention. She had wee Noah when she was fifteen. That's why my ma got Lizzie out of the roof space: to knock a bit of sense into me."

You're scribbling madly to keep up with Chloe. "You said your mum was fourteen when she had your sister. Can I ask where her parents were?"

"My ma was in care. Her mammy and daddy got blown up in a bomb back when the Troubles were on. There was nobody left to take her in."

You couldn't have written this better yourself. You are picturing the editor's face when you present her with the backstory to end all backstories. "It's a new spin on *Angela's Ashes,*" you'll say, anticipating a follow-up article: the mother, the sister, intergenerational trauma spread out over three and a half thousand words. You try to rein your excitement in. Sympathy is required. You force yourself to think sad thoughts: your nice granny dying, the Christmas special of *Call the Midwife,* the time you left your laptop on the Tube.

"I'm so sorry to hear that, Chloe," you say. "Your family's been through an awful lot."

The head goes down. You can't see her face. *Dear God,* you think, *please don't cry.* Maybe you'll give her the extra fifty quid anyway.

"So, I'm guessing you'd been carrying Lizzie around all day," you say, changing the subject as best you can. "If I remember right, you can't leave those dolls for even a second. Is that why you took her to the riot?"

Chloe nods.

"And was your mum upset about what happened? She must have heard. She's probably seen the photographs."

"Naw," says Chloe. The head comes up, and you can see she's grinning. "My ma thought it was hilarious."

You pause, pen hovering over your notebook. "Hilarious?" you say.

"Aye, she was for chucking Lizzie in the bin anyway. She was redding out the roof space when she found her. And I was all like 'Ma, don't be throwing that out. You could put it on eBay. It's probably worth something. I don't think they make them anymore.' Did you ever see that program *16 and Pregnant*? It used to be on years ago."

You nod. You're not sure where this is going now.

"Me and my mates watch it all the time. You can get it on one of them catch-up channels. It's hilarious, so it is. They give out those dolls to the pregnant ones so they know what they're in for when their babbies arrive. Anyway, when my ma found Lizzie, I thought the girls would get a kick out of her. We were all going down to the riots, so I brought Lizzie with me. It was grand until she started gurning. When they cry, there's no way to turn them off."

"Hold on," you say. "You said your mum gave you the doll because she didn't want you getting pregnant."

"I did," says Chloe. "Sometimes I lie."

"Was your mum even a teenage mother?"

"Naw. She was twenty-five when she had our Tanya. She never got her figure back after that."

"And was she ever taken into care?"

Chloe shakes her head, smiling.

"And the Troubles?"

"The Troubles really happened. It's on Wikipedia and everything. You can look it up on your phone."

"Yes, I know about the Troubles. What I'm asking is, did you lose your grandparents in a bomb?"

"Naw, Granny Mo's still going strong. Granda had a stroke before I was born."

"Why did you tell me all that crap?"

"For a laugh," she says. She's actually laughing when she says this. "Look at you, drinking it all up."

You put your notebook into your pocket, next to the extra fifty quid. There's no way in hell she's getting it now. You'll use it on a taxi to the airport instead.

"Here, do you want that picture of me and Lizzie?" she asks, holding up her mobile phone. "It'd look good with your article. Give me twenty quid and I'll email it to you."

◆◆

You call the airport. The last flight to London leaves in twenty-five minutes. You haven't a hope of making it. You yell at the woman on the phone. "It's only ten past five. How can there be no more flights to London today? What sort of backward shithole is this?" The woman calmly and pedantically explains that they're currently operating a reduced flight schedule. She hangs up when you start cursing, when you say you'll never be back in Belfast again.

You phone the Ibis. You are asked if you'd like the same room again.

You say, "No. I want a different room tonight. A room with a view. Could you possibly stretch to that?"

"Of course," says the lady on reception, and assigns you the same room on the second floor.

You spend the evening eating takeaway pizza: jumbo, enormous, four-person size, with extra toppings and three sides. You know before you bite into the first greasy slice that you'll spend the latter part of the evening hanging over the toilet bowl.

Just after eight, the subeditor emails to ask how you're getting on. Deadline's looming, and Sam's already filed her copy. Good for Sam. Sam always lands on her bloody feet. You email back, "Brilliant! Fantastic! All good here! Just finishing up. Copy soon." You go back and delete the exclamation marks. The subeditor's not an idiot.

You pull up the photo on your laptop. With the fourth slice of pizza wilting in your hand, you scrutinize each part of the image now that you have hindsight on your side. The boys with football scarves wound round their mouths. The peace wall looming in the foreground. The adults flanking either side. The baby suspended overhead. You scroll through their faces. You try to see what you need to see. Hopelessness. Frustration. Legitimate fear. It's not forthcoming. You look again. The boys are shadows, faceless and nameless. The baby, a ludicrous kind of thing. The bystanders are captured in brute ignorance, not yet understanding what they've seen. Those blank faces might fold into horror, anger, or deep, deep sadness. The next five seconds could go any way. It isn't a moment that's easily written. Nothing in this city is.

You open a Word doc and begin to type, tapping one-handed at the keyboard. "Chloe was born on the Loyalist Shankill Road. Her mother fell pregnant when she was fourteen." You will do your best to make a story out of it. You are a journalist. It is your job.

# BAT McELHATTON LEARNS TO DRIVE

Bat McElhatton doesn't phone ahead. He doesn't even bother texting, though he's more than capable of texting. His brother-in-law—the one who works in the EE shop—has sorted him out with a special mobile: big buttons, raised type, and a speaker setting, which means he gets his messages read to him by a fella who speaks in a weird robot voice. Bat thinks it might actually be a robot; there's that many things it doesn't say right. Like "Ahoghill," which it splits into three separate words: "A-hog-hill." And "lashing," which it doesn't recognize and automatically changes to "clashing." This makes no sense. No sense at all. You wouldn't stay in because it was clashing. It isn't a thing you'd actually say.

Bat McElhatton doesn't phone to say he's coming. If he does, Slim will pretend he isn't in. He'll get his ma to cover for him. *Sorry, son, you've just missed Matthew. He's running a wee message for me.* Even if Slim answers his phone, the minute he hears what Bat's after, he'll be all, *Uch, mate, sorry. If you'd given me a bit of warning.* He'll have somebody wanting to go over three-point turns, or some wee girl panicking because her test's in the morning and she's nowhere near ready for it.

Half the town goes to Slim for driving lessons. He isn't registered or anything. But he has a clean license and his ma's Fiesta, and he only charges a tenner an hour. The real instructors—the ones with signs and foot pedals on the passenger side—charge three times this and sometimes more. Slim doesn't need to. He only gives lessons on the side. His actual job is being a bin man. He also does alloys and puts stereos in. For ten quid, cash in hand, he'll take you down Sainsbury's car park after it shuts or, if you've already got the basics, over to the industrial estate. There's no real traffic round Pennybridge, only other learners and the odd drinks lorry lumbering into the cash-and-carry, slow and heavy as an unmilked cow.

Bat McElhatton times his arrival perfectly. He's standing outside Slim's front door, ringing the bell at precisely five minutes to seven. He knows Slim will have the dinner in him. He'll be sitting with a cup of tea, watching *Hollyoaks* on Channel 4. Slim never misses an episode of *Hollyoaks*. He is what you'd call a superfan. The lads try to wind him up about it—"Sure, it's only wee girls watch *Hollyoaks*"—but you can never get a rise out of Slim. "It's the best thing on the telly," he'll say, "best-looking women, anyway." A few years back, he started calling it *H'oaks* for short.

Slim's ma answers the door. Her name is either Olive or Olivia. Bat can never remember which one it is. To be on the safe side, he always calls her Mrs. Cleaver, and she always responds in the very same way: "Mrs. Cleaver's my mother, and you'll never meet a more bitter auld bitch. You can call me Olive, son." *Or is it Olivia?* Bat can't remember. *Probably Olive.* There are other Olives knocking about. Olive Houston and Olive Clarke, who goes to Slimming World with his ma. Olivia, on the other hand, is a horsey sort of name. You don't get many Olivias round here.

Bat sticks to calling her Mrs. Cleaver. If nothing else, she'll think him polite.

Mrs. Cleaver doesn't even acknowledge Bat. As soon as she clocks him, she turns and gulders over her shoulder: "It's Barry. For you. He's at the door." Barry is Bat McElhatton's actual name. Barry Clifford McElhatton. Barry after somebody his ma went to school with. Clifford for her wee brother, who came off his motorbike and died. His ma knows it's a bit of a mouthful. They're nice enough names, but all together, they don't go. It didn't stop her putting the full whack down on his birth certificate. *Barry Clifford McElhatton.* Sometimes, when he winds her up, she'll pitch all three at him in quick succession—BARRY CLIFFORD McELHATTON—like a series of well-placed blows.

Bat spent fourteen years trying to swap his name for something a bit less rare. In the end, he had to swallow his pride and ask the lads to help him out. You couldn't give yourself a nickname. It wasn't how the system worked. They all had other names themselves. Andy Bell was always Dinger. His wee brother, Curtis, was lumbered with Chime. Chris went by Loaf because all the way up through primary school, he'd got nothing but plain butter sandwiches in his lunch box. They called Steven Thompson, Roastie. At ten, he'd looked like a roast potato. By fourteen, his skin had improved, but the name stuck. Slim was Slim because he was fat. Bat knew he'd never really be one of the lads until he got himself a stupid name. He'd have preferred to have had one thrust upon him, but he wasn't above asking. Life had taught him not to hang back. If you didn't ask, you didn't get.

They were kicking a ball against the back of the community center when he finally brought the matter up. This would have been July or August, five or maybe six years ago.

"Here," Bat said, "I need a nickname. Barry's a shocking thing to be called." They all stopped kicking. He could feel them turning to stare at him. He knew they were shooting looks at each other. Rolling their eyes. Like: *WTF?* Bat could sense when they were doing this.

"What about Baz?" said Roastie. "Baz or Bazzer?"

"Naw, that's shite," said Loaf. "There's millions of Bazzers. We should call him Bat."

"Bat?" asked Slim.

"As in blind as a . . ."

Bat could hear them giving Loaf daggers. A couple of them started scuffing the gravel with their trainer heels. One of them—Dinger, he thought—actually gasped and then tried to turn it into a cough. There were things you could take the piss out of; other things you couldn't touch. Like Loaf's wee brother who wasn't all there. Like Roastie's ma who was always half-cut. And Dinger's birthmark. And Bat being blind.

"It's class," Bat said, "pure genius, mate," before Loaf had a chance to take it back. "I love it, so I do. *Bat McElhatton.* It's got a nice ring to it. Like I could be a paramilitary or something with a name like that. *Watch yourselves lads, or Bat McElhatton'll put your knees in.*"

After that he was always Bat. Or Batters. Or Batman. Or the Bat Controller. There were any number of variations. It was only the mothers—both his own and the lads'—who ever called him Barry these days.

"How's your mother keeping, Barry?" asks Slim's ma. She doesn't pause long enough to let him answer. She keeps right on talking, filling the silence until Slim appears. Bat's used to this. He knows his presence makes people nervous. Sometimes they talk at him, like Slim's ma. Sometimes they ask questions and answer for him, as if he isn't right in the head. It's only happened a couple of times, but the odd eejit has even talked to the dog, hunkering down beside Judith's big furry head to ask her where they're off to or make some comment about the weather. The dog has yet to answer back.

Bat makes no attempt to interrupt. He's here for Slim, not Slim's ma. In the background, he can hear Slim rising from the sofa and turning the telly off, shuffling through the kitchen and down the hall. Mrs. Cleaver keeps talking, gabbing away, until her son is standing at her side. "Is your poor old granny still hanging on? Your ma's a saint, so she is, looking after youse all. Not that you need much looking after these days. Matthew tells me you've got yourself a wee job. It's just answering phones, isn't it? Sure, at least it gets you out of the house. And it's nice to have a bit of money of your own. Good for you, son, that's what I say. You've never let anything hold you back. Your mammy must be powerful proud of you . . . Well, here's our Matthew coming now. Are the pair of youse heading out?"

"Naw," says Slim.

"Aye," says Bat.

Slim's ma beats a tactical retreat. "I'll leave youse to it. *Corrie*'s starting. Tell your mother I was asking for her."

Bat hears her padding back toward the living room, soft footsteps suckering against the lino. He can tell she has the slippers on. Slim comes out and pulls the door behind him. He fumbles in his pocket. Bat hears the lighter nip and flare. Then Slim inhales. Five seconds later, the smoke is up Bat's nose and in his eyes. Slim doesn't speak until after the second drag.

"How's the form?" he says.

"Grand," says Bat. "And yourself?"

"Aye, grand," says Slim, and, having dispensed with the pleasantries, asks his friend what he wants. It's not like Bat to turn up unannounced. With the dog and the vest and everything, it's a whole palaver every time he leaves the house.

"Are you free this evening?" asks Bat. "Like right now?"

Slim is. He's just had a fella cancel on him. He weighs up his options. He'd had no intention of going out. Couple of cans in front of the telly. Maybe nip to the shop for a choc ice later; his ma likes a choc ice for a treat. To be very honest, he's been looking forward to a wee night in. Then again, he's not seen Bat for a week or two. And it's a nice enough evening; too nice for lying about in front of the telly. *Aye,* Slim thinks, *I could be persuaded to head out. A wee dander down the road to McElvey's. A couple of pints. There's worse ways to put an evening in.* He knows Bat always appreciates a bit of company. Since his da passed, it's only him and the ma at home.

"Naw," Slim says, "I've nothing on. Are you up for a pint down the road?"

"Not tonight," says Bat. "I came round to ask you something, Slim. Would you teach me to drive? Obviously, I'll pay for the lessons, whatever's your going rate."

Slim laughs. He takes a long drag on his cigarette, lets the smoke out slowly, and laughs some more. "You crack me up, Batters," he says, and cuffs him fondly around the neck. "Stand you there till I get my jacket. I'll tell Ma, we're away down the pub."

"No. I'm serious, Slim. I want you to teach me how to drive."

Slim tries to squeeze another mouthful of laughter out. It won't come. It sticks in his throat and starts to choke him. Bat's not joking. Slim can tell. He has a way of lifting his chin and looking up when he wants to make a serious point. He thinks he's making eye contact. He's actually looking over Slim's shoulder, talking straight at the wheelie bin. Slim has a final long suck at his cigarette, then screws it out against the pebble dash. He has no notion what to say. Well, he knows fine rightly what he should say. *Wise up, Bat. Have you lost your mind?* But he'll have to phrase it differently; say it kindly, like a woman would say it. Make sure he doesn't annoy poor Bat. For a second, Slim wonders if he should call for his ma.

He's known Bat forever. Literally. Bat lives round the corner, next to the park. When they were babbies, their mas would take them out together, pushing their buggies round the duck pond. Bat's always been the way he is, but he's never forced it on the rest of them. He's always been content enough, hanging around on the edge of things. When they were younger, he never asked for a turn on Roastie's Nintendo or a spin on Dinger's new mountain bike. He just sat there quietly in the background, laughing whenever the rest of them laughed. When they started going out, he never suggested coming with them, up to Kelly's or down the Fort on a Friday night. Bat never asked, so they never offered. They all knew there were some things he couldn't do. They weren't bad to him. In fact, folks often said how good they were; you wouldn't expect it of teenage boys. Their mothers had clearly brought them up well. They'd ask Bat along to the pictures and over to the Showgrounds to watch the Sky Blues. To the pub, where he sat in the midst of their banter, nursing his pint and grinning away. They went out of their way to include Bat when it would've been that much easier to leave him at home.

Slim's always assumed Bat is happy, that being included's enough for him. Sure, he always says he's grand. He's usually smiling. And when somebody's always smiling and saying they're grand, sure, you just assume they are. Bat's never asked for anything before. Slim wonders why the sudden change. Maybe Bat's only now realizing how shite he's actually got it. The big lad's never known anything else. Which is what people say when they see him and Judith, shuttling slowly around the town. "It's a pity of poor Bat McElhatton. God love him, he's always smiling. Sure, he's never known anything else." Nobody would say this to Bat's face. The lads never bring up what's wrong with him. They never ask what it's like or how he feels. Not because they aren't interested; there's a rake of things they'd love to ask. They just don't know how to say them without making Bat feel like a specimen. Even after all this time, they still don't know how to talk to him. Slim wonders if he should've asked years ago, when they first started knocking about. It's easier for weans to say daft things and take them back. Afterward, you can still be friends. It's not that simple when you're older. Everything cuts.

Slim knows Bat's not really looking for driving lessons. He's asking something bigger of him, something that can't be said in words.

He thinks about that summer it never stopped raining when they all hung out in Dinger's garage. They'd built a go-kart using the wheels of his wee sister's pram and a couple of ancient kitchen chairs. They had a fallout—an almighty row—over whose house they'd keep the go-kart in. Roastie said, "Well, it definitely can't stay at Slim's. There's no room for it." And they'd all started saying his house was poky. He didn't even have a garage or any sort of garden for playing in. Slim's house was the smallest house of anybody they knew. Then one of them said it was probably because Slim had no da. Loaf's da wasn't on the scene either, but at least

Loaf knew who he was. He got presents off him for birthdays and Christmas, and sometimes he got took to the caravan. Slim was that cross, he'd chucked a hammer at the go-kart. It left a big crack in the plastic seat. He told them all to go to bloody hell, which didn't sound as good as it had sounded in his head. This made him more raging than he'd been before. He'd stomped away off to sit on the curb. He was nine that summer. Nine was a particularly huffy age. After a few minutes, Bat came out and sat beside him. He didn't say anything out loud. He just sat next to Slim and, after a while, handed him a bit of scrunched-up loo roll. Slim hadn't realized he was crying. He's always wondered how Bat knew.

Bat often notices things the rest of them miss. Not just everyday stuff, like when the weather's about to change or what people mumble when they don't think anyone's listening. He'd phoned to see if Slim was all right when the GCSE results came out and he'd a D in maths instead of a C. Slim knew he wasn't for going back to school, but he was still disappointed about that D. And when his ma got made redundant, and he got looked over for the BB's five-a-side team, the others never mentioned it, but Bat had noticed and said something like, "Uch, mate, that's shit." Which didn't really change anything, but Slim had appreciated it anyway. It was nice to know you weren't being ignored.

Slim has read on the Internet that blind people are better than normal people at using their other senses, mostly hearing and smelling. They figure out ways to compensate for not being able to see. He's not sure if there's any truth in this. Bat's the only blind person he knows, and Bat hasn't got extra-sensitive ears or any other superpowers. He's just good at paying attention. He always sees how people really are.

Slim takes a longish look at Bat. His eyes land on the slip-on runners with their easy-access, elasticated sides. The gray marl jogging bottoms sagging round Bat's knees. The sensible fleece in compost green. His ma still picks his clothes for him. The look's not changed since he was a child. But his face is shadowed with stubble now, and he's fairly filled out since he started going to the gym. His hairline's not dissimilar to Slim's. It's crept back into a McDonald's arch. Bat's not a wee lad anymore. When Slim looks at him, he sees a fella much like himself; better-looking, if he's honest, though the outfit's screaming middle-aged dad. Slim looks at Bat. It's a long time since he last looked at him.

He leans over and grips Bat's shoulder firmly. He looks his friend straight in the eye. It doesn't matter that Bat can't see him. The gesture's entirely for himself. "You know I'd take you out if I could, mate," he says. "We'd have a laugh. But it wouldn't be safe for either of us."

"Maybe not before," says Bat. "But things have changed."

"What do you mean, things have changed?"

"I can see now, so I can."

"What?"

"I know it sounds mental, Slim. I've not got my head round it yet. But I'm not blind anymore."

"You're joking," says Slim. He knows he's not. He can tell by the way Bat's squared his shoulders inside his fleece. He's deadly serious. Slim doesn't know what to say.

"So, my ma's cousin's friendly with this woman from Kilrea direction. Her sister does faith healing out of her conservatory. Basically, you pay her money, and she prays for you. We went over there last weekend, me and my ma and her cousin Eunice. I thought it was a load of bollocks, myself. The kind of shite Ma's always falling for. I only went so I wouldn't upset her. She's been wild weepy since my da. But the faith healing worked. Honest to God, Slim, it actually worked. Your woman done all this praying and mumbling. She put holy oil on my head and rubbed it in. After, when I opened my eyes, I could see a bit. The next day, I could see a bit more. Every day since, it's got better. My ma thinks I'll be a hundred percent by the end of the month."

Slim doesn't know how to respond. He's all up in his head thinking, *This is crazy.* It's like something you'd see in a film. One of those true-life ones about romance or cancer that his ma likes to watch in the afternoon. It isn't just what Bat's saying, it's how he's talking that doesn't sit. Bat is usually a man of few words. Slim's never seen him this animated. He's like a wee lad on the Skittles. Hands dancing about all over the show. He can barely hold himself still. Bat opens his mouth and takes a deep breath. He's about to start into another spiel. Slim cuts him off before he can speak.

"And what's the doctor say about it?"

"I haven't been to the doctor yet. I'm waiting to see my consultant up in Antrim. The first appointment I could get's not for a fortnight. The waiting list's a mile long these days."

"Could you not take a run up to Casualty?"

"Sure, it's only meant for emergencies, Slim. I wouldn't want to bother them."

"I'd say this is an emergency, Bat. You've been blind for twenty-odd years and now you can see. That's a miracle in my book. Pure holy Jesus, Bible stuff. Them Casualty doctors'll be bending over backward for a look at you."

Bat laughs. "Aye, you might be right there."

Slim watches his face closely as he laughs. He's looking to see if Bat's normal now. *Does he look like the rest of them?* He wants to see it, but he can't. Bat's eyes are just like they've always been: darting back and forth beneath his pale eyelashes as if he's squinting and blinking at the same time. Slim can't let Bat behind the wheel, but how on earth's he going to say this? There's no nice way of putting it. He doesn't believe Bat's healed at all, and if Bat's not healed then he's still blind and Slim can't take a blind lad out for a drive. That's the brutal truth of it. He just needs to find a softer way to say it; something to hide the truth behind.

"Why've you still got Judith with you?" he asks, seizing upon Bat's ancient guide dog. "And the vest and the cane and everything? Sure, you don't need it anymore."

"Force of habit," says Bat. "I'm that used to putting everything on. And Judith won't let me out of her sight. I think I'm stuck with her. I can't see them making me give her back." He reaches down to place his hands over the dog's ears. "Between you and me, mate, she'll be retiring soon anyway."

"What about your provisional?" asks Slim. He knows fine rightly he's grasping at straws. "You'll need a provisional license before you start taking lessons. It's the law."

"Since when did you care about provisionals, Slim? Sure, you'd Dinger's wee sister out last week, and she doesn't turn seventeen till the end of next month."

"That's different, Bat," Slim says. He hopes Bat won't ask him how it's different. Because he knows it's not.

"Look, if you don't believe me, just say so," Bat snaps. "I'll just wait till I get signed off by the consultant. Then I'll go to one of them dear bastards over in Galgorm."

"Uch, now, don't be doing that," says Slim. "I believe you, Batters. If you say you're better, that's good enough for me. Sure, give your eyes a few more weeks, then I'll take you out for a spin."

"Can we not start now? Sure, you've nothing on, and honestly, my eyes are grand. Just run me through the basics. Let me get a feel for the motor. We'll not go farther than the end of the road."

There's a different tone to Bat's voice now. He isn't whining or wheedling. He's confident, like a salesman running through a sure-fire pitch. He's got Slim backed into a corner. He knows it. And he's using this knowledge to his advantage, pure battering Slim down with it. There's an accusation hovering. If Slim says no, he's a cruel bastard, refusing his friend this one wee thing. He's a bad friend. Maybe even a bad person. The sort of person who can't see past another person's disability.

"I'm not sure, Bat," Slim mumbles.

"Uch, come on, mate. Ten minutes. Just to the end of the road and back. What's the worst that can happen? Sure, I'll not even get into second gear."

Bat's already walking to the Fiesta, striding forward confidently as if he knows its exact position in the drive. If Slim didn't know better, he'd think Bat's sight is as good as the next man's. But he can't help thinking that his ma's Fiesta always sits in the very same place. It's too late to raise any concerns. Bat's already halfway down the drive.

"What about Judith?" Slim asks. "Should we leave her with my ma?"

"Naw," Bat shouts from the driver's side. "She'll not stay with a stranger. She'll only cry and get on the whole time we're out. Just put her in the boot. She'll be grand in there."

Slim wonders if Bat understands dimensions. He's never seen the inside of a Fiesta's boot, nor how it compares to a fully grown golden retriever. It'll be a squeeze, especially if he can't get the dog to lie down. But Judith's an awful placid big dog. She's used to being trailed around, tucked underneath tables, and tripped over. She raises no objection to being stuffed sideways into the boot.

As Slim's manhandling Judith inside, Bat feels around for the door handle. He opens it and slides into the driver's seat. While Slim's not watching, he runs his fingers over the wheel and dashboard, the gearstick and seatbelt clip. He carefully pictures where everything is. He reaches over and turns the stereo on. It's playing one of Mrs. Cleaver's ABBA CDs. He gets a three-second blast of music, *There was something in the air that night,* and flicks it off before your woman can wail *Fernando*. ABBA's always done his head in. Especially the sappy songs. He'd turn on the radio, but he'd need to ask Slim to do it for him, and if he asked for help, the game would be up.

Bat's got the whole thing down to a T. He'll drag it out for another minute—act like he's going to sink the pedal and take off down the Doury Road—and then, when Slim's about to grab the handbrake, admit he's only taking the piss. If Slim doesn't see the funny side—and Bat's pretty sure he'll see the funny side—he'll offer to buy him a couple of pints. He'll tell him the whole thing was Roastie's idea.

They came up with the plan a few nights ago, when they were round Loaf's house for a barbecue. It wasn't much of a barbecue. A load of Carlsberg. Potato salad out of a tub. Two dozen of Cookstown's finest, charred to a cinder on one of them disposable numbers they sell for a pound in Poundstretcher. They'd rolled their sausages up in sliced white pan and slathered them in tomato sauce, called them hot dogs, and were happy as Larry to be out in the sun, getting pissed. Everybody was there except Slim. He was taking some woman through her hill starts. Being absent, he couldn't defend himself when they all started laying into him; not in a mean way, friendly like. They were just laughing about the *Hollyoaks* thing and the way he'd take his ma to the lady hairdresser's and get his own hair cut while he was there. "He's a rare one," said Dinger, and they all agreed, in a fond sort of way. Like how you could rip your own wee brother a new one, but you wouldn't let anyone else say a bad word.

It was Roastie's idea to send Bat round for driving lessons. "Go on, Batman. It'll be a hoot. If you keep a straight face, dear only knows how far you can take it." Dinger suggested Cullybackey. Loaf thought they could make it to the North Coast. It was all big talk. By this stage, they'd worked their way through the Carlsberg and started into the harder stuff. It was all just blather until Bat said, "Aye, all right. Why not? I'll go over next week and see if I can talk him into it." It hadn't taken much to talk Bat round. It was one thing to be included and another, less familiar thing to find himself front and center; an essential component of their plan.

Slim slips into the passenger seat and pulls the door tight behind him. He brings a waft of stale fag smoke and Lynx deodorant into the car.

"Did you get Judith sorted?"

"Aye," Slim says. "There's not much room in that boot. I couldn't get the parcel shelf out. But she should be grand for ten minutes if she doesn't try to stand up."

"Right," says Bat.

"Right," says Slim.

Neither wants to make the first move.

"Seatbelts on," says Bat.

"Seatbelts on," repeats Slim. In tandem they reach over their shoulders and drag the seatbelts across their chests. "Are you sure you're up to it?" asks Slim.

"Absolutely," says Bat.

"All right, then. Whenever you're ready. Stick the keys in the ignition and turn Big Red on."

Slim passes the car keys across the handbrake, placing them in the center of Bat's upturned palm. Bat closes his fingers around the Fiesta's key with its fat plastic keyring of the Blackpool Tower. They all have the same one in different colors, a wee present from Loaf's ma the year she went to the Illuminations with a rake of women from her lodge. Slim is slow to withdraw his hand. He's always careful passing things to Bat. He's more deliberate than he usually is. He hesitates for a half second until he's sure Bat's got the hold of the car keys. Then he pulls his hand back and places it on his thigh. His fingers dig nervously through his jeans, leaving tense red marks in his flesh.

"On you go, whenever you're ready." He tries not to see Bat fumbling to fit the key into the ignition. He tries not to think about any wee children who might be wobbling along the road on their bikes or old folk crossing or next door's psychopathic cat, which is forever darting out in front of cars.

Bat's not thinking about the very same things. The cats. The old folk. The little children bashed and bloody beneath his wheels. Bat's pushed it all to the back of his mind. He's concentrating on Slim's voice. The steady way he has of talking, like water running out of a tap. It's easy to believe what Slim's saying because Slim talks like he believes in you. Which is probably why folks go to him for their lessons. If Slim tells you you can drive a motor, well, you get to thinking you probably can. It's not just the driving. It's other things too. There's been so many times he's made Bat feel like a door has opened out of himself. He doesn't have to say that much. It's the way he says it—all flippant like—as if he's certain, sure, you'll be all right.

Bat thinks about last Christmas, the night they were all round at McElvey's, playing pool. Slim had come over and pulled up a barstool and said there was a wee blade over by the cigarette machine—a good-looking lassie in a tight black dress—who couldn't take her eyes off him. "Not that I'm surprised, Batters," he'd said, "you've a touch of the Beckham about you since you got the hair sorted out." At first Bat hadn't believed him, because there'd never been any girls before. But Slim had promised he wasn't winding and insisted they go over and talk to the girl and her mates. And they had, and Bat had bought her a pint and asked her all sorts of questions about her work and where she went on her holidays. It wasn't that hard. He just copied stuff he'd heard on the telly, and he seemed to do it right. Before she left, she'd taken him round the back of McElvey's—leaving Judith to guard his pint—and kissed him up against the recycling bin. It had been the first proper kiss of Bat's life. When he'd come back into the bar, the others all went, "Yeeeooooo," and told him he was taking a reddener. Slim just leaned across the table and said, "See, mate, I told you she'd the eye for you."

Now here's Slim telling Bat he can drive; urging him to get a move on. There's so much he has to learn: three-point turns and parallel parking, reversing round a corner on a hill. It'll not be easy, but he knows he can do it as long as Slim keeps saying he can. Bat can picture them together next summer, when he has the R plates off. They'll go up the Port and cruise around, eating chips and eyeing up girls. They'll take their mas down to Newcastle on a wee day out or up to Belfast for Christmas shopping. They'll make a playlist of banging tunes and just drive about for a laugh. Once Bat feels more confident, he'll save up for his own wee car. He can picture it all. He can actually see it in his head.

"Right, let's get this show on the road," says Slim. "Turn your engine on."

Bat reaches under the wheel, finds Blackpool Tower with his fingers, and turns the key in the ignition. The Fiesta splutters into life.

# CARAVAN

The caravan has been squatting in the yard for as long as Caroline can remember. It sits in the corner between the water pump and the trough: a touring caravan, really only big enough for two. She thinks it belonged to an uncle once and that he is either dead or moved to Canada, unable to take his caravan with him. It is shaped like a beluga whale: fat head, towbar for a tail, one great window like a glass eye peering over the fence and into the fields beyond. It looks sad and a little ashamed, as all moving creatures look once they've run aground.

Though Caroline is too young to remember, the caravan was once colored cream, beige, and custardy yellow in broad corrugated stripes. The weather has worn the brightness out of it. Now it is the all-over color of fingernails. Its roof is green with moss and a spattering of spindly plants which sprout each spring and shrivel by June, incapable of thriving on nothing but bird shit and rain. In the winter, cats crawl behind its brick-blocked wheels to shelter from the wind. During the autumn, it is fairly clogged with leaves. In the summer, it belongs to Caroline and her little sister. Entirely. Only. For a few short months.

They approach the caravan like prodigal sons returning after winter long. They fling its window wide and prop the door open with a brick. They try to scoop the fusty smell out with flat hands and cushions and, when this doesn't work, cover the stink with air freshener lifted from the downstairs toilet: blue sea smell, or cloying lilac, sometimes sprayed together in a thick, nauseating mist. After a few days, the inside air becomes breathable again. Then they move in, filling the caravan with Barbie dolls and bears, coloring-in books and tiny bottles of nail polish got free with magazines. They eat as many meals as possible in the caravan, folding up the double bed so it becomes a table, laying this table with cutlery and placemats. They pour orange squash out of a teapot like it is actually tea and they are grown-up ladies, supping this tea with fancy biscuits.

They make flower-petal potions in the caravan's stopped-up sink and siphon their perfume into old medicine bottles. They talk about taking a stall at the market and selling it: fifty pence a bottle, three small bottles for a pound. Every afternoon they nap in the caravan, curled up beneath unzipped sleeping bags on the table, which is once again a bed. They have every spare pillow in the house out here. Every blanket too. Their mother despairs, good-heartedly, and sometimes brings a choc ice out to them, or a slice of Swiss roll on a saucer. In the evenings, they return home to sleep in their own wee beds. But every waking moment is spent in their *other house*.

Mum plays along, knocking on their door like a stranger every time she ventures across the yard to visit. She lets them use her old saucepans and bowls for cooking pretend meals. She says not to worry if they get ruined. They almost all get ruined with mud and petals and leaves mulched to a grungy paste. Caroline's brother is not so understanding. He rolls his eyes and says, "The pair of youse have too much time on your hands." He's fourteen now and has a job in the stables down the road, mucking out the horses and cleaning tack. Most mornings he's up and out of the house before Caroline's even awake. Last year it was him and her joined at the hip, and Emily was the baby. Now he drinks instant coffee and talks to her dad about things that are happening on the news. Caroline feels awkward around him, like she does sometimes with the cousins they see only at Christmas. She's jealous of the way he fills his seat at the table, eating the same things the adults eat; jealous and also a little afraid. All this is ahead of her. She's not quite ready for it.

Every so often Caroline's dad threatens to get rid of the caravan. "It's a bloody eyesore," he'll say, "sitting in the corner of the yard, taking up room." It would make good money for scrap. He'd buy the girls a swing set from the proceeds and new bicycles to replace their outgrown ones. Caroline's little sister howls like a struck cat every time he mentions selling their caravan. She climbs all over him, hugging, kissing, and whining in his ear, "Please don't get rid of the caravan, Daddy. It's our house. We live there." He laughs when she gets on like this, and ruffles her hair, and because she's the baby—his favorite of the three—says, "Okay, wee Bird. I'll keep the caravan for one more summer." And he always does.

Every summer, it is a novelty to peel open the caravan's plasticky door and step inside. To rediscover all the little cupboards tucked beneath its seats and find there toys and plastic doodahs misplaced for a year. To open the pale orange curtains and tie them back with string. To make the bed into a table and slide it into a bed again. To take your lunch off a picnic plate balanced on your knee. Every summer, for as long as she can remember, Caroline has looked forward to the caravan like she looks forward to lowering the same old Christmas tree, still strung with last year's lights, carefully through the attic hatch and getting the colored baubles out. There's comfort in the familiar and a kind of pinchy thrill in knowing such joys are limited to one serving per year.

This summer, Caroline doesn't feel the same old excitement. It's the first of July. School finished yesterday, though they've hardly opened a book all week. The weather's fine and looks set to last. This is the best day of the year to be a child. The whole summer stretches in front of her. Eight full weeks of cartoons in the mornings and outside eating, grass stains, sunburn, and staying up long past bedtime. Yet Caroline's already weary of it. She's been in and out and had a good hoke round the caravan. By midmorning she's already done with it. It is different to her this year. Not the same as it was at nine or eight. It's smaller than it used to be, dirtier, and less unknown. She finds herself bored by the tiny cupboards, the folding bed, the compact versions of everything you'd find proper-sized in a real house. The smell turns her. Sour wool. Leaf mulch. Damp. It clogs in her nose and brings on a coughing fit. She lifts an old magazine from the counter and takes it outside where the air isn't so clammy.

She sits on an upturned bucket, flicking through out-of-date articles about pop stars and clothes that girls were wearing this time last year. She picks a scab until it bleeds and blots the wet with a piece of kitchen roll. In the caravan behind her, she can hear Emily buzzing round the little kitchen picking things up and putting them down. Oohing and aahing, pretending she's discovering everything for the very first time. There are over four years between Caroline and her sister. This morning it could be a century. On the other side of the yard, she sees her dad come out of the toolshed. He has a roll of hose looped loosely over his arm. He's off to clean out the cowshed. He spots Caroline sitting by the caravan and strides over. "That's some face you have on you," he says. "You'll be scaring the crows."

Caroline tries not to smile. She can't quite manage to hold her anger up, not with Dad standing there grinning, making light of it. She squints up at him, her mouth all watery and unsure of itself. "I'm bored," she says.

"You're what?"

"Bored. There's nothing to do round here." She sweeps a hand across the yard, taking in the outhouses, the front field, the dirty caravan behind her, as if to say, *See for yourself. There's nothing here to occupy a child.* "Can we not go on holidays this year, Dad? Everybody in my class is going on holidays. Why do we never go away?"

"Uch, now, Caroline, we've been over this before. I can't get away from the farm, and there's no money for holidays at the minute. Maybe next year. Sure, youse have the caravan to play in."

"I'm too old for playing house," snaps Caroline. "I don't want to spend the whole summer in a stupid caravan."

Her own mouth takes her by surprise. She hasn't, until this moment, realized she's not a child anymore. But here she is, shouting it out across the yard, so it must be true.

"Ah, right," says her dad. "I suppose you are getting on a bit. What age is it you are now, Caro . . . twenty-one? Twenty-three?"

"Ten," says Caroline, "nearly eleven," and can't keep herself from smiling again. "I'm almost a grown-up."

"You are indeed, my girl. It'll not be long till you're up and out of the house. Sure, you must be two feet taller than you were last year. I can see now, you're beyond playing with dollies."

"Exactly."

"But you're hardly old enough for a summer job."

"No, not just yet."

"So, you're in need of something to occupy you while you're out of school."

"Uh-huh."

"Listen, I tell you what. You've nearly two months off. I'll give you a wee project. If you can get that caravan licked into shape—I mean really, properly done up—I'll give it to you. You can have it all year round, not for a playhouse, you know. For your own room."

"And I wouldn't have to share it with Emily?"

"No, no, it'd be all yours, pet. A wee bit of privacy for you, now you're almost a grown-up. Would you like that?"

"I would," she says, and pictures the cramped attic room she shares with her little sister: the Beatrix Potter wallpaper and stuffed animals avalanching off the top bunk every time Emily turns in her sleep. All their underwear muddled up together in a drawer so she sometimes goes fishing for her own pants and comes out with Emily's wee girl knickers, still covered in rainbows and teddy bears. There is nothing she'd like more than a room of her own; a door she could close and bolt against everybody but herself.

"Now, this isn't a game," her dad says. "It's a proper job. I want to see you putting the effort in. If that caravan's anything less than perfect, you'll not be getting it."

"I'll work hard, Daddy. Wait'll you see how nice it looks."

"Right you be. I'll have my eye on you, Caroline. All summer. And don't be saying anything to your sister. She'll have a pink fit. I'll tell her later, when the whole thing's settled."

Off he goes, striding across the yard in his muck-spattered wellies. The end of the hose has begun to unwind. It drags behind him like a snake, leaving a line in the gravel so you can see where he's come from. Caroline steps up and into the caravan. She stands in the middle of its mess, one foot in the kitchen, one foot in the living area/bedroom, and clasps her hands in front of her. She has a picture of her mum standing just like this, broad-shouldered and determined in front of a particularly mountainous load of laundry. "Right," she says to herself as much as Emily, who's fiddling about with dishes in the sink, "this place is a state. Let's get it sorted out."

By midafternoon she's procured buckets and bleach, a mop and ancient tea towels to be used as cleaning rags, brushes, dustpans, bin liners, and a wad of old *Chronicle*s, which her mum says are the very thing to use on glass. She's found furniture polish, feather dusters, and a wire brush to go at the grease-encrusted hob, plus a sixty-five-foot extension cord so the hoover can be run all the way across the yard. She piles everything in front of the caravan. It looks like her mum's cleaning cupboard has finally exploded, scattering bottles and brushes all across the yard. She looks at her little sister. The thrill of cleaning has already left Emily. She's bored and looking to her coloring-in books for distraction.

"It's a game," says Caroline. "We're going to play proper mummies, doing spring cleaning." Emily looks skeptical. "You can do the hoovering," says Caroline.

Her sister lights up like a birthday candle. She's not allowed to use the hoover at home. She is, all of a sudden, in. They start by emptying everything out so they can see just how bad the caravan is.

That night, Caroline takes the caravan to bed with her and does not sleep. She turns the possibility of it this way and that until she convinces herself that having a caravan will actually be better than having a bedroom of her own. She thinks about the little cupboards and the bed, which is also a table; the orange curtains, which she plans to replace with new curtains handsewn from scraps. Seen in the new light of ownership, the caravan is no longer small and slightly squalid. It is the most exciting thing that's ever happened to her. More exciting by far than breaking her arm in P4 or going to Scotland once, on the ferry, or even the acquisition of a new baby sister, which, though exciting at the time, has proved to be more of a liability than a blessing.

Some of her school friends have their own bedroom. Some even have a whole set of bunks to themselves just in case they want to host a sleepover. None of her friends have their own tiny house. None of them have a working fridge or cooker. Caroline falls asleep planning how she will write about the caravan in her "What I Did This Summer" essay. How she will stand in front of her class and read this essay aloud. How they will all, every single one of them—even rich Philip, who has a TV in his bedroom—look at her with pure, impossible-to-disguise jealousy when she reads, "Now I live all by myself, in my own caravan."

All summer Caroline scrubs and cleans. She gets down on her hands and knees and goes under the table, behind the seats, and inside the cupboards. She scrapes out mouse droppings and spindly spiderwebs, fly corpses so old and sucked out they're like unsoaked raisins. In most places the dust has solidified into a crust. She scrapes at it and sometimes has to use a knife to work it loose. The dirt gathers under her fingernails and can't be shifted. All summer long her skin is covered in a thin film of dust. When she breathes in, it feels like she is breathing through cardboard. She is always filthy. She doesn't mind. By mid-July she can see the clean coming through the dirt. She presses on.

Emily loses interest. She says the caravan isn't fun anymore. Caroline has evicted all her dolls and teddies. Crayons are no longer allowed inside, for fear they may leave marks on the Formica. They don't even have picnics in the caravan now. Caroline is afraid of spills. She's worried the food smells will get into the upholstery and stale. She insists that all shoes are heeled off at the door. There's too much mud on a farm, and she doesn't want it trekked across her good clean floors. At first Emily is annoyed. She whines to her mother: "It's not fair, Caroline has taken over the caravan. She's not sharing." But Emily is only six. She has a head like a bowl-stuck goldfish. For a week or so she moans and huffs, pitching clods of dried-out cow dung at the caravan to spite her sister. By late July she's forgotten all about it.

Emily makes a den in the coal shed, a second den in the ditch at the top of the front field, and practices her flower-petal alchemy alone. She spends the holidays running a school for stuffed animals in the toolshed. She starts a snail farm in an old kettle. She teaches herself to snowboard, going down the back-field hill on one of her brother's ancient skateboards. Every so often she sticks her head into the caravan to ask, "Do you want to make magic potions with me, Caro?" or "Can we play vets?" Caroline looks up from her cleaning, then smiles like a harassed housewife and says, "I'd love to, Em, but I've so much to do here. I just can't."

Caroline hauls all the soft furnishings out of the caravan and runs them through the washing machine. Seat covers. Curtains. Cushions. The elderly linen tablecloth they've been using on the foldy table. She learns how to use the tumble dryer and iron things properly on the ironing board. She is short for her age and has to kneel on a chair to get up to the right height, but even this does not put her off. She makes new curtains from a pair of old pillowcases. They are pink with pale yellow flowers threaded across the fabric in a trellis design. She sews the curtains herself, hand-hemming them with a needle and thread. When they're finished and hung, she takes immense pleasure in the way the sunlight swims through the gauzy fabric, baptizing the entire caravan in a warm pink glow. She picks primroses from the top field and arranges them in a jar on the window shelf. They match her curtains perfectly. She replaces her primroses weekly, watching carefully to catch them before the edges turn brown and papery. She doesn't want anything stale or ruined in her new house.

Her dad checks in from time to time. "Well, Caro," he'll say as he's going out to the Land Rover or pushing a wheelbarrow full of feed sacks across the yard, "how's the caravan coming on?"

"It looks great, Daddy," she'll say. She'll let him peek in through the window, though she won't permit him inside, not with his mucky boots on.

"Grand job, Caro. I love what you've done with the place."

"Do you like my curtains? I sewed them myself."

"Gorgeous altogether. I'll bet the Queen herself doesn't have curtains that fancy . . . And you'll be all set to move in by the end of the summer."

"I think so."

"Good girl."

Sometimes over dinner, he'll ask Caroline how she's getting on in the caravan. They'll only be able to talk in loose circles. They don't want Emily hearing and working out what's going on. Her dad has a particular way of touching his nose and nodding at her little sister, which is code for *Watch what you say in front of her.* Everyone in the family understands this code. Her mum never brings up the caravan. Sometimes when they're talking about it vaguely at the dinner table, she'll get up and leave the table or mutter, "Come on, Thomas, change the subject."

When Caroline manages to get Mum alone, so she can ask about the best way to clean windows or get grease splatters out of cushions, there's no twinkle in her talk. None of the usual banter. All her answers are straight to the point, and she doesn't ask questions. This strikes Caroline as odd. Her mum is usually full of questions. She wonders if she's tired. Or expecting another baby. She remembers how distracted she got just before Emily arrived.

All through July, Caroline works on the inside of the caravan. Once it's sorted, she moves on to the exterior. She gets the hose out of the toolshed and goes scrubbing at the caravan's corrugated walls. It is a shock to discover the cream, beige, and custardy-yellow stripes are still there, faded but discernible beneath so many years of grime. She scrubs with a hard brush until the colors come up and her caravan is like a little block of sunshine sat in the corner of the yard, smiling. She paints a wooden sign and props it by the door, "Primrose House," with a carefully copied portrait of a primrose drawn in the lower left-hand corner. After some deliberation, she has decided to call it a house rather than a caravan, "house" being a word that reeks of permanence. She arranges two plant pots on either side of the sign. These contain sunflower seeds. It's the wrong time of year. Dad says they won't grow. But Caroline likes the idea of proving him wrong. She has a feeling the sunflowers will sprout. She is full of good feelings these days.

The caravan is finished then. It doesn't look as good as new, but Caroline thinks it looks pretty smart for a thing that's been sitting outside for almost a decade. It is only ten days until the end of August. There are hardly any holidays left. Caroline is pale as paper from spending all her sunny days inside. She hasn't seen any of her friends or gone adventuring through the fields. There is a pile of library books sitting by her bedside, untouched for the last month. But it's been worth the effort. Every time she has reservations, she thinks about the first week of school and the "What I Did This Summer" essay. She knows that she's made the right decision.

She waits until the whole family is gathered to announce that the caravan's finished. She thinks it best to make an occasion of it. Emily should be told sooner rather than later. And she wants her brother to know what she's accomplished; to see she's not a child any longer, messing around with dolls and made-up games. She wants her mum to hear and say, "Well done, Caroline. I'm really proud of you." Mum makes a point of saying she is proud when one of the children accomplishes something remarkable, or even something quite ordinary which they've worked hard at. "My mum and dad never told me they were proud of me," she explains. Caroline understands that this is also why Mum hugs and kisses them constantly and shouts, "Love you," out the car window when she drops them off at school.

"I finished the caravan," she announces as soon as Dad has said grace.

"Good woman," says her dad.

No one else speaks, but Caroline notices her brother and Mum catch each other's eye across the casserole dish and look down quickly.

"I've cleaned the outside and the inside and made new curtains and a sign for the door."

"I know," he says, "it looks great, and it kept you occupied all summer long. You weren't bored at all, were you, Caroline?"

"No, Daddy," she says and can't understand why her mum isn't picking the conversation up. "So, when can I move in?"

Her dad smiles. All teeth. All thin-stretched lips and mustache. He laughs, but it doesn't sound like a laugh. It sounds like someone squeezing a laugh through a too thin space. It comes out sounding more like a cough. "When can she move in? Do you hear that, Susan? This one thinks she's going to live in the caravan."

A heavy silence descends upon the table. Caroline struggles to cut through it. None of her words feels sharp enough. "But you said I could, Daddy," she whispers. "You promised, so you did."

"You didn't think I was serious? Sure, you must've known I was only pulling your leg, Caro. You're ten years old. A wee girl of ten can't live outside in a caravan all by herself. There's no heat in there, no electric either."

"Jesus," says her mum, "I told you she actually believed you, Thomas. I told you you were taking this too far." She leans back in her chair suddenly, distancing herself from her husband. The tablecloth snags on her belt, tugging the fabric toward her so everyone's water glasses judder, slopping tiny mouthfuls of water onto the table.

Caroline raises a finger and drags it through the wetness, leaving marks. She needs something to focus on, otherwise she'll cry. "But you promised," she repeats, staring hard at the tiny bobble of water as it soaks into the tablecloth fabric and falls flat.

"Why am I always the bad guy?" says her dad. "Can nobody in this family take a joke?"

Nobody says anything. Nobody moves.

"Well, I won't sit here being glared at like I've done something wrong. I'll take my dinner in the TV room."

He lifts his plate and storms out of the room, returning seconds later for his forgotten cutlery. Upset by Dad's raised voice, Emily begins to cry. She is not good with scenes. She gets up and runs from the table, not caring about her left-behind dinner congealing on the plate. Caroline's mum follows her. Then it is just Caroline and her brother left at the table, poking at the edge of their shepherd's pie.

"Seriously, Caro," he says, his voice thick with sarcasm, "you're such a baby."

Caroline has never felt less like a baby in her life. She's fifteen years older than she was this morning and, all of a sudden, so very tired she can barely get the fork to her mouth. She can see the whole summer has been wasted, and there'll never be another summer like this. Next year she'll be eleven. She'll be on her way to big school. She won't be the same as she is now. This has been the last pure summer of her life, and her father has taken it away from her.

Caroline wishes she was able to hate her dad. It might help to pin the blame on him. But she hasn't the energy to be angry. And she knows she won't be able to keep it up. No matter what Dad does to hurt her, no matter how many times he lets her down, in the end he always manages to win her round. He'll make her laugh. He'll start singing "Sweet Caroline." He'll come back from the village with a wee thing for her: a quarter of pear drops or a Wham bar. And though she'll still be angry in her head, she'll feel her body betraying her. Grinning. Laughing. Reaching out for whatever peace offering he's presented. Voicing her reluctant thanks. Dad always gets the better of her.

It's not like Caroline doesn't know he loves her. She's certain enough of that. Sure, isn't he never done telling everyone who'll listen what a great wee girl she is. It's just that sometimes she wonders what sort of man her dad actually is. She sees the way Mum looks at him. Lately, she's seen the same looks in her brother too. She's heard people in the village talking. "That one's a chancer, so he is. I wouldn't trust him as far as I could throw him. Tommy's nothing but a blow." It's hard to see him as a person. Caroline's stuck seeing him as a dad, and dads are always biggish men. She tries to remember the good times. There have been good times in the past, times when she's seen the whole of her father. And thought him a person worth looking up to. Not just as a dad but also as a man.

Caroline's mind settles on a day two summers ago. It had been piping hot that week. Mum filled the old blow-up dinghy with water so Emily and Caroline could plouter about in their swimsuits. Later, Dad had come up from the field stripped to the waist, the line of his shirtsleeves still visible despite his suntan. He'd stopped at the gate and shouted in, "What's this, a boat run aground in my own front field and two wee stowaways hiding in it?" And they'd squealed in delight, because he was doing his Big Bad Wolf voice and advancing toward them, arms outspread like an ogre. Then he took the inflatable dinghy—an ancient thing they usually kept for the beach—by the rope attached to its nose and swung the whole contraption, Emily and Caroline included, round and round so fast they were coasting above the cornfield, actually floating above the stalks. Gravity flung the pair of them heel over elbow toward the farthest end of the dinghy, and Caroline was, for a moment, lighter than air or the weight of their two bodies combined. She'd felt as if they could easily take off into the blue August sky and disappear, but she'd known that this would not happen because her dad was holding on to them. He would never let them go. He'd seemed like a giant that afternoon. A man worth looking up to.

Now Caroline does not know if she's remembering the moment right at all. Perhaps her feelings are made up, lifted from the photo Mum took that day. She bends her head over her untouched shepherd's pie. She closes her eyes. She tries to picture the photograph. Here is a broad-shouldered man in a cornfield, spinning an orange boat round and round, sailing it through the golden corn. Here are two small girls clinging to the boat, their faces smudged with movement so Caroline can't even be sure if she's smiling or terrified.

# TROUBLING THE WATER

The rumor about the Templemore Baths was essentially circular. Which is to say that this one told that one, that one passed it on to the next, and within a few days, it had made a complete circuit of the Knit and Natter. Nobody could've said who started it, though Agnes was the likeliest candidate. Agnes had a source in the council: a great-niece in cleansing services. She was the go-to for complaints about missing wheelie bins or the dog dirt that kept appearing in the bus shelter, each deposit individually bagged like a portion of butcher-bought mince.

Kathleen suspected Agnes was the instigator, although it had been Mary who'd called to ask the lend of her magic loop, and to let Kathleen know the paramedics were in with Marty round the corner (*not Marty Barr, the other Marty, with the leg*), and to tell her chocolate digestives were on two for one in SuperValu, oh, and on the off chance, had she heard anything funny about the Templemore Baths? Kathleen knew—from the slight change in pitch—that this was the real reason for Mary's call.

It was not the first time Kathleen had encountered a rumor like this. People assumed it was only country folk who went in for the weird stuff; that if you lived in a city with modern conveniences such as satellite television and all-night Tesco, you'd be too sophisticated to go in for such nonsense. Not a bit of it. The East was full of old ladies who spun tall tales: Margarets, Maureens, and Marys (pronounced "Meery" to rhyme with "cheery," thus differentiating them from the other sort of Mary, the ones named after the Mother of God). Mother of God, these women loved to gossip. There was no keeping a good rumor down, and Kathleen had heard a fair few good ones in her time.

There was the one about the young fella in Ballybeen who'd been run over by joyriders only to wake up on the undertaker's slab, bruised and confused but, ultimately, grand. Apparently, the granny was a champion prayer, a tight wee Baptist woman with a beret permanently clamped to her crown. They said her earnest petitions had brought the wee lad back. Then there was the lady who walked among the headstones in Dundonald Cemetery and the equally dead RUC officer (half his face missing from a car bomb) who frequented the Park Avenue's lounge. There was the woman with the cure for asthma in Ballyhack, and the auld lad who sat outside McDonald's. He'd do your future for a Smarties McFlurry. He was accurate, they said, up to a point. Officially, it was the other sort who done the weeping statues and miracles. Pragmatism might well have been preached from Protestant pulpits, but in the streets and fussy wee living rooms of East Belfast, folks still believed in things unseen. There wasn't much else to hold on to round here.

The rumor about the Templemore Baths was new to Kathleen. She was familiar enough with the Baths themselves. They'd been clinging to the better end of Templemore Avenue since 1893. Red-bricked, chimneyed, and blessed with a somewhat incongruous spire, the building didn't immediately scream swimming pool. The passing stranger—and there were very few strangers passing through this part of the city—might well have taken it for a Victorian cloth mill or a place of worship. Inside, the facilities remained reassuringly old-fashioned. The stench of bleach and chlorine sat crisply on every tiled surface. Drafts swept uninterrupted from one end of the building to the other, and all the heating pipes were crusty. A deep rectangular pool dominated the inner sanctum. The ceiling above was high, windowed, and impractically arched, so the air above the water remained permanently icy. In winter, the swimmers could see their breath fogging in front of them as they butterflied up and down the lanes.

Individual changing cubicles lined the pool's edge, so it was only a short swimsuit-clad shuffle from the door to the water. The old ladies appreciated this. They didn't like to be observed, varicose-veined and bulging, in their saggy one-pieces and clip-beneath-your-chin caps. The old boys didn't give a rat's ass how they looked in their trunks yet swam in the Baths because they were cheap and handier than busing across town to the big municipal complex on the Boucher Road. Through the day, when the weans were in school, it was really only old ones who swam there. Yes, you might stumble across the odd pregnant lady or a young mum dragging a toddler across the shallows, clumsy and howling in orange armbands.

And there was, of course, the rougher element: young fellas on sticks like bandy-legged lambs hobbling to the pool's edge, lowering themselves painfully in. The physios said swimming was good for them, low-impact and all that. There was very little else you could do, exercise-wise, once you'd had the kneecaps off. It was a pity of these young fellas. Or was it? Sure, they only had themselves to blame. The old women gave them the side-eye as they swam past, and knew not to bring anything valuable down to the pool. You couldn't really trust a locker, could you? Those kinds of lads would be in and out and away with your purse before you'd even got your key out.

The Knit and Natter ladies were Templemore regulars. They came for aqua aerobics on Tuesday morning and afterward retired to a coffee shop round the corner. The place was staffed by young ones with special needs. Though the coffee wasn't as good as Costa, and sometimes you'd have to go up and repeat your order to the supervisor, they liked to be seen doing their bit. Tuesdays weren't an official Knit and Natter session. These took place on Thursday afternoons and Monday mornings. They were held in the community center and presided over by Julie, who was employed to run projects for old folk. The ladies could count on Julie to keep them well supplied with tepid mugs of Nescafé, Jammie Dodgers, and the inevitable evaluation forms which appeared after every session.

Julie was meant to be expanding the ranks, but nobody ever joined the Knit and Natter. To its credit, they'd only ever lost two members: Marlene, who'd died of cancer in her lady parts; and Susan, who'd started doting and moved into her son's granny flat. The lack of new recruits bothered Julie. Especially after the council sent her on a course about inclusion and diversity. It didn't bother the Knit and Natter ladies one wee bit. All eight of them had known one another since girlhood. They'd no desire to recruit outsiders. They met twice a week to knit and gossip and take advantage of the community center's central heating. They wouldn't want strangers in the mix. All but Linda (who was constrained by her oxygen tank) reconvened on Tuesdays for a subsidized swim.

It was Wednesday when Mary phoned Kathleen. They wouldn't be back in the Baths for almost a week. Mary wasn't saying Kathleen should make a point of going down there unscheduled or anything. Mary wasn't even claiming there was any truth in the rumor. She was only letting Kathleen know what people were saying. She was just being a good friend, for she knew Kathleen was crippled with the arthritis, not to mention poor Bill. To be honest, it was Bill she was really thinking of. She didn't like to put it so bluntly, but they both knew he didn't have that long left. And daft as the whole thing sounded, sure, there was no harm in trying. You'd try anything when it came close to the end, wouldn't you? Hadn't she put her own dying mother in the car and driven her all the way up to Ballymena to see that faith healer? It hadn't made the blind bit of difference, but at least Mary could content herself knowing she'd tried. There was a comfort in knowing you'd done everything you could.

The conversation went on like this for several minutes. The telephone receiver began to sweat uncomfortably against Kathleen's ear. Mary's calls were always delivered in a similar roundabout style. There was a nugget of news in there somewhere; you just had to wait patiently until it emerged. Kathleen caught Bill's eye across the room. He was a good sort. He'd muted the TV as soon as the phone went off and rolled his wheelchair up close to the screen so he could read the subtitles. She mouthed the word "Mary" to him and pointed at the phone. He rolled his eyes ceiling-ward before returning to the news. The light from the screen drew the color out of his face. He was particularly pallid today. The last round of treatment had left him wild papery-looking. Like a boiled potato left too long in the pot. Kathleen needed to get Mary off the phone so she could get her husband up to bed before he was too exhausted to help her.

"What are you going on about, Mary?" she asked, interrupting the other woman midflow.

"There's a girl swimming at the Baths on Friday mornings," said Mary, "a foreign girl."

"What sort of foreign?"

"I'm not sure. Eastern European, I think. It doesn't really matter. Anyway, they say this girl's got some kind of cure. If you're in the water when she's swimming, it comes off on you."

"Bollocks," said Kathleen. Bill was starting to fall asleep, and she was running out of patience.

"Honest to God, Kathleen. Our Liz was down there last Friday when the girl went in, and afterward there wasn't a speck of psoriasis on her. You know yourself she's been plagued for years. And the young one on the butcher's counter at the SPAR said his wife took their baby in when that girl was swimming, and I swear to God, it fixed her squinty eye. I even heard somebody over on the Beersbridge Road got rid of their *cancer*." She dropped her voice to a whisper as she spoke. This was clearly for Bill's benefit, though Bill was already flat out and snoring. "I'm just saying," Mary continued, "don't rule it out, Kathleen. If I was in your position, I'd try anything."

"It's not true," said Kathleen. "Somebody's just made it up. The thing about the pool and getting healed is in the Bible. It's one of Jesus's miracles."

"Is it? I don't know that one myself. Well, if it's in the Bible, then it must be true."

"Aye, for Bible times, maybe. Not for now, in East Belfast."

"Ah, you're probably right there, Kathleen. If Jesus was going to do a miracle nowadays, he'd go somewhere a wee bit classier than the Templemore Baths. There's that waterslide park over in Lisburn. The grandweans are never done going on about it. It's got a wave pool and all. I'd say Jesus'd probably go somewhere like that."

"He would indeed," said Kathleen, and, shortly after, hung up.

She tried to put the Templemore Baths to the back of her mind. She knew it was nonsense. Or pure coincidence. Swimming was good for sick people. Doctors were always banging on about gentle exercise. Everybody felt better for having been to the Baths. It was nothing to do with the foreign girl appearing. Nothing at all. But then again, what if the rumors were true? They were living in strange times. Bill was only after telling her a fella in England had given birth to a baby, and in the States, there were Holy Rollers claiming they could raise the dead. Sure, you didn't know what to believe anymore. At the end of the day, thought Kathleen, was there any real harm in taking her husband to the Baths? Better to chance your arm and be disappointed than miss out for fear of looking daft. She didn't sleep a wink all night for considering it and, by breakfast time, had decided, yes, they would go down there on Friday morning, though she'd have to make it look coincidental; like it was nothing to do with the girl being there.

Half the Knit and Natter had had the same idea. By the time Kathleen got Bill out of his chair, into his trunks, and transferred into the special hoist, the other ladies were emerging from their own cubicles. Agnes, with her blood pressure. Mary, who was a martyr to lumbago. Deirdre and Evelyn, who had so many complaints between them, Kathleen could never keep track of who was crippled with what from one week to the next. They lingered round the pool like elephants toeing the edge of a watering hole. Nobody wanted to be the first one in. It was important to maintain an air of nonchalance. You couldn't let the others see you'd come here looking to get healed, for you'd only feel a right eejit when it didn't happen. There'd been a similar standoff last November when Poundland ran a Black Friday special on selection boxes. They'd all turned up at ten to nine, ready to grab enough for every one of their grandbabies and, confronted by the others, felt the need to mask their desperation. They'd made a sterling attempt at pretending to be there for toothpaste or toilet cleaner and only stumbling upon the selection-box offer by sheer chance.

This morning they eyed each other suspiciously across the water and mumbled their excuses. Agnes was trying to lose a bit of weight. Mary had mixed her days up and come down to the Baths thinking it was aqua aerobics day. Evelyn and Deirdre claimed the doctor had prescribed swimming to ease their various complaints, and, spotting a perfect opportunity, Kathleen jumped on the back of their excuse. She said the specialist had told Bill the very same thing. She looked to her husband, hoping for an alibi, and, when he didn't offer one, stood lightly on his naked foot so he got the message. Yes, he said, nodding, the specialist thought the water might help with his pain. The specialist had said no such thing, but the two of them had been together long enough to understand when backup was required.

Kathleen hadn't told Bill that she hoped a dip in the Templemore Baths might cure his terminal cancer. She'd found herself incapable of voicing the words. Though they seemed almost plausible in her head, she knew out loud they'd sound limp and ludicrous, like the punch line to a cracker joke. Instead, she'd appealed to her husband's romantic side. As teenagers, they'd spent many hours down the deep end of the Baths. The East, with its tiny houses stacked one on top of the other, offered very little privacy for courting couples, and they'd soon learned how to keep their faces casual and impassive while, beneath the waterline, they touched each other through their swimsuits in blatant disregard of the sign forbidding heavy petting. Kathleen and Bill had fond memories of the Baths. She'd asked him for one last dip, for old times' sake. Afterward she'd take him to S. D. Bell's for a fancy cup of coffee and a bun. It was not like Kathleen to ask for anything, so Bill had conceded immediately and been somewhat baffled to find the other Knit and Natter ladies intruding upon their romantic day out.

It was obvious that all four women were waiting for the foreign girl to appear. Kathleen understood their logic. She'd done her homework: fished the old King James Version out of the bookcase and read the story before leaving the house. If this girl was anything like Jesus—and that was the assumption to end all assumptions—they'd have to wait for the spirit to trouble the water. Or, in local parlance, the cure wouldn't take if they got into the pool before her. If Agnes's furtive glancing was anything to go by, the girl was already here and changing in the cubicle farthest from the entrance. Kathleen could picture her in there dragging her hair up into a high ponytail, contemplating a wee cappuccino after her swim, not for a minute anticipating six senior citizens waiting to suck the power out of her the instant she dived in. *Poor wee lassie,* thought Kathleen, *the young are never fully aware of their own capabilities.*

When she emerged, the girl was plainer than Kathleen had imagined, a bit hefty round the thighs and just as pale as a born-and-bred local. In all honesty, probably paler, for the local girls were always slathered in fake tan. She did not look like a miracle. She looked like the kind of woman who cleaned toilets for a living or worked in one of those vaping shops. Still, you couldn't judge people on looks alone. Kathleen herself had been at school with a girl who'd ended up a novelist, and a more homely-looking girl she'd never seen.

She glanced across the room. Agnes was already inclined toward the pool's edge, her weight resting on her front leg like a runner poised at the starting blocks. Mary was all business too, her face folded in grim concentration. *So, it has come to this,* thought Kathleen. They were pitching themselves against each other, for it was only the first to hit the water who'd get the good of the miracle. Everybody else would just get wet. Having a husband who was genuinely dying didn't seem to give Kathleen any natural advantage. It was going to be every Knit and Natter lady for herself. *Damn them all,* she thought. She deserved this more than they did. Or, rather, Bill did. There wasn't a one among them as poorly as him. And did you ever hear Bill complaining about his aches and pains and all the tablets he had to take? No, you certainly did not. Bill just quietly got on with dying. There was a lot to be said for that. As the girl curled her toes around the pool's lip and prepared to dive, Kathleen wrapped her arms around her husband's flabby belly and, with all the strength she could muster, jumped.

They hit the water a split second after the girl. The other four followed immediately, dully plopping into the pool like a handful of dropped stones. For a second the water was white with froth. It puckered and then settled slowly as five gray heads bobbed back to the surface, spluttering wildly. Agnes. Mary. Deirdre. Evelyn. And Kathleen. They blinked the chlorine out of their eyes. They looked like they wanted to stab one another, though their lips were smiling and their mouths were saying, "That was some splash, wasn't it? It's a wonder there's any water left in the pool."

Bill was not so buoyant. Kathleen watched on in horror as he sank to the bottom of the pool and lay there feebly, like a thing resigned. If she'd only been a little fitter, a little younger, a little stronger in the arms, she might have hauled her husband out, but Kathleen was turning seventy-four on her next birthday. She was well past the hauling stage. Despite her best intentions, she knew there was nothing she could do to help Bill. Bill required the assistance of the on-site lifeguard, a dose of oxygen, and a long weekend in ICU. He would not see the end of the month. Poor Bill.

The Knit and Natter ladies noted his declining condition and did not ask Kathleen if the Baths had been any help at all, if there was any truth in the rumor about the foreign girl. They said nothing at all to Kathleen but, in her absence, dissected the matter at some length. Mary especially felt terrible for having given the poor woman hope. She'd be more careful in the future about what she passed on. Well, she'd try to be more careful, at least.

Kathleen felt bad too, but her guilt was different. It was not so easy to dismiss. She'd done her best to help Bill. Or had she? Perhaps some selfish part of her had wanted the miracle for herself. Her body had rushed ahead of her good intentions, all fourteen and a half solid stone of it. It had been her heels that pierced the water first, her legs, her arms, her arthritic limbs that had soaked up all the cure. She'd felt it almost instantly. A hot white feeling

# IN THE CAR WITH THE RAIN COMING DOWN

There's a standoff in the front yard. No significant progress can be made until the men decide who's driving. It's the same every time we go anywhere together.

There are six cars in the yard. To say they've been parked would be giving the drivers too much credit. They look as if they've been dropped from a great height and have come to rest at outlandish angles, sniffing each other's bumpers like a pack of frisky dogs. The men are debating which cars will be required today. They've ruled out Matty's wee Nova. He's taken the backseat out for transporting feed. The whole car stinks of sheep and teenage boy. You wouldn't want to be cooped up in it, not in this clammy heat. The Escort's out too. It's filthy with dog hair. William, my father-in-law, keeps it for his collies. He's never once thought of cleaning it out. Sure, what would be the point? This leaves four cars in the running: Brian's big Audi, our—more modest—Audi, Cathy's Golf, and the Peugeot 407 William keeps for driving Susan to church on Sundays. It will require two cars to transport us all. We are nine these days, soon to be ten. Next time we head out together, we might need a third car. Baby seats take up a lot of space.

The men have distanced themselves from the women. They have their hands in their pockets, jiggling keys. They're not looking at each other. They are intentional about this. William has a suit jacket on, a dress shirt, and a tie. I recognize this getup. He used to wear it to church a few years back. It has seen better days. The elbows are shiny from being leaned on. There's a button missing from the cuff. It's too formal for a day like today. He'll be sweltered. He won't be able to kick football with the boys. The boys have made no such effort. Buff and Brian are in T-shirts and tracksuit bottoms. Matty's wearing a pair of shorts, a branded polo, and a hoodie knotted loosely round his shoulders. He's taken to wearing his shirt collar up, copying the lads at the Rugby Club. He's the youngest, the only one still living at home. Surrounded by his sons in their trainers, William looks stiff and faded, like a man lifted from another time.

William insists he will drive. Brian is equally insistent that he won't.

"It's your birthday, Dad," he says. "Let us chauffeur you about for a change."

Young William (or Buff, as we call him) says, "I don't mind driving either."

He says this so quietly nobody hears. I hear. He's my husband. I'm used to him. Even so, I miss half the things he says. Buff's a wild mumbler. Susan once told me he had a speech impediment when he was younger. He's never told me this himself. That's not to say it isn't true. There are lots of things Buff doesn't tell me. He's not having affairs or gambling or anything like that. It's the embarrassing things he keeps to himself. Diarrhea. Parking tickets. The time he tripped over the entrance mat in Tesco and fell into a stack of cereal packets. I only heard about that because Jill next door was coming through the door behind him.

I'd like my husband to be more assertive, especially around his family, but it doesn't come natural to him. I shout across the yard, "Buff could drive, so he could. We're only after filling the car up." Sometimes I have to do the asserting for him.

We women are standing at the door. We are glaring at the men. Four of us are wearing versions of the same thing: cutoff trousers, a T-shirt, sandals, and some sort of cardigan. Susan's gone for a calf-length skirt instead of cutoffs: mint green with cream and blue brushstrokes running across it in waves. I've never once seen my mother-in-law in trousers. I don't think she owns any. We women are losing patience with the men. We are clucking and fussing like caged chickens. There's a fresh cream sponge to be considered. It'll be going off in this heat.

"Don't be causing a scene, William," shouts Susan. "Just let the boys drive."

William turns to look at his wife. He raises a hand to her. "Wheesht, Susan," he says.

I've seen him pull the same move with cows.

Susan rolls her eyes. She mutters something under her breath. It could be "Amen"—for she's a very religious woman—or it could just as easily be "Men." My money's on the latter. It wouldn't be the first time I've heard her snap at William; only under her breath, of course. She'd never let him hear her giving cheek. She smooths the pink anorak draped over her forearm. Even on a warm day like today, Susan considers it tempting fate to leave home without an anorak. When this anorak's not hooked round her handbag strap, she carries it in front of her like a wine waiter's towel, shielding her belly and upper thighs. Susan is the sort of woman who doesn't like to be seen. This is not to say Susan doesn't see absolutely everything. She's like God Himself; you couldn't get anything by her. She glances upward now, past Brian's wife, Michelle, and the monkey puzzle tree that dominates the front lawn.

"There's a cloud," she announces solemnly. "It's going to rain if we don't get a move on."

I squint at the sky, angling my eyes north toward the coast, where we'll be heading as soon as the car situation's sorted. Sure enough, there is a cloud—a single fist-sized puff of white—interrupting the blue.

"Uch, it's only a wee cloud, Susan," I say. "I think we'll be grand."

My sister-in-law Cathy and her partner glance at each other and smile. The pair of them are always getting on like this. Smiling. Touching. Kissing each other in unusual places such as shoulders and earlobes. They are stupid happy. I wouldn't want to be a lesbian myself, but I envy Cathy all the same. Buff's never looked at me the way Clodagh looks at her, not even at the start, when we were shifting secretly behind the chicken sheds. Back then Buff said we were like Kate Winslet and your man in *Titanic,* and I said that was a very romantic thing to say (which, for Buff, it really was), though I couldn't, for the life of me, see the similarity. *Romeo and Juliet* would've been a better comparison, but Buff hadn't seen the film of it.

Cathy and Clodagh have piled all our picnic stuff up against the wall. They're standing in the middle of the mess, holding hands, waiting to see which cars to put it in. Cool boxes, biscuit tins, deck chairs, and rugs are all stacked next to the enormous Thermoses Susan's borrowed from the church. One's filled with tea. The other's got plain hot water in it because she prefers Nescafé with her sandwiches.

Michelle's done a Victoria sponge. She's already made a palaver of lifting it out of the boot. "Don't be looking too closely, ladies," she said, opening the cake tin and shoving it right under her mother-in-law's nose. "I literally flung this together last night. It's like a dog's dinner." Dog's dinner, my arse. Michelle's cake is like something you'd see in the *Bake Off* final. I've not bothered baking myself. Since the baby, I haven't been able to. The very sight of a raw egg turns me. It's the slime I can't be doing with: the way the white clings to the shell like loose snot. I've bought all our picnic stuff from Marks & Spencer. Correction: Buff's bought everything from Marks & Spencer. I gave him a list. He's good like that, offering before I have to ask. I can tell he'll be hands-on with the baby too. He's as excited as I am, in his own Buffy sort of way.

Susan's just noticed the Marks & Spencer bag. She pokes at it with the toe of her pewter sandal. She's made an effort for William's birthday. Her toenails are painted pink to match her fingernails, though the effect's muted by a layer of nylon tights: bamboo color, with a thick seam cutting across her nails.

"It's nice for some," she says. "I wish I could afford to buy everything out of Marksy's."

"Sorry," I say, "I've been that busy with work."

I've no idea why I'm apologizing.

Clodagh hears us. She catches my eye and smiles kindly. I wonder if she already knows; if Buff's told Cathy, and Cathy's told Clodagh, and the word's already out. We'd agreed we were going to tell the whole family together this afternoon, after the birthday cake. I smile back at Clodagh. She rolls her eyes in

Susan's direction. She mouths the word "Bitch." I almost laugh out loud. No, I decide, Clodagh doesn't know. She's just being nice. She can't stand Susan either.

I like Clodagh a lot. She's fit right in with the rest of us. Granted, the older generation's a bit stiff around her. Susan calls her "Catherine's wee friend," and William will up and leave the room if they're sitting too close or holding hands. But neither of them will ever say anything to the girls. They're too scared of where the conversation might lead. You start being honest with each other, and it's like opening what's-her-name's box. You never know what'll come slinking out. Despite the politeness, you can tell they'd prefer it if Clodagh was somebody else: a man, ideally. It's not just the lesbian thing that's grating on them. Clodagh's the other sort too. Her family's from Letterkenny. They've a hardware shop down there, in the Free State, as Susan insists upon calling it. You have to give the girl her dues. She has some balls, taking up with the likes of Cathy. I've no notion how they met. Before Clodagh, Cathy only ever brought farmers home: big pink-faced lads with boot-cut jeans and Caterpillar boots. God knows where she fell in with a lesbian. I was grateful when she did. I thought it'd take the heat off me. It didn't. There's a pecking order when it comes to my mother-in-law's affections. Even lesbian lovers rate higher than me.

Clodagh bends down and peers into the open mouth of the Marks & Spencer bag. She sticks her hand in, rifles around, and emerges with a packet of Percy Pigs.

"Good woman, Vicky," she says, beaming up at me. "These are, like, my all-time favorite sweeties."

"They totally are," confirms Cathy. "That one'll do anything for a Percy Pig."

"Anything," says Clodagh, flashing Cathy a very suggestive look. "Here, what would you do for a Percy Pig, Sue?" she asks, waggling the packet under my mother-in-law's nose.

Susan is flustered. She knows she's being mocked. She just doesn't know how to respond.

"No, thank you," she says. She slips a second arm under her folded anorak and pulls it toward herself defensively.

Clodagh continues to wave the Percy Pigs about. She's doing a funny dance, wiggling her backside as she emits a series of snuffly pig noises. Cathy is cracking up. I am cracking up. Susan is trying to smile and not quite managing it and holding her anorak so tightly it's going to need ironing later. She'd like to be in on the joke, but she doesn't know what the joke is. She looks toward Michelle, hoping she'll wade in and help. But Michelle is on her knees checking the state of her Victoria sponge. (Not good. Not good at all. The whole thing's started to slide in the heat.)

"It's going to rain," Susan announces abruptly. "We need to get going." An edge of panic has crept into her voice. It sticks a little on the third syllable so "to" and "rain" sound strangled, as if she's coughing and speaking at the same time.

Clodagh can see the joke's gone far enough. She stuffs the Percy Pigs into her cardigan pocket. "Don't be getting your knickers in a twist, Sue," she says. She sticks her thumb and index finger into her mouth, forming a circle beneath her tongue. She blows hard. The noise that comes out is somewhere between a wolf whistle and the sound William makes when he's calling the dogs. The men stop talking. They turn to stare at Clodagh.

"Right, lads, let's head," she shouts. "Buff and Brian should drive. Their cars are bigger."

It is as if God has spoken. The men stop arguing instantly. They nod at Clodagh and, without saying anything, disperse. I can't decide whether it's the tone she's taken or the fact that she's an outsider. Surely it can't be anything to do with her being a lesbian. These men don't usually take instructions from women. I'd be jealous if I wasn't half in love with Clodagh myself. I've known my father-in-law for the better part of two decades, and I could never take that tone with him.

William gets into the dog car. He backs it up so there's room for both the Audis to edge past. Brian, Buff, and Matty start loading the picnic stuff into the open boots. Clodagh stands in the middle of the yard, directing operations. William and Susan will go with Brian and Michelle, the birthday boy riding up front, next to his son. William gets into the passenger seat immediately. He doesn't even bother offering it to his wife. It's a country thing. You'd not expect a man to sit in the backseat. It wouldn't be dignified.

Our car's not as flashy as Brian's, but the backseat is roomier. We'll take Matty and the girls. It'll be a squeeze, but that'll hardly bother Cathy and Clodagh. Matty comes stumbling across the yard with a rug and two deck chairs. "Shotgun," he shouts.

Buff lifts the chairs out of his brother's arms and places them inside the boot. "Do you mind if Vicky sits up front, mate?" he asks. "She gets a bit bokey in the backseat."

"'Course," says Matty, "so long as I'm not stuck between the dykes like a big gooseberry."

Susan's ears prick up. She pauses—one leg into Brian's Audi, one leg out—and gives Matty a withering look. "That's no way to talk about your sister and her friend," she says. "Show a bit of respect."

I'm shocked on multiple levels. Mostly, I'm surprised to

discover that Susan knows a word like "dyke." I wonder where she's heard it. Maybe on Sky. William's finally upgraded to satellite. If you ask William, he'll say the Sky's for the young lad. He'll claim he never watches it himself. Buff says he's hooked on the American programs. He's big into *How I Met Your Mother*. He has the whole series prerecorded.

We finish loading up the cars and climb in. Brian sticks his head out the window. I have to open my door to hear him. Our electric windows are on the blink.

"I'll go first," he shouts across to Buff. "We'll head for the Whiterocks. Keep your phone on in case there's a change of plan."

"Okay," says Buff. I turn to relay this message to Brian. He already has his window up. He revs the Audi and takes off at speed. By the time Buff turns our car and edges carefully down the lane, avoiding the suicidal cats who fling themselves under the wheels of passing cars, Brian's Audi is long gone. He'll be at the Whiterocks before we've even made it to Ballymoney. Brian drives like a lunatic.

Buff is careful behind the wheel; cautious, even. He passed his test on the third attempt and claims this makes him a better driver. He has never had an accident. At least he's never hit another vehicle. He does have a tendency to drive into stationary objects: bollards, walls, curbs. He's not good at judging distance—something to do with his prescription lenses—but at least he never goes fast enough to do any real damage. As we drive out of the village and turn onto the dual carriageway, he begins to accelerate, slowly and meticulously working his way up through the gears till he hits sixty and goes no further.

Matty leans through from the backseat. "Put the foot down, Buff," he says. "You're driving like an old woman."

"Sixty's fast enough," says Buff.

"It's not a bloody funeral."

"I won't be going any faster than sixty, Matthew. If that doesn't suit, you can get out and walk."

"Naw, mate. I'd be scared of overtaking you." He turns to claim a congratulatory high five off Cathy. She puts him in a headlock instead.

"Leave the Buffster alone," she says. "It's not his fault. The oldest sibling's always the sensible one. It's just the way it is."

"Now, Catherine, by 'sensible' do you actually mean 'boring'?" asks Matty, squirming free of her grip.

They're always taking the piss out of Buff. It's usually good-hearted. Sometimes I even join in. They mock his driving, his dress sense (which is, to be honest, nonexistent), his mumbly way of speaking, his love of the Carpenters. My husband is an easy man to mock. Usually, it doesn't bother me. Families are supposed to wind each other up, aren't they? It never seems to annoy Buff. He's used to it. Today I'm not in the mood for their winding. I am annoyed on my husband's behalf.

"Leave Buff alone," I snap. "He's going slow because of the baby."

"What?" says Matty.

"There's a baby?" says Cathy.

"Wow, congratulations," says Clodagh, already two steps ahead of the others.

"I thought we were going to wait till everybody was together," says Buff.

"Sorry, love," I say, placing my hand over his hand where it's resting on the gearstick. "It just slipped out." I turn to face the backseat. "Yeah, it's early days, but it looks like we're going to have a wee one in January." I remove my hand from the gearstick and pat my stomach lightly. The motion's already instinctive.

"That's amazing news," says Clodagh.

"Well done, big lad," says Matty, squeezing Buff's shoulder. "I didn't think you had it in you."

"I'm going to be an auntie," says Cathy. She tries to hug me from behind, stretching her arms round the passenger seat's headrest, almost throttling me in the process.

Clodagh whips out the Percy Pigs. "I think this calls for a celebration," she says. "Percy Pigs all round." She passes the packet into the front seat. I turn the music up. "Rainy Days and Mondays" comes on. It's not a particularly upbeat choice, but the only two CDs Buff has in his car are *The Best of the Carpenters* and *The Carpenters Covered*.

I glance over at my husband. He's watching the young ones; he still has an eye on the road. The other's trained on the rearview mirror. He's holding the steering wheel carefully with both hands. He is smiling. Buff's not given to shows of emotion, but I can tell he's made up right now. We've not discussed how the announcement will play out. We don't want a big fuss. Neither of us enjoys being the center of attention. Still, it's great to see how excited the backseat contingent is. This baby's a big deal for us. We've been waiting a long time for it. By "waiting," I mean "trying." By "trying," I mean doctors' appointments and schedules, prescriptive sex, and four rounds of IVF. We've spent all the money we were saving for the loft conversion, and the conservatory, and the new kitchen. It has been worth it, though. The minute those wee lines appeared on the test, I knew it had all been worth it.

I won't forget that morning in a hurry. Buff was waiting for me when I came out of the loo. I was still holding the stick. I had it bundled up in a wad of toilet roll. I tried to tell him it was positive. I was crying so much I couldn't get the words out. Poor Buff, he wasn't sure whether they were good or bad tears. He'd seen me come out of the toilet bawling that many times before. He took the test out of my hand; it was covered in pee, but he didn't even bother with the toilet roll. He stared at it for ages, his big face all screwed up in concentration.

Eventually, he looked up at me and said, "Two lines is good, right?"

I nodded.

"We're having a baby?"

I nodded again. I probably should have said, *We've a long way to go yet, love. Wait till we talk to the doctor. It might not work out.* But I knew in the pit of my belly, this one was going to stick. Sometimes you just know a thing is inevitable. There's a heaviness to it. It was like that with me and Buff. The first time I saw him at the bus stop, I just knew that was me forever: stuck with him, in a good way. We were sixteen when we started going out. We're thirty-four now. It shouldn't have taken so long to get to this point, but nothing's ever come easy to us. Well, nothing except getting together. That felt like falling. We couldn't have avoided each other even if we'd wanted to.

"I can't believe we're finally having a baby," Buff said, holding the test in one hand.

I wrapped my arms around him. He held me differently, sort of gentler, like he was scared of crushing the baby. I'm a good bit shorter than he is, so when I whispered, "I can't believe it either," the sentiment was lost. All my words disappeared into his chest, while my ear—angled, as it was, toward his chin—caught everything he said ("God, I can't wait to tell Mam and Dad"). I wished I hadn't heard, for it stung to know that even during this, the most intimate of moments, his parents were first and foremost in his thoughts. I let it go. I didn't want to ruin the moment. I understood where he was coming from. I've always understood. My parents aren't great either.

Buff's the oldest, but he's never been their first or favorite. When he's in one of his moods, he'll say, "They only had me to practice, so they could get everything right with Brian." It's probably not true. It feels like it is. Buff's the screwup. Brian's the golden boy. For every shitstorm we've muddled through—my redundancy, Buff's psoriasis, the bungalow subsiding, the baby stuff—Brian's enjoyed unmerited success. He's currently on his sixth promotion. If he keeps progressing at this rate, he'll be CEO before he's forty. He has a big house and a holiday home in Portstewart, a full head of hair, and a washboard stomach. He's even managed to bag the only woman in County Antrim who looks like a lingerie model and gets on like a minister's wife. In short, Brian's the kind of son William and Susan actually wanted. They're not bad people. They love Buff too, but it's a different kind of love. It's always angled down. With Brian, they're constantly looking up.

The baby will change everything. A grandchild will level the playing field. When we drop our bombshell, we'll be front and center for a change. I can picture the look on their faces. I can pivot like a TV camera round every single one of my in-laws, framing them for a second in my mind. I know who'll be smiling and who'll look like they're sucking lemons. I can tell you right now how it's going to play out this afternoon. Sure, haven't I pictured this moment a hundred times? Haven't I wanted it for Buff almost as much as I've wanted it for myself?

They'll all be sitting about on picnic rugs; everybody splayed out on the sand; everybody except Susan, who always insists upon a proper deck chair. She uses her arthritis as an excuse. I suspect she thinks her backside's more refined than everyone else's. She'll be sat there like Lady Muck, with the anorak draped over her shoulders Superman-style. The hood may or may not be up. This will depend upon how imminent she believes the rain to be. She'll be the one who pours the tea and butters the pancakes and says every thirty seconds, "Is everybody all right for something?" It is Susan who will decide when it's time for William's birthday cake. She is the matriarch. Her role is long established. Nobody, not even Clodagh, is brave enough to mount a challenge.

Cathy will light the candles and come at her daddy with whatever's left of the Victoria sponge. This too is set in stone. As the only girl child, it's always been her job to present the birthday cake and start the singing. "Happy Birthday to you," she'll begin, and everyone will quickly join in: "Happy Birthday to you. Happy Birthday, dear William/Dad/Mr. McKinley" (under my breath, I will substitute "Granda" for "William" and feel the wee hairs on my arms begin to rise).

Once the cake's cut and everybody's said, "It's absolutely delicious, Michelle," and Michelle's made a point of batting their compliments away like persistent bluebottles, Buff will clear his throat awkwardly and maybe get to his feet. Buff is inclined to be overly formal on occasions like this. "So," he'll say, "Victoria and I have a wee bit of news. Another birthday present, so to speak. There's no other way to say it, Dad, but you're going to be a granda soon." They'll all smile and ask questions and want to hug us. It will be like how it is when the fans rush onto the pitch after a football match and lift the winning team up in the air, chanting. In my head, it will be exactly like this when we tell them.

It is not like this at all.

Somewhere between the Ballymoney roundabout and Ballybogey, it begins to rain.

Susan is miles ahead, bundled up in the backseat of Brian's car, yet I can hear her pointing out the obvious. "See," she'll be saying, barely able to suppress her own smugness, "I told youse it was for raining. We'll not be able to picnic now." She'll be enjoying this in her own dour way.

In our car, it is Cathy who notices the rain first. "Shite," she says, "Mam was right. It is for raining."

Buff switches the wipers on at the lowest setting. The rain smears across the windscreen in dense, spit-thick streaks. It's really only drizzling. We are optimistic in our car. We have reason for optimism today.

"It's just mizzling," I say.

"It'll pass," says Cathy.

"Sure, we've all got coats with us," says Clodagh.

"It's not as dull-looking over there," says Buff. He inclines his head toward the coast. "See, that wee patch of blue. That's where we're heading."

In the backseat behind Buff, Matty's phone goes off. His ringtone is a fella with a thick Belfast accent yelling "Yeeeeooooww," stretching the word out so it sounds like some kind of animal noise. He got it off one of the lads in the Rugby Club. It's really annoying. We're on the third "Yeeeeoooowww" before he manages to fumble the phone out of his pocket and press it to his ear.

"Uh-huh," he says, flapping his hand about to indicate I'm to turn the Carpenters down. "It's not too bad here, Shelly. Just drizzling, really. Uh-huh. She does. All right, then, if Mum thinks it's best. We'll be there in five. Naw, make that ten. Buff's driving."

He hangs up and slips his phone back into his pocket. "Michelle says it's lashing at the Whiterocks," he says. "Absolutely pissing."

"Will we go somewhere for a coffee instead?" asks Clodagh.

"Aye," says Cathy. "There's a nice new place on the Prom in Portstewart."

"That's far too sensible for the McKinleys," says Matty. "Mum says we're not for wasting all the food she's prepared. We'll have the picnic in the car."

"Seriously?" says Cathy. "We're not weans anymore. There's hardly any room in here."

Matty shrugs. "Mother's spoken. We're having a car picnic. And damn it, Catherine," he adds, mimicking Susan's dour drawl, "you'll enjoy every second of it."

Everyone laughs, even Cathy. "Remember the time we went to Ayr on the ferry and we ended up having a picnic in the layby next to the sewage plant?"

"How could I forget a magic moment like that?" says Matty.

"You pair were probably too wee to remember," says Buff, addressing them in the rearview mirror, "but Dad once took us all to North Wales for a holiday, and it rained the entire time. You wouldn't believe how many picnics we had in the car that week. Youse two always got put in the boot to make room for the rest of us. It was different back then. You could put your children in the boot if you'd a big enough car."

"Am I wrong here, Buff, or did we once have a picnic in a multistory car park?" asks Cathy.

"We did indeed, Catherine. That would've been in Conwy, on our way to the castle."

"And am I completely mad in thinking that Mum set the deck chairs out down the side of the car?"

"No, you are spot on there, Catherine: deck chairs, cool box, china cups for the tea. Our mother knows how to picnic properly, even when she's serving sandwiches out the back of a clapped-out Astra."

Clodagh has been noticeably silent throughout this exchange. I can see her wee face in the mirror. She looks perplexed.

"Is it a Protestant thing?" she asks. "Having your picnic in the car? 'Cause it's not something my folks do."

"Naw," says Cathy quickly.

"I don't know," I say. "Maybe."

"Absolutely," says Matty. "Nobody actually enjoys a car picnic. It's just something you have to endure. Must be a Protestant thing."

Everyone laughs except Buff. He turns to look at me. I can tell exactly what's bothering him. His face is like a window. I can see right through him.

"Don't worry," I say. "It'll be grand. We can still tell them. We'll just wait for the right moment."

"But it won't be like we planned it."

"It'll be grand," I repeat. I pat Buff's thigh. I smile reassuringly. "Sure, it doesn't matter how we tell them."

He doesn't look convinced.

"Your folks are going to be over the moon," I say.

He nods a little. He's about to let himself smile.

"And even if they're not as excited as we want them to be, sure, it doesn't matter, Buff. It's our baby. Who cares what they think?"

The instant the words are out of my mouth, I can tell I've said the wrong thing. Buff's mouth sets. His hands grip the steering wheel so tightly I can see the white of bones knuckling through his skin.

"I care what they think," he says. His voice is raw as ripped paper. He's practically shouting. The backseat contingent has definitely heard. The air is heavier inside the car now. It takes ten minutes to drive to the Whiterocks, and nobody attempts to break the silence. When we arrive in the car park, Buff pulls up next to Brian's Audi.

Michelle's standing beside the open boot, an umbrella clutched in one hand and, in the other, a Tupperware full of white-bread sandwiches. She's chatting to Susan. The boot has swallowed her head and torso. The only part of my mother-in-law that's visible is her backside, bent and straining beneath the confines of that god-awful skirt. I can't see what she's doing in there: filling teacups, no doubt, or slicing up wheaten, creaming individual meringues for dessert.

They've started without us. Behind the fogged-up windows of the Audi, I can see Brian tucking into what might be a chocolate éclair. William has a mug in his hand. I can't see for condensation, but I'd be reasonably certain it's his favorite John Deere one. He won't take his tea in anything else.

The women are seeing to the men before they eat, themselves. "I'll go and give them a hand," I say.

It's not so much duty as habit. Buff does nothing to stop me. He'll expect me to bring the tea to his door. It doesn't matter if I get drenched in the process. Tea making's a woman's job. I don't resent the assumption. He knows better. It's not how we are, together, in our own wee house. But here, there's his father to consider and his brothers too. I wouldn't want him losing face in front of them. As soon as the motor's stopped, I open my door. Michelle was right. It is absolutely lashing. I open the glove compartment and remove my umbrella. I stick it out the door and force it up before I slide out.

"Do you want some help?" asks Clodagh.

"Naw," I say, "no point in us both getting soaked. I'll bring the food over to youse."

I give Cathy a bit of a look. Clodagh's a guest. I wouldn't expect her to help. But Cathy's one of us. She should've offered, at least. I close the passenger door and pick my way through the puddles to the back of Brian's Audi.

"Sorry we took so long," I say.

Michelle gives me a watery smile. "We started without you," she says. She isn't apologizing. She's merely stating a fact. "Do you want a sandwich?" she asks, extending the Tupperware box. "There's paper plates in the boot."

"Aye, I'll take some over to the ones in our car."

I take the Tupperware from Michelle and go into the boot for the plates. It is immediately apparent that Susan has not heard us arrive. You can hear almost nothing with your head ducked under the parcel shelf. She starts when she sees my face come looming toward her. She almost drops the mug she's filling. It's a bone-china number with a pheasant printed on the side. A wee slurp of hot tea goes slopping over its edge, lands in the open sugar bowl, and forms a brown crystallized lump. Susan clearly hasn't noticed, or she'd be in there picking it out with a teaspoon.

"Goodness, Victoria," she says, straightening up, "where did you appear from?"

"We just arrived," I say. "I'm after some plates." I switch hands in order to hold my umbrella over Susan's head. My own hair's getting wet now, but I don't want my mother-in-law adding thoughtlessness to my ever growing list of faults.

"They're in there, next to the cool box," she says. She makes no effort to assist me.

"Right. Thanks." I reach in, straining to make sure Susan's still protected by my umbrella. I lift out a wad of paper plates. "It's a pity about the rain."

"I told youse it was going to rain. We might've missed it if we'd left earlier."

"Uch, well," I say, "we'll not let a bit of rain ruin the afternoon. We've a lot to celebrate."

"We do indeed," says Susan; her whole face lights up. She's like the inside of a fridge when the door opens, sort of glowy. She smiles over my shoulder at Michelle. Though I can't see her, I can feel Michelle smiling back. I wonder if she knows. Maybe Buff's told Brian, and Brian's told Michelle, and Michelle's told Susan. It'd be just like Michelle to tell Susan. Michelle's way more calculating than she lets on.

"What do you mean?" I ask tentatively. "William's birthday?"

"Aye, well, of course there's William's birthday to celebrate," says Susan. "But there's the baby too. I've only just heard."

"You have?"

"Aye, I suppose I'm probably the last to know."

I shrug. I'm not sure who knows and who doesn't know anymore. Over Susan's shoulder, I watch Matty draw a sad face in the condensation. They're probably starving in there. Any second now, they'll wind the windows down and start baying for sandwiches.

"How did you find out?" I ask.

"It was my fault," interrupts Michelle. "I let it slip."

*Bitch,* I think. I manage to keep this thought to myself. Later tonight, when we're on our own, I'll have a good old moan to Buff. He doesn't mind me giving off about his sister-in-law, though he never joins in himself.

Susan slips an arm round Michelle's almost nonexistent waist. "I'm glad you told us, sweetheart," she says.

"I thought you should know. Brian said I shouldn't tell you, but it's a big deal—your first grandbaby—I thought you should know straight away, Susan."

"It's so funny the way it came out," Susan says, smiling. "Wait till you hear what happened, Victoria. The pair of us were in the boot here, getting things sorted, and I said to Michelle, 'Michelle, you have to try one of these cream cheese and grape sandwiches. I got the idea for them from *Bella* magazine. They're absolutely gorgeous.' Then Michelle says to me, 'I can't eat cream cheese at the minute, Susan, because of the baby.' And, well, that's how it slipped out, Victoria. Isn't that hilarious?"

I nod dumbly. My head feels far too heavy. If I wasn't holding the stupid umbrella over Susan, I'd have my hands under my chin, taking the weight of it off my neck.

Susan mistakes my silence for interest. "She's not that far gone, are you, Michelle?"

"Only eight weeks, Susan. It's early days."

I am thinking eight weeks is far too early to be telling folks. I've lost babies at nine weeks and eleven. I wouldn't go shouting about an eight-week baby. It's far too soon. It might not last.

"I'm glad you've told us," Susan continues, pouring the tea as she talks. "I mean, you wouldn't want to be telling everyone at this stage. But family's different, isn't it, Victoria?"

"Yes," I say. "Family's different."

I look over at our car. Buff's wiped a hole in the condensation. He's peering out of it, his mouth hung open like a doddery auld one. He has a particularly gormless look off him when he's hungry. *My poor husband,* I think. He doesn't know yet. He's sat there waiting for me to bring him a ham sandwich and, after that, a slice of buttered wheaten, and he is genuinely happy in himself; happier than he's been in years. He still thinks the day is ours.

I am overcome with feelings for my husband. There's a bit of love in there and a lot of pity and a thing that I believe to be righteous anger. I pull the umbrella away from Susan's head and cover my own. I purposefully angle the umbrella's edge so a big plop of water drips off and runs down the back of her neck. It is no real consolation, but I can't say it doesn't give me a little rush of pleasure to see Susan start and whack her head off the parcel shelf, sloshing hot coffee over her cardigan sleeve.

"Whoops," I say. I stop myself from apologizing. "I'm just going to take Buff his tea. Congratulations, Michelle. I'm delighted for you and Brian." I say this last part in the same voice I use for offering the bereaved sympathy after a funeral. I am steady. I am serious. I am perhaps a little too somber.

I take Buff's tea over to him. I lean through the open window to offer him his choice of sandwiches. I can see they've already been picked over. Brian and William have lifted all the chicken ones. I watch Buff make his selection, choosing the best of the leftovers. It's not like me at all, but I'm suddenly struck with the need to kiss him, right there, in front of everyone. It's not something we usually do. Neither is it desire. It is simply meeting a need. I take his big head in my hands. I kiss him lightly on the lips, and I call him by his real name. "William," I say, "you are the best." This will mean more to him than saying *I love you,* or *I'm proud of you,* or any of that sappy shite. It's first place Buff's after. God love him, he's only ever been second.

We'll not tell the in-laws today. The moment's gone.

When the rain eases off, we'll circle round Brian's car with the rest of them: the young men standing, Susan and William on the deck chairs, us girls resting up against the open boot, our backsides competing for space. When the birthday candles are blown out and Brian says he has something to tell us, I'll walk over to my husband's side. I'll take his hand and squeeze it tightly. I'll not have to say anything. He'll know, as I know, not to mention our baby. Today is Brian and Michelle's day. We can't take away from their news.

We'll congratulate the pair of them. We will measure our words carefully, saying enough to cover ourselves but no more. We'll accept a slice of Victoria sponge on a clean paper plate and eat without pleasure. Two bites in, I'll assure Michelle that the cake's absolutely grand, that the heat's not got to it at all. Between the nine of us, we'll devour the whole thing. Then, noticing the way the men are scraping at their plates, I will say, "There's a wee Marks and Spencer coffee cake in there. I could open it if youse are still hungry."

Susan will look at me like I've two heads and say, "We don't need another cake, Victoria. Don't be opening it. Take it home with youse and put it in the freezer."

I'll say, "I brought it for William, for his birthday. Why don't youse take it home with you?"

"William doesn't like coffee cake," she'll say.

I will be overcome by the desire to stab her with my disposable plastic fork. I will be able to feel the press of it jabbing into her throat, right beneath her hairy chin. I will picture the red blood dripping onto her pale pink anorak; the stains it'll leave on that pastel skirt. My mouth will be full of vicious words, things I've always wanted to say to her. Buff will squeeze my hand then, just a little squeeze: a reminder rather than a restraint.

"I could go for a bit of coffee cake," he'll say. "What about yourself, Matty? Hoke it out of the cool bag there, Vicky."

I will understand then that Buff has been holding me all this time, ages and ages, in his own gentle way. I am holding Buff too. I have been holding him tight—so tight and close—since the first moment I clapped eyes on him, standing there next to the bus stop in his too-small school uniform. I have wanted to hold on to this man. I have wanted him to hold on to me. We may well be holding on by the skin of our teeth, but neither of us has any notion of letting go.

# ONE-HANDER

It was in the fridge when they got back from visiting Granny and Gramps. Laura saw it as soon as she opened the door. It was sitting on the shelf where she kept her cheese and margarine, splayed out on a plate she didn't recognize. The plate was a seventies mustard brown. Laura's crockery was all white. As were her sheets. Her carpets. Her walls and both the sofas in the living room. She wanted the house looking like a perfume ad. Minimal. Stark. Classy. Neat. It was hard to keep the place pristine. Darek worked on a building site. He was always bringing it home on his boots.

Laura poked her head into the fridge. She was after milk for the tea. She was not expecting a bloody hand. And the hand was nothing if not bloody. Red and dripping. Raw as meat. All five fingers distinctly arranged as if offering her a wild high five. Blood pooled beneath the palm and around the wrist. This blood was a slightly darker shade than the blood that was smeared across its fingers and beneath its nails. The whole foul package was bound up in a layer of tight clingfilm. Chilled flesh pressed against see-through plastic. Swaddled. Squidged. Barely contained. It looked like something you'd buy from the butcher's and chop up for a quick stir-fry. Laura noted the largeness of it—a man's hand or a mannish woman's—then the nausea caught up with her.

She closed the door and took a second to steady herself, leaning up against the kitchen island where the day's dishes were stacked, waiting on someone—most likely her—to unload the dishwasher and load it again. She considered calling the police and instantly dismissed this thought. They'd hear her name, which was also her daddy's, and assume she'd brought this on herself. In a way, she knew she had. Taking up with Darek. Moving him in. Not even trying to hide the fact. The police would enjoy pointing this out.

Darek was already installed in front of the telly. Laura could hear him scanning Netflix for something to watch. A two-second burp of music. Canned laughter. Then people screaming in American accents. Darek liked the American shows. The accents were easier. The local accent was an absolute bitch if you'd not grown up here. "Sorry, love," she shouted in. "We're out of milk. Are you all right with black tea?" This was a lie. There was plenty of milk—half a quart of green top nestled up against the salad dressing—but there was no way Laura was going back into the fridge. She didn't need another eyeful. The image of the hand was already implanted on the back of her brain.

"Tea?" she repeated, keeking her head out the kitchen and down the hall. Either Darek did not hear or couldn't be bothered to reply. Laura fired the kettle on anyway. She needed something to do with her hands. She was already nervy from the run-in at Granny and Gramps's. The hand had tipped her over the edge. Her whole body was trembling, her legs like water with the shock and a feeling akin to relief. She'd been waiting so long—almost six months—for something awful to catch up with them. It had felt like a sort of loosening to open the fridge and discover the hand; to have it over and done with at last.

And a severed hand was not the worst thing they could have left her. A hand could be dealt with quite easily. Wrapped in a bin liner. Shoved to the bottom of the wheelie bin. Pitched off the Albert Bridge tomorrow morning on her way to work. *Yes,* thought Laura, *it could have been an awful lot worse.* She'd been bracing herself for a bullet or a petrol bomb. A dollop of dog shit shoved through the letter box. If she didn't consider the arm that had previously owned the hand or the person attached to this arm, she could almost dismiss it. She could find it funny or, if not funny, then ludicrous in a grotesque sort of way. Like something from a horror movie. *Wasn't there a film about a severed hand? A green wizened-up thing that was possessed?* She'd watched it once with her brothers, back when they were in primary school. She'd laughed at it and not been scared. Laura wasn't a squeamish girl.

Her family had no time for squeamishness. As a child, she'd seen things she shouldn't have seen. Other bloody, violent things. In the backyard. The garage. The bathtub. Through a crack in the bathroom door. Then they'd come for her daddy and put him away. The house had been quiet for a while, until her brothers joined the local contingent. One was fifteen, the other sixteen. Her ma had cried her eyes out the night they told her and begged them to have a bit of sense. Her ma's sister—Auntie Liz—said it was the boys taking after their daddy that'd driven her ma to an early grave. Laura hadn't stuck around. She'd moved out as soon as she could. By nineteen, she'd her own wee place in a different estate. She'd let her ma visit but not the boys. She didn't want them seeing where she lived, though she knew they could find out easy enough. She didn't want them dirtying up the place. It was so clean, so white, so very different from the house where she'd grown up.

Laura leaned against the fridge door, displacing magnets, takeaway menus, and a photo of Darek's niece and nephew in their school uniforms. She forced herself to picture a stranger creeping round her kitchen, rooting about in her cupboards, positioning the hand where she'd see it, moving the Dairylea triangles to one side. She tried to be okay with this. It was just about manageable if she knew the hand would be the end of it. There was every possibility it would. She'd been threatened now. Put in her place. Intimidated, as they said in the papers. There wouldn't be anything after the hand. "That'll be the end of it," she muttered as she dunked the tea bags and got the chocolate digestives out of the larder, taking them through to the living room. Her hands were still shaking, making ripples in the tea, but she was a good bit steadier than five minutes ago. She'd deal with the hand in the morning; get rid of it while Darek was still in his pit. There was no need to tell him. Sure, he'd already had enough to deal with, what with folks bad-mouthing him at the bus stop and the graffiti appearing on their front wall. She'd bin the hand, or bury it, or pitch it into the bloody Lagan. Once it was gone, things would be grand.

They sat through a cop show Darek liked, neither really watching. Laura sipped her tea and picked at loose threads in the throw. Darek scrolled through Twitter on his phone. There was an atmosphere in the room. It had nothing to do with the hand. They'd dragged the heaviness home from Granny and Gramps's. They had yet to acknowledge it. Laura had not apologized for her grandfather's behavior, and Darek had not said, *What the hell's wrong with your family, Laura? Are they all psychopaths?* This conversation was yet to be had. Talking most likely would have helped. It would have lightened the mood, at least. They might even have made a joke of it: Laura saying, as she'd said when the graffiti first appeared, "What did you expect, Dar? You're married to the mob now, so you are."

Sure, you had to keep laughing or you'd fall apart, though it wasn't one bit funny, the things they'd written on her wall. Or finding a bloody hand in her fridge. Or the way Gramps had looked at the love of her life as he'd stood on the welcome mat, petrol-station carnations in hand, saying, "I'm so pleased to finally meet you, sir," introducing himself as Darek, which was so close to being Derek, just one vowel shy of a proper name. Gramps had instantly lit upon it. And the accent which, even after eight years here, had yet to fully assimilate. "Are you daft, wee girl?" the old man had said, fairly spitting the words at her. "Taking up with a bloody Pole. I'm guessing he's the other sort too. Have you forgotten who your daddy is?" Laura had wanted to say, *Chance'd be a fine thing*, but Gramps was already depositing a gob of phlegm on Darek's shoe. He was already slamming the door on them.

"Right," Darek had said as he'd stood there contemplating another closed door. He was far too used to this sort of thing, accustomed enough to fall back on humor: "I'm guessing we're not getting any dinner. McDonald's drive-through on the way home?" He'd reached for her hand, but Laura wasn't in the mood. She'd shoved her fists into her anorak pockets. She'd turned on her heel and stomped back to the car. She was angry, partially with Darek, who should've been more upset than he was. Most of her anger was for herself. She'd drawn a line beneath the lot of them—her daddy, her brothers, her poor dead ma—yet had hoped her grandparents might be softer. That they might accept

Darek for what he was: a decent fella who treated her well. They were older. On the telly, old ones were usually softer on their grandkids.

And maybe, possibly, Granny was. She might not think the same as Gramps. But Laura had seen with her ma how hard it was for women to get round the men who stood in their way. They could think all the soft thoughts they wanted to think; that didn't mean they could act on them. Sure enough, while they were sitting in Connswater Macky D's eating their nuggets in icy silence, a text had come through from Granny Mo. "Sorry love. Your granda has an awful temper. *Derek* seems lovely. Very handsome and his English is great. Maybe we could meet for a coffee sometime in town. Just the three of us." Darek had asked her who was texting, and Laura had said it was Sharon from work. She'd deleted the text without replying. It was easier not to complicate things. Her family was awful; awful, awful, with no exceptions. In the future, she'd steer well clear. Darek was her family now.

She'd fully intended to talk it over once they got home, but she'd not anticipated the hand in the fridge. Now Laura hadn't the energy for a deep and meaningful. She just wanted to slob in front of the telly, drink her tea, and go to bed. It wouldn't come to an argument—Darek wasn't the arguing kind—but talking about her family would scoop the guts right out of her. She had work first thing. And the hand to deal with. She'd be worth nothing in the morning if they sat up half the night crying and trying to reason it out. Instead, she rested a hand on Darek's thigh and leaned her head against his shoulder. She hoped he'd read solidarity in this gesture. That he'd know she was not on her family's side. Laura was not now, nor ever had been, a Wilson in the traditional sense.

When the episode ended, they went up to bed. Darek did not speak of the things Gramps had said. Laura did not mention the hand in the fridge. They brushed their teeth, standing side by side at the bathroom sink, and afterward, climbed into bed. It was three months since Darek had moved in, six since they'd started seeing each other in a serious way. Sex was now reserved for weekends and the odd Thursday night if they'd been out and had a drink. Most evenings followed a similar script. Ten minutes of reading separate paperbacks. Quick kiss. Lights out. "Sweet dreams, I love you." "I love you too." Tonight it was only when Darek began to snore that Laura realized they'd forgotten the kissing bit. It was only a small kiss—a tight, closed-mouth peck of a thing—but the timing seemed significant. Or perhaps, she reasoned, it was just a coincidence. The honeymoon couldn't last forever. There was always going to be a kissless night.

It took her hours to fall asleep. The police helicopter was out again. Laura could hear it strumming above the roof. It itched at her anxiety. Her feet were boiling. Her face felt like it was on too tight. She was up to pee three times and didn't get over till almost four. When she did, she dreamed of her daddy, and her brothers, and Gramps as he'd looked when she was wee, and all the fellas she'd ever gone with: Billy and Kyle and Stevie Duncan and the other Stevie with the mustache. They were standing round her in a circle, calling her all the names of the day. Her daddy's voice was the loudest. She was a bitch and a slut, a calearied wee bint, whoring herself out to the Poles. He was ashamed to have raised a daughter like her.

In the dream, Darek could not get close enough to help. He was outside the circle, calling her name. He hadn't a hope of getting in. There were too many men in his road. They all began to slap her, one at a time. They'd big leery grins on them. She could tell they were pure loving it. They took aim and hit her hard between her shoulder blades. They spread their fingers really wide so the sound of flesh meeting tight back flesh was bullet-loud, not dissimilar to a round of applause. When Laura was wee, they'd hit each other this way in the playground. It was meant to be a laugh. Afterward, they'd pull up their shirts and examine each other for handprints. They'd called this "game" the Red Hand of Ulster, a local spin on the Chinese burn. You'd to do your best not to cry no matter how much the slapping hurt. As the men lined up to hit her, Laura felt the pain as a real hurt. She also knew she was dreaming. Soon she'd wake up in her own wee bed.

She woke at six, dripping in sweat, slipped out of bed without waking Darek, and showered quietly, keeping her head out of the water. She didn't want to risk the hair dryer. She had to be out before Darek woke. Her hair could go another day if she put it up in a ponytail. The hand was just where she'd left it, next to the margarine. As she slid it out—plate pinched between fingertips to avoid the blood—she kept her gaze loose and vague, looking past the ugliness. She swept the hand, plate and all, into a Tesco bag. Then placed it inside a second carrier, a Marksy's one this time. The plastic was thicker. You couldn't see through it as easily. She washed her hands twice with bar soap, put on her coat, and headed out.

There was a big dumpster three streets away. It was half full of rubble from a house that was getting an extension put in. Laura had clocked it yesterday. This morning it'd come straight to mind. As she approached its rusty yellow belly, she glanced up and down the street for observers. The street was empty. Every house had its curtains drawn. Most folks hadn't even got their lights on yet. Laura pitched the bagged hand deftly in. Leaning over the dumpster's edge, she dragged a lampshade and a sheet of plywood over the bag, so no part was visible. Then she wiped her own hands on her trousers and, satisfied that this was the end of it, strode on toward the Albertbridge Road.

She was far too early for work—the system wouldn't let you clock in until eight—so she stopped in Starbucks, treating herself to a cappuccino and a *pain au chocolat*. Laura felt good, better than she'd felt in ages. She sipped her expensive coffee and scrolled through her Instagram feed, liking the odd thing a friend had posted: cats, babies, birthdays, the usual shit. She lol'd at some funny memes and felt genuinely okay in herself. The hand was gone. That would be the end of it. When she stumbled across the news story (which was only just breaking at this point), she scrolled right past it, not for one second associating it with herself or the thing she'd just dumped in a neighbor's dumpster.

It was lunchtime before she heard. She was in the staff room, picking at a pasta salad, when the hand came on the midday news. If she'd not been looking up at the time, she'd have missed it altogether. She'd have made it through the afternoon, happy and oblivious. At the sight of it, Laura rose as if in a trance. She crossed the staff room in three long strides until her face was no more than a foot from the TV screen. From this distance, it was possible to be more rational. Dismembered hands were much of a muchness. It was not necessarily the hand from her fridge. It could be any man's hand, recently removed and slathered in blood. She knew it wasn't. This was her hand they were discussing. She felt this knowledge as a physical sensation, a kind of shrug in the pit of her belly. The same dropped-gut feeling she'd felt the night they came for her dad. She'd known—just known—that this was it as soon as she'd heard the doorbell go. Sometimes, with the big revelations, your body caught on before your head. Laura fumbled for the remote and turned the volume up. She'd not been listening to the story. She'd already missed two thirds of it.

The news anchor was standing on the side of the Newtownards Road, the Freedom Corner murals garish and threatening behind his back. "That was Professor Magowan from Queen's University," he said, "giving us a brief background on the history of the Red Hand. I'm joined now by a local community leader." The camera panned out to reveal a big baldy man, both arms covered in a swirl of tats. He was glaring down the barrel of the camera as he held aloft a perfectly white flag.

In the corner by the microwave, Jim from accounts was reading the paper. He glanced up to see Laura standing in front of the telly. "Now, that," he said, "is the weirdest shit I've ever seen, and I've seen a lot of weird shit in my time." He shook his head and made a sort of tutting sound. "In my day, people respected each other's culture. They didn't go round destroying other folks' stuff. I don't know what the world's coming to." This was sanctimonious bollocks. Jim was only fifty-eight. He'd grown up at the height of the Troubles, when there'd been scant respect for each other's cultures. He was inclined to make these sweeping generalizations. The world was going to hell in a handbasket. Things weren't what they used to be. Back in his day, people were nicer, the nights were longer, the world was a generally better place. Another man spouting such platitudes might've seemed grandfatherly, but Jim was not a likable man. He was prickly and pedantic. He was an awful know-it-all. Which wasn't the worst thing a man could be. It was just the tone he took. Overbearing. Patronizing. Sometimes slightly lecherous. He took this tone with Laura now.

"You do know about the hand?" he said.

"Yes," said Laura, then checked herself. It was probably better to play dumb. "No," she countered, "what hand are you talking about?"

"The Red Hand of Ulster," said Jim. "The actual one."

"What about it?"

"Apparently, it's disappeared. Did you not see the news this morning? Folks are talking about nothing else."

"No," said Laura. She hadn't seen the morning news.

She turned her attention back to the lunchtime bulletin. The item was already over. They'd returned to the studio. Your one with the hair was shuffling her papers and handing over to the sports anchor, who was coming live from Windsor Park. His comb-over waved wildly in the wind.

"What do you mean, the Red Hand of Ulster's disappeared?" Laura asked. "Sure, it isn't real? Is it? Is there an actual hand in a museum or something?"

"Are you joking?" said Jim.

Laura wasn't sure if she was joking or not.

"Uch, Laura, you know the Red Hand's just a story they tell to weans. If you ask me, it's a load of rubbish. Not that I'd ever tell them boys that." He nodded toward the TV screen, invoking the big baldy fella and his Loyalist tats. "These days," Jim continued, "the Red Hand's nothing more than a symbol. The trouble is, your lot don't have anything but symbols left. Flags and symbols, that's all they've got. They're all up in arms this morning because their precious hand's disappeared. It's like they've lost a bit of themselves."

Laura resisted the urge to point out that "her lot" was not "her lot" anymore. She didn't want a slanging match. She knew that

Jim would like nothing better. "Sorry," she said, "I'm still confused. What do you mean, the Red Hand's disappeared?"

"It's gone," said Jim. "Vanished. Scarpered. Done a runner. There's not a single Red Hand to be found in Ulster. All the flags are missing their hands and the red cross too, all the crests and signs and official letterheads. Even the Ulster Hall's lost the wee red hand that used to sit above its door."

"Seriously?" said Laura.

"Seriously," said Jim.

"Has somebody nicked them?"

"The police don't think so. How would you ever get all them hands off all those flags and signs and whatnot. Sure, there's hundreds and thousands of them, and they've all vanished. It's like they were never there in the first place. Pure David Blaine stuff. Some sort of magic trick, they think. Your lot's blaming Sinn Féin, or maybe the priests. It could be some sort of curse against the Prods. The Red Hand's a massive deal to Prods. You'll know that yourself, Laura. Sure, your daddy was always waving it around."

Jim was right. Her daddy had made a point of always getting his photo taken in front of, or holding, a big Ulster flag. There was a picture of her and her brothers at the Twelfth, taken when she was only three or four. Her ma had drawn Union Jacks with face paint on their right cheeks and, on the left, a wee red hand, the fingers fat and sausagey, like the cartoon notion of a hand. That'd been the summer before they lifted her daddy. When he'd seen them done up for the parade, he'd made them pose for a photo. Her ma said he had it up on his wall in the prison. He'd written on it with a permanent marker: "Loyal Sons of Ulster," as if Laura didn't count.

As a child, Laura had never been taught the story behind the Red Hand. They'd not gone in for Irish legends in the Protestant primary she'd been sent to. Her daddy would've had a conniption if he thought his wee ones were getting a grounding in Gaelic shite. God, Queen, country, and a bit of maths was all he'd required of the education system. Anything more might corrupt his weans. Over the years, Laura had tried to educate herself. Not just on the stories. She'd also read up on the Easter Rising and the history of the South. Daniel O'Connell. Charles Stewart Parnell. Michael Collins and the rest of the lads. She'd gone out of her way to enjoy trad music, though it never really sat right with her. She could hear her daddy at the back of her head, taking the piss in a fake "Oirish" accent. *Fiddledy-diddledy-dee Fenian music. What's next, Laura?* Riverdance*? Yon's music for fruits, so it is.*

Darek would sometimes ask Laura what was what when it came to Irish stuff: history and places in the South, how you said words in Irish, simple wee words like "hello" and "goodbye." Mostly, Laura didn't know. She felt a deep sort of shame for her ignorance. Darek knew lots of Polish stories. He was dead set on passing them on to his niece and nephew. They should know who they were and where they came from, though his sister wanted them raised as Belfast kids. She sent them to Scouts in the C of I and also up to Irish dancing, which happened in the Parochial Hall. She'd taught them how to slur their consonants and sharp their vowels like local weans. She'd named them Lyndsey and Christopher and made them take their father's name. Darek thought this a crying shame.

Laura agreed with Darek. She was determined to learn more about her own heritage. And by this she meant all of Ireland, not just the tight corner she'd grown up in. She'd got a book out of

Ballyhack library. It was meant for children, but it covered all the basics. Laura liked the pictures. They helped the stories stick in her head. She'd learned enough to pass herself on Cú Chulainn; Medb; Conchobar; and the giant, Finn McCool, whom she'd already encountered on a school trip to the Giant's Causeway. The book had skated over the Red Hand of Ulster. There were that many versions of the story. Laura tried to remember the details now and could summon only the vaguest notion of what the legend actually entailed. Two big lads, maybe three, had been fighting to claim Ulster as their own. *Were they in boats or on horses?* She couldn't recall. But she did remember the first to lay hand on the land would have the run of it. One smart-arse with a sword saw a loophole in the arrangement. He'd cut his own hand off at the wrist and pitched it onto Ulster's soil and, in doing so, become either king or lord of the place. Laura couldn't remember which one it was. She could have asked Jim, but she didn't want him to think her unduly interested in the hand.

"You're right," she said, turning toward him, "that's not the kind of story you usually get on UTV."

"Aye," said Jim, "it puts me in mind of the time they thought the shipyard cranes were getting bigger. Do you remember that, Laura? It'd have been back in the late nineties, just before the peace kicked in?"

Laura didn't. She'd been nine in '98. She couldn't remember anything except Gramps saying Good Friday might get her dad out on early release. It hadn't, of course. He was still inside, and Laura was not in the mood for reminiscing about the good old, bad old days. She cut Jim off before he could launch back into the shipyard cranes. "Well, that's my break over. I'd better head on before the boss docks my pay."

She left the staff room fully intending to return to work. Somewhere between the ladies' toilets and her desk, the red hand caught up with her. Laura could feel the weight of it lying heavily across her forehead. It was not unlike the clamped sensation she'd come to associate with the migraines she got just before her period came. Though the very notion was ludicrous, Laura was convinced that the hand in her fridge wasn't just any dismembered hand. She'd taken possession—albeit unknowingly—of the actual Red Hand of Ulster and casually chucked it into a dumpster. Now half the country was on the warpath, claiming a direct attack on Protestant identity. Twitter was fit to inform her there were riots planned for later that night and a protest already gathering at City Hall's gates. It was unclear exactly what they were protesting. This hadn't stopped them protesting before.

Laura knew they'd be looking for someone to blame, and this responsibility fell at her feet. Because she was her father's daughter. Because she'd taken up with a Catholic Pole and did not see the harm in this. Because she would not—*no, could not*—let Darek go, she'd compromised the Ulster Protestant way of life. This line of thinking made no sense. And felt entirely logical. The very thought of it made her seething mad. Laura didn't know how to rectify the situation or whether she even wanted to. If the Red Hand of Ulster couldn't be traced back to her fridge, she was happy enough to see the end of it. The North would be much improved if all the flags and symbols disappeared. Despite this, she still felt anxious about the hand. To be on the safe side, she'd skive off work for the afternoon and make sure it was actually gone.

The dumpster was no longer outside the house. Laura saw this as a good sign. She imagined it en route to a rubbish dump or recycling plant, carting the hand even farther away from

She burned it in the drum of their barbecue, first dousing it liberally in lighter fluid, then watching it shrivel up into a coal-black husk of its former self. She raked out the ashes and chucked them into next door's yard and, when she returned to the kitchen, knew before checking that the hand was already back in the fridge.

Finally, in desperation, she placed the hand inside a shoebox and placed the shoebox in the boot and drove it south as far as she could, until she was no longer in the North. As she sped through the suburbs of Belfast and inched her way along the Westlink, down the motorway past Lisburn, and round the outskirts of Banbridge, Laura couldn't help noticing the absence of hands. A hundred or more white flags fluttered from lampposts and front walls. She saw these flags as a form of surrender, a nod toward the idea of truce. There were no white flags outside Newry. Laura hadn't expected there to be. Once over the border, she pulled into a car park and shoved the hand, shoebox and all, into the first rubbish bin she saw. She cleaned her hands with a packet of wet wipes and made it home in less than an hour.

Darek was waiting on the doorstep, lighting a cigarette from the stub of the last. Laura thought he'd given up. He'd found the hand inside the fridge. He wanted to call the police but was wise enough to check with her first. The hand might have something to do with her dad. He'd not yet made the link between this hand and the lead story on the evening news. In fairness to Darek, this would have been quite the leap.

"There's a hand in the fridge," he said as soon as Laura was out of the car. "Why's there a bloody hand in the fridge?"

Laura sat down beside him on the front step. She told him the blunt facts of the hand. How she'd found it. How she'd tried to dispose of it. Then she told him about the news and the missing red hands and the empty flags. He did not laugh. He did not even look like he was thinking of laughing. Laura was very grateful for this. He smoked another cigarette and reached for her hand. And when she'd finished speaking, he said, "Right, well, something's got to be done with the hand. We can't just leave it in the fridge." He also said, "Next time, you need to tell me. You can't keep a thing like this to yourself." Laura promised she would. She hoped there would never be another time like this.

It was dark by this stage, dark enough not to be seen by the neighbors, and far too cold to be sitting outside on the front doorstep. "I'll sort this," said Darek. "Let me sort this out for you." Laura said no, they would deal with it together or not at all. She liked the sound of her voice saying this. It felt like a grown-up thing to say. They rose and went into the kitchen together. Darek lifted the hand out of the fridge. Laura helped him remove the clingfilm. It was slick with blood and condensation. She dropped it straight into the bin. They walked to the back door together—Darek holding the hand in his hand—down the steps, and across the yard.

The security lights from next door came on. Darek looked like an angel, transfigured in the buttery glow. He stood at the fence which separated their house from the wasteland beyond. He drew his hand back and, in this moment, looked utterly mythic. Like something lifted from her library book. Laura had never fancied him more. Then his whole arm sprang suddenly forward. He pitched the hand as hard and far as he possibly could. It flew like a comet, blood trailing in its wake, and disappeared into the dark. "That's that," he said. And Laura believed it actually might be. She let Darek kiss her on the mouth. She let him put his hands on her. She wasn't bothered about the blood or the mess he'd make of her good work clothes. When she came indoors and checked the fridge, there was nothing inside but the usual things: milk and orange juice, margarine and cheese, a tub of low-fat coleslaw that was two weeks past its use-by date.

# COASTERS

## (AFTER JOHN HEWITT)

They've been here twenty-five minutes, and Donald has yet to lay eyes on an actual plant. As per usual, they've run aground in the homeware section. It's less than a fortnight since their last visit. To look at Rosemary, you'd think she hadn't been here in years. She has the glasses on and the handbag shoved up high on her shoulder. It flaps in and out like a chicken wing as she works her way around the shelves. She lifts each item in turn and sizes it up before setting it carefully back in place. Occasionally, she flings a comment in Donald's direction. "Isn't that just gorgeous? Sure, you'd never get the use out of something like that. Sixty-two pounds fifty! It must be made of solid gold." Donald lingers by a rack of personalized keyrings which are also pens. There's no Donald keyring. There never is. It's all Jades and Dylans and Aoifes these days.

Since his retirement, Donald's become an expert in lingering. Rosemary has him trailed round every shopping center in Ulster. Buttercrane. Abbey Centre. Bow Street Mall. The Quays. The Flagship. The Fairhill. They're much of a muchness outside Belfast. Rosemary tells people they enjoy shopping together. The reality is decidedly less egalitarian. When Rosemary wants something, Donald gets his wallet out. Once it's paid for, it falls to him to carry the bag. Rosemary requires two free hands to continue lifting, rubbing, and patting things.

Donald never strays more than ten feet from his wife. It's important to maintain an association, otherwise people might think he's wandering round Dunnes or Menarys of his own volition. It's not quite as bad in a garden center. A man could feasibly be here by himself. Though not right here, by the aprons and biscuit tins and kitschy placemats. Rosemary's the dickens for this kind of tack. Their house is coming down with trite sentiments emblazoned on scabby-looking bits of wood. "It's the dog's house, we just pay the mortgage." "Home is not a place, it's a feeling." "Dance like nobody's watching." Donald can't remember Rosemary ever dancing. Did they even dance on their wedding day? She only bought the "dancing" plaque because it was done in duck-egg blue and cream, this being the color aesthetic of their en suite.

Rosemary's holding something up to show him now: a set of six coasters for coffee mugs. "Look at these, Donald." She reads out the quote: "'You can never get a cup of tea large enough or a book long enough to suit me,' C. S. Lewis. That doesn't sound very like C. S. Lewis to me. You know C. S. Lewis, the Narnia man? Do you think he actually said that, Donald? Sure, it doesn't sound like him at all." Donald resists the urge to say, *I'll just give him a ring here and ask, shall I?* Instead, he gives her a noncommittal shrug. Rosemary's not really looking for his opinion. She's already moved on to the Cath Kidston mugs.

Donald gazes wistfully at the electric doors. Beyond these doors is a partially covered area where they display the garden furniture, planters, and pots. Beyond this section are water features and, beyond the water features, plants. Donald would love a wee wander round the plants. It's almost March. The days are stretching. He's in the garden most evenings now. Last week, he took a notion for a new raised bed. He's already mapped out an area near the patio. He's in need of some shrubs to fill it out.

For a second, things look up. Rosemary steps away from the rustic-look teapots. She's leaving homeware. *Hallelujah.* Donald prepares to steer her toward the door. He doesn't touch her physically. He's developed a way of leaning in when next to his wife, like a collie dog herding sheep. This technique has proved quite successful in the past. He tries it now. *Come on, Rosemary. There isn't much time.* Kenneth and Sandra are due any second, and Kenneth's the sort of man who always arrives promptly, if not ten minutes early. He likes to leave a bit of a buffer in case of something unforeseen. Traffic. Weather. The hand of God. Donald surreptitiously checks his watch. They have five minutes, tops. If he can just keep edging Rosemary toward the door, there's a chance—a small and rapidly diminishing chance—of actually seeing some bloody plants.

Donald is old enough to remember the days when garden centers were chiefly concerned with selling plants. A few had tiny cafés tucked on the side, almost as an afterthought. Some had a display rack or two of garden-related accessories. Poured-concrete birdbaths. Fancy wellies. Homemade jam. But the greater part of the site was always reserved for greenhouses, polytunnels, and carefully laid-out rows of bedding plants. Wheelbarrows. Trellises. Ornamental stones. Seed packets, racked and hanging from individual hooks like room keys in an old-fashioned hotel. Saplings. Sprinklers. Fertilizer. Garden centers were not clean places.

You didn't dress up to purchase plants. You came in your wellies and your gardening clothes. You put a tarp down to protect your boot. No, a garden center was not an excuse for a wee day out. You came to pick up what you needed. Then you went home. In Donald's opinion—and nobody's asking for Donald's opinion—the modern garden center has lost the run of itself.

He glances around the room. It's mostly ladies of a certain age: the pewter-sandal-and-cardi brigade. They're not here for hardy perennials or topsoil. They've come for a nosy round the gift shop and, afterward, coffee, perhaps a bun. There's nothing quite like the feed you get in a garden center café: a heady mix of good home cooking and portions that cater to farming appetites. Donald's not complaining. He's a frequent partaker himself. Every other Tuesday morning, they meet Kenneth and Sandra here at ten to avail themselves of the pensioner's special: any regular coffee and a plain or fruit scone for two pounds fifty. *Two pounds fifty! Sure, you can't be bad to that. The same thing costs a fiver in the shopping center café, and they do piddly wee prepackaged scones.* The sign says you're required to produce a valid bus pass, but nobody's ever asked to see theirs. Sandra occasionally huffs about this. As the youngest present—a mere seventy-two—she claims it's insulting not to be asked. Donald has nothing against the café. He just feels that any feature which isn't a plant should be a secondary concern in a garden center. It's not a "coffee center" or a "handcrafted-tat center."

Rosemary's no more than ten yards from the doors now. Miraculously, she's still moving in the right direction. Like a cruise missile or a homing pigeon. But slower. Much slower. Still, Donald lets himself hope a little. He can see the outline of a bird table looming behind the glass door. A stack of terra-cotta plant pots. He lets himself picture the plants beyond. He's thinking about a rhododendron—a big blousy number with deep cerise flowers—when disaster strikes him a double blow.

First Rosemary's eye drifts left and falls upon a table of Christmas decorations. They're ludicrously early. Or slightly late. Or perhaps—and this possibility troubles Donald—some kind of ever-present Christmas display. *Jesus,* he thinks, *is there any call for a thing like that?* He'd ask Rosemary for her opinion, but she's already fondling a festive penguin that sings Cliff Richard when its beak is depressed. As it's launching into its second round of "Mistletoe and Wine," Kenneth appears. He's three minutes early. "Sorry we're running a bit late," he says. "I came on ahead so youse wouldn't worry. Sandra's just locking up the car. We're to go on in and grab a table before the café gets too busy."

And that is that. There'll be no plants for Donald today.

Rosemary sets the penguin down. The time for patting things is over. She's hell-bent on a latte now. She steers the two men through the gift shop. Past scented candles and gardening clogs, organic soaps and racks of Beanie Babies with their freaky-looking headlamp eyes. Donald has to admire his wife's technique. In thirty-five seconds, she's made more distance than he's managed all morning. Rosemary's formidable when she wants to be.

The café's hiving. It always is on a Tuesday morning. Today it's even worse than usual; there's a bus run just arrived from Larne. The queue's all the way along the counter, round the corner, and out the door. There must be thirty old ones in front of them, each buying coffee individually, fumbling around in purses and pockets to find the exact change. *Why do old ones always insist upon exact change?* It'll take an hour to process them all.

Donald lets his eye drift along the line. He notes the rollators, the walking sticks and corrective footwear, the hearing aids and oxygen tanks. The poorly fitted, sloppy dentures. Being a dentist, albeit retired, he's particularly sensitive to bad dentures. He feels no affinity to the group. Yes, he's a pensioner and they're pensioners too, drawn together by their mutual interest in cheapish scones. But Donald's definitely not an elderly man. He's only very recently retired, and Rosemary insists on dressing him young: boot-cut jeans, lace-up brogues, a nice plaid shirt, and a cardigan. Without thinking, he leaves a five-foot gap between himself and the two auld dolls in front. He'd consider paying full price for his coffee if it meant distancing himself from the walking dead.

Sandra's equally unsympathetic. "Jesus," she says, appearing behind them suddenly, "it's like *One Foot in the Grave* in here." She sends Kenneth off to claim a table. There's a sign specifically saying "Please don't reserve tables." Sandra assumes it doesn't apply to them. Kenneth always does as he's told. "Here, take my coat," she says, "so it looks like there's somebody already there." "Good idea," adds Rosemary, "here's mine as well." Donald automatically decants his anorak. Kenneth heads off, laden down. The line shuffles two places forward, so they're almost in reach of the plastic trays. Donald makes a quick calculation in his head. At the rate they're moving, it'll be half an hour before they get to the till.

He could easily make a quick circuit of the outdoor plants and return in time to claim his scone. He needn't even admit what he's doing. He could mumble something about using the gents' and afterward claim the line was long. He looks at Rosemary. She's informing Sandra that Emily is pregnant again. Sandra's rising to the bait: "I thought they were for waiting till wee Martha had started school?" Rosemary's nodding. "Aye, that's what they told us, anyway." Her jaw is set. There's nothing Rosemary enjoys more than being perturbed. More so when there's an audience to hand. *Best not to chance the plants,* thinks Donald. *Not while Rosemary's in one of her moods.* The queue shuffles forward. If Donald stretches a little, he can reach the trays. He lifts two from the rack that are still sweating with dishwasher steam. There's nowhere to set them, so he tucks them awkwardly under his arm. He can feel the dampness soaking into his cardigan sleeve.

Kenneth returns. "They told me off for keeping a table." His arms are full of everybody's coats and handbags.

"Who told you off?" snaps Sandra.

"That woman over there. In the blue uniform. I think she's with the nursing home lot. She said we weren't allowed to reserve tables when there's so many people in front of us."

"Uch, Kenneth, you should've stood your ground. That woman has no right to move you. She doesn't even work here. I'll go over and have a word with her."

"There's no point, love. Somebody else has our table now."

The queue shuffles forward, making room for Kenneth. He slots in between Sandra and a glass-fronted rack of hot cheesy croissants and sausage rolls.

"The queue's moving quickly," he says optimistically.

"Aye, so are the scones," says Rosemary. She's up on her tiptoes, peeking over a sea of silver heads, monitoring the rapid erosion of the scone mountain at the end of the line. "There's only three fruit ones left."

"Maybe they have more out the back," counters Donald.

Rosemary and Sandra turn on their moderately elevated heels. They look at Donald like he's gone in the head.

"When the scones are done, they're done," says Sandra. "That's why you have to get here early on Tuesday mornings."

"We'll be grand," says Kenneth, ever the peacekeeper, "there's a whole basket of plain ones left."

All four of them prefer a fruit scone—though Sandra usually picks her raisins out—but Kenneth's already spinning the situation in his head. A plain scone's exactly what he's after this morning. He'd fancied a change anyway. Kenneth is the sort of man who can talk himself into anything if it means avoiding a fuss. Donald takes a long look at him. "Pathetic" is the word that comes to mind. Standing there, arms full of ladies' anoraks. And the burgundy cords. *What sort of man wears burgundy trousers?* Sandra has him dressed like an overgrown toddler; all matchy-matchy. *It isn't right. It's demeaning, that's what it is.* Donald wonders if people see him similarly. Maybe he should be a bit more forthright. He's thinking about suggesting they come back later when the café's calmed down. *Will we take a wee dander round the plants?* He's just about to open his mouth when the Tannoy system crackles into life. It's a woman with a thick Broughshane accent. You can tell she's trying, and failing, to put on a slightly posher voice.

"Do we have a doctor on the premises? If there's a doctor or any kind of medical professional in the building this morning, could they make their way to the front till immediately."

A dry mumble oscillates down the line. Everyone's quick to speculate. Somebody's had a heart attack. Or a bad fall. It's a woman gone into early labor. Apparently, this is a reasonably common occurrence in garden centers. Overdue women are known to visit these places just to bring themselves on. Somebody knows somebody who knows a girl who actually had her baby in the water feature section at Hillmount. It wasn't planned at all. Though the staff, delighted with the publicity, presented her with a fifty-pound gift voucher and a free meal for four. There was a picture of her and her week-old baby in the *Newsletter* a few months back.

Rosemary settles on a more obvious explanation. "One of the old ones must've taken a turn."

"Dear love them," says Sandra, "though you have to ask, was it wise bringing that lot out to a place like this? There's a few of them there look awful frail."

"Are you for going, Donald?" asks Kenneth. (Kenneth's never been great at reading a room.)

Donald hadn't been thinking of going, but now Kenneth's put the idea in his head.

"He's not a doctor," snaps Rosemary. "He's just a dentist."

"And he's retired," adds Sandra. "There's nothing he could help them with."

"I just thought," mumbles Kenneth, "well, they said any medical professional. A dentist—sorry, Donald—a retired dentist might be better than nothing, if there's nobody else around."

A lesser man might've been offended, but Donald is heartened by this description. "Better than nothing." It lacks expectation. The pressure's off. So long as he doesn't make the situation worse (i.e., kill the patient), his presence could be seen as an asset. And it would be nice to feel useful for a change. Donald hasn't felt useful for such a long time. Not since he built the patio furniture last Easter, and that was nearly a year ago.

He pictures himself volunteering to help. *I'm a dentist*—no need to mention the retired part—*if you haven't got a doctor, maybe I could help. I'm better than nothing. Ha ha ha.* It wouldn't be too difficult to come up with a few vaguely medical things to say. *Has anyone checked the airways? Let's get her into the recovery position.* Something loosely related to pulse. If delivered in the correct authoritative tone, people would assume he knows what he's doing, though he's learned most of this spiel off *Casualty*. He could roll up his sleeves in a reassuring fashion. He could pass out Polo mints while they wait for the ambulance to arrive. He could look the patient in the eye and say, *Hang in there, you're going to be fine.* There are any number of things Donald could contribute to the crisis, which, while not particularly helpful, certainly wouldn't do any harm.

The queue lurches forward. They're now standing next to the salad bar. Eight plastic tubs are arranged behind a sign which reads, "Choice of three salads with any main." One tub contains limp-looking iceberg lettuce leaves. The remaining seven are mayonnaise-based concoctions of unclear provenance. Donald finds himself staring at something which is most likely coleslaw, though it's quite an alarming purple shade. *I should offer to help,* he thinks. *It is, inarguably, the right thing to do. And offering,* he reminds himself, *wouldn't necessarily equate to actual involvement.* They've probably found a doctor already. If Donald gets as far as the front till and finds a doctor has beaten him to it, well, it wouldn't be the end of the world. In fact, it could be the very excuse he's looking for. He could keep on walking through the gift shop and out the doors, past garden furniture and water features. He could spend fifteen minutes with the plants while the other three wait in line for his scone, believing Donald to be a benevolent man. *Bingo,* thinks Donald. *I'll offer to help, then I'll nip outside for a look at the plants.*

"I should probably offer to help," he says.

"Do you want me to come with you?" asks Kenneth.

"They won't want a dentist," says Rosemary.

"There might not be anybody else."

"Look around you, Donald. It's a garden center on a Tuesday morning. They'll be inundated with retired GPs."

"Still, I should at least let them know I'm here . . . just in case, love."

"You'll lose your place," snaps Sandra.

Rosemary nods in agreement. And that's the end of that.

On the other side of the café, Donald notices a man in a green staff fleece, approaching the lady from the nursing home; he leans across the table and whispers something into her ear. Her face doesn't move. She keeps right on smiling. She's grinning away at all the old folk in her care. Donald can't help noticing her too-big teeth: *inexpertly applied veneers.* Her eyes aren't smiling. Her eyes look insane. She grabs her handbag—it's more of a sack than a handbag, really—rises quickly, and follows the man out of the café.

"It's definitely somebody from the old folks' home," Donald mutters. Nobody is listening to him.

Rosemary is telling Sandra about the C. S. Lewis coasters. "I mean, does that sound like the sort of thing he would say? Sure, C. S. Lewis was all into his holy stuff."

"I think they put any old shite on mugs and what have you," says Sandra. She launches into an in-depth description of a mug she recently received for Mother's Day. It says "World's Best Grandma" on it, though she's told her daughter-in-law umpteen times that she's Nana, not Grandma or Granny or even Gran. "You understand where I'm coming from, Rosemary, don't you?" she says. "Granny's an old woman, and I'm still young."

Rosemary sympathizes, although she gets Granny Ro from Martha and Gran from Philip's kids. "If I was you, I'd just say thank you and put it at the back of the cupboard, where you never have to look at it."

The two of them laugh.

Donald looks at Kenneth. He considers instigating a conversation. Kenneth has two conversational modes: agreeing with whatever the other person says and analyzing the weather. Of the two, his forte is definitely the weather. Kenneth can take a casual comment about what it's doing outside and riff on it for up to an hour: "It's not a bad wee day. It's grand out there. Nice bit of weather, isn't it? Better than yesterday, though not nearly as pleasant as last weekend. I've heard it's to change tomorrow morning. Still, it's nice, the day, isn't it?" It would be impressive if it did not feel so much like a niggling toothache. Donald decides to hold his silence. He has to be in the right mood for Kenneth, and he's not in that mood today.

The queue wobbles forward. They arrive at mains, though it's far too early for lunch. Metal lids hover over empty metal trays, eight of them floating above the lukewarm water of the bain-marie. Donald reads the label affixed to each lid. They're not staying for lunch, yet he finds himself deliberating between chicken with peaches and lasagna. *Lasagna,* he decides, *but just by itself, no chips on the side, so it won't ruin my appetite.* Rosemary always makes something with potatoes on a Tuesday night. The two old ladies in front of him are playing the same fantasy lunch game. They don't think much of the vegan chili. Both the chili and the vegan parts. To be honest, Donald wouldn't mind a chat. He could ask the old ladies if they've seen the plants yet. Old ladies are often fond of plants. The one on the left's Miss Marple–esque. He can picture her gloved, with secateurs in hand. It could be quite nice to stand in line in a garden center discussing actual plants for a change. He could pretend he was on *Gardeners' Question Time*.

Rosemary and Sandra are a brick wall, since they started into their daughters-in-law, and poor old Kenneth is on a mission. Every thirty seconds or so, he keeks his head around the queue, ducking back to update the rest of them on the scone situation. "Only one fruit left, but there's still loads of plain. There's only ten folks ahead of us now." Donald's impressed by Kenneth's technique. For a man of almost eighty, he's positively skittish, periscoping his head up and out every thirty seconds. He looks like a country-lane driver contemplating an overtake. For a second, Donald has a vision of the next five years: spending every Tuesday with Kenneth and Sandra, slowly morphing into a man who wears burgundy cords and fixates on discount scones, never again making it to the plants. He places his hands on the counter to steady himself. He's eye to eye with a glutinous mound of premixed egg salad. It's custard-pale and freckled with scallions. Donald feels a little sick.

"I think I should check if they need any help," he announces. Nobody reacts. He repeats himself a little louder. "I'm going to offer to help."

"If you have to," says Rosemary with a sigh, "but I really think you're wasting your time."

"You're definitely wasting your time," echoes Sandra. She snatches the damp plastic trays from Donald and holds them awkwardly in front of her as if they are an enormous imposition. Sandra's good at looking put upon.

"Good man," says Kenneth, briefly breaking eye contact with the scones to give Donald his blessing. "Will I get your cappuccino in a takeaway cup in case they need you to go in the ambulance?"

Rosemary interrupts, "He'll not be going in any ambulance. We've Martha to pick up at quarter past twelve."

Donald slips away, avoiding further discussion about takeaway cups. He navigates his way through the café, stepping over rollators and abandoned handbags. In the absence of the woman from the nursing home, chaos has descended. Two wee girls in pink overalls and navy hoodies are doing their best to restore calm. They look to be about fifteen. They float between the tables distributing reassurances and paper hankies. All the old ones are clucking and fussing. Everybody's talking loudly at once. A hearing aid shrills, and the coffee machine lets out a loud, steamy fart. By the cutlery station, an old lady with an Asda bag for life is taking advantage of the chaos. Donald watches her swipe two large handfuls of soup spoons and a ketchup dispenser. She pops a sugar sachet into her mouth and smiles to herself as she starts to chew.

Donald leaves the café and makes his way through the gift shop. As he's passing the toilets, he's still intent upon offering to help. He's undecided in homeware. By the time he reaches scented candles, he's convinced himself there's little point. Rosemary's right, the place is probably wall to wall with retired GPs and ENT consultants enjoying a morning off. They'll be falling over themselves to volunteer. GPs, in particular, love a spot of off-duty "do-goodery." He'd probably only embarrass himself. In comparison to an actual doctor, dentists are like vets or massage therapists: same ballpark, different game. *No,* thinks Donald, *they won't have any use for me.*

Thus reassured, he takes a sharp left by birthday cards. He storms past some Christmas penguins and a pair of cross-eyed wicker reindeer, straight through the big electric doors, into the gentle drizzle outside. He pauses next to a vintage-look streetlamp and savors the moment of sweet liberation. He feels like an animal escaped from the zoo: one of those sad-faced monkeys Bellevue is forever misplacing. It is much easier to breathe out here. He glances around, pivoting on his heels for a 360 take. There's not the slightest whiff of a radiator sachet or a scented candle. The air is thick with mulch and the menstrual stench of glass-bound plants. This is where the garden center actually begins. Donald is taken with the notion to buy everything.

Donald doesn't buy diddly-squat. How on earth would he hide a plant from the other three? Plus, Kenneth's minding his jacket, and his wallet's in the inner pocket, poised to pay for Rosemary's scone. Donald's only window-shopping. This doesn't stop him taking his time. He moves slowly through the polytunnels, through the gravel beds and carefully shelved industrial greenhouses with their three dozen different kinds of tomato and squash. He runs his hands through scratchy heathers. He bends to bury his face in a lilac bush and permits himself a good noseful of some long-buried memory: his late mother's perfume, perhaps, or a French holiday. He examines bulbs and pats at sodden corpselike bags of compost. He passes judgment on geraniums. *They're not up to much, and the nasturtiums are already past their best.* He lusts after a trailing clematis. He pictures it climbing the trellis against his back wall. He takes a surreptitious pinch off a rhododendron—such a gorgeous-looking specimen: Ribena purple with glossed mint leaves. It's not quite a cutting, but it might just take if he gets it replanted straight away. Donald has no problem justifying the theft. *It's not really shoplifting, because plants grow back.*

After twenty minutes, he knows he's beginning to take the piss. Still, he has to tear himself away from the plants. It's half eleven. In ten minutes' time, Rosemary will start to talk about heading. It can take her up to half an hour to effect an exit. There'll be umpteen things she just has to tell Sandra before they leave. Not that this will stop her from phoning Sandra after dinner to continue the conversation at some volume while Donald tries to watch the news. Donald makes his way back through water features and garden furniture. He steps through the electric doors and is immediately assaulted by the smell of synthetic cinnamon. An instrumental version of "Unchained Melody" tinkles through the PA system. It's either panpipes or flute. Donald feels like his face is on too tight. He nods to the wicker reindeer as he passes, takes a sharp right at birthday cards, and is just approaching scented candles when he spies the paramedics by the till.

There are two of them: a man and a woman. She's all cropped hair and coiled energy, like the TV ideal of a paramedic, trim and eager in her green jumpsuit. He's fat and beardy, his backside bulging through his trousers as if he's got a pillow stuffed down there. She's on the walkie-talkie. He's talking earnestly to the woman from the nursing home. His big beardy head is bent toward her. He has one hand resting on her shoulder, the other clenched tightly by his side. Donald can tell the woman's crying, though her face is turned away from him. It's the way she's clutching the two wings of her cardigan together. Women do this when they're upset. He takes a few steps forward, moving in the direction of the café door, and, as he moves, notices the trolley tucked down the side of the till. The body humped beneath the blanket. The blanket drawn over the face for privacy's sake. The toes sticking out at the other end. Old-lady toes encased in bamboo-colored tights. The seam rimming across the scabby toenails. Donald looks to see if a doctor's present. There's a woman in a chiffon scarf hovering about fifteen feet away. She's standing next to a display rack of genuine Victorian boiled sweets. He tells himself that she looks like she could be a GP. In his guts, he knows she's not.

He makes his way back through homeware, past the gents' and the ladies' and the toilet that covers both disabled people and nappy changing. He pushes the glass door of the café open. He can tell before he steps inside that the atmosphere's changed in the last half hour. All the old folks have fallen silent. A couple of the women are crying into white paper serviettes embellished with the garden center's logo. A man in a flatcap is pacing up and down between the tables, shaking his head in disbelief. The two wee lassies in the pink overalls are trying to get everybody up and into their coats. One of the café girls has emerged from behind the counter and is doing her best to assist, coaxing withered arms into cardigan sleeves, decanting half-drunk lattes into takeaway cups, murmuring hopeless platitudes: "Come on, now, love, the bus is waiting. The best thing is to get you all home and settled. You'll feel better when you're back in your own wee house."

Kenneth waves to get Donald's attention. The three of them have bagged the good setup next to the window. It comprises a coffee table and two squidgy sofas on either side. It's impractical for anything that requires a knife and fork, but perfect for lingering over coffee and scones. Sandra's always angling for this table on account of the sofas and the uninterrupted view of the front car park. It's highly contested. They rarely get it. On any other Tuesday, Sandra would be looking exceptionally smug.

"Well?" asks Rosemary as Donald lowers himself onto the sofa beside her.

"She died," he says, though he's sure they've already picked this up.

"Uch, love," says Rosemary, patting his knee.

"You done your best," says Sandra, "and at the end of the day, that's all you can do."

The other three nod sympathetically. Donald can tell the women are already thinking about how they'll recount the morning's events to their friends. Will they tell it funny or go for the pathos angle? There's tremendous fodder in a thing like this.

"What was it, Donald?" ask Sandra. "A heart attack, I suppose?"

Donald shrugs and dips his chin in and out of a noncommittal nod.

"Aye, I thought so. Sure, there's nothing you can do with a heart attack. Nine times out of ten, they're gone before the ambulance even arrives."

Kenneth slides a plate across the coffee table. It contains a fruit scone, two foil-wrapped dominoes of butter, a knife, a napkin, and a single serving of strawberry jam.

"There was only one fruit scone left," he says. "We kept it for you."

"Thanks," says Donald. He shouldn't be hungry, but he's ravenous. He attacks the scone with tremendous enthusiasm, slathering each half in butter and excavating Rosemary's jam pot when he gets to the bottom of his own. He drinks his cappuccino, which, despite Kenneth's best efforts, has not held its heat.

"Get that in you, Donald," says Rosemary, "it's almost twelve. We'll have to head soon. I was just letting the nursing home contingent get out before us."

"Dear love them," says Sandra. "They'll be one less of them getting on the bus now."

All four turn to look out through the window. There's a snake of old ones shuffling slowly across the car park. The driver's out of the bus and helping the girls to manhandle them up the steep steps one at a time. At the back of the bus, there's a kind of winch for the nonambulatory. They watch as a large man in a wheelchair ascends jerkily, inch by stuttering inch, as if suspended on a forklift's prongs. Having reached a height of around five foot, he suddenly disappears inside. It looks like the bus has eaten him.

Sandra and Rosemary turn away from the window.

"I think that's almost all of them on the bus now," says Sandra. "We should head before the lunchtime rush descends."

"I think I might get those coasters for Angela," says Rosemary. "We're for her and Bill's on Friday night. It'd save me going into the town for flowers."

"You might as well, Rosemary. For handiness' sake."

"Coasters or mug? They've the same thing written on a mug. I'd get her both, but it might seem a bit like overkill, and it's not an occasion or anything. What do you think, Sandra, should I go for the coasters or a mug?"

"Definitely coasters, Rosemary. A mug's more of a birthday sort of present, you know, for an individual friend. The way I see it, everybody can get the good out of a coaster."

"What?" says Donald. His eyes are still trained on the spot where the man has just been. Squinting into the sun has left a perfect imprint of the wheelchair's silhouette burned into his retina.

"The C. S. Lewis coasters, Donald, the ones with the thing about books and tea. Do you not think they'd be perfect for Angela? Sure, she's mad about tea. I'm going to buy them for her on the way out."

Donald is just about to tell his wife that tea's not an Angela-specific obsession. Every woman in Northern Ireland has an unhealthy relationship with tea. Rosemary might as well say Angela is big into money or sleeping or television and buy her branded crap accordingly themed. More to the point, he'd like to tell her that nobody actually wants more coasters. They must have a dozen sets themselves at home. Coasters are the sort of thing you get for Christmas and immediately off-load onto somebody else. Like a kind of circular economy. See also: bath salts, Black Magic chocolates, and those godawful Willow Tree ornaments with their creepy absent faces. Only an idiot would set out to purchase coasters. You're meant to acquire them and pass them on. Donald's about to point this out to his wife when he remembers about the clematis plant.

"That's a lovely idea, pet," he says. "Angela's always going on about tea. She'll think those coasters are hilarious. Here, take my wallet. I'll meet you up front. I'm just going to nip outside and pick up a wee plant."

Five minutes later, Donald and Rosemary reconnect by the till. He has a rhododendron balanced against one hip and a clematis on the other. He'd like to have lifted a few heathers too, but this would have required a trolley. He doesn't want to chance his arm. Rosemary's got her coasters and an old-fashioned mason jar full of fudge. "For Bill," she explains. Donald just nods. He puts it all on his credit card and, as he's leaving, slips a fiver into the collection box for the Alzheimer's Society.

"Why'd you do that?" asks Rosemary. They've a direct debit set up to Cancer Research and another one to Save the Children. They don't, as a rule, give to anything else.

"I don't know," says Donald. "I just felt like it. Sometimes it's nice to give something back."

# FAMILY CIRCLE

The baby came down the river in a Family Circle biscuit tin.

All wedged in she was, with newspapers and a pair of once-white hand towels twisted round her middle like a kind of bandage. She looked similar to just-born Jesus in paintings. "Swaddled" was the word for this.

The baby could not have tipped herself out. Not with elbows or much squirming. The baby didn't even try. She enjoyed the closeness of the biscuit tin. The way the walls of it pressed tightly against her and burbled when the river ran over pebbles. This shifting nearness reminded her of the previous place, though it had been dark in there, a great deal warmer, and less loud.

The baby mostly slept and, when she wasn't sleeping, looked. There was much to be seen in every direction.

The river didn't sleep. It could not hold itself still or stop without assistance. The river ran one way. One way only. From medium-sized mountain to much bigger sea. This was the way with rivers. East went the river, directly east slicking through three villages and a pine-stenched forest, a bridge, a second bridge, and the farmland belonging to two brothers who did not speak.

Like a bold word it went, slicing their one field into two.

"This be your side," the river said, "and this be yours, and don't be having any fool notions of a bridge."

This was suitably fine with the brothers. They were not at all taken with bridges/rowing boats/mobile telephones or any such means of making contact. They were great fans of the distance: distance and separation, and not having to take your Christmas dinner in the company of your eejit brother or his wife. One brother had not looked directly at the other in almost a decade. Nor had they spoken save to say "Get your bloody cows out of my field" every so often on the telephone, yelling, always yelling, for this was the only language they both spoke. They craved distance and borders and knowing which bit of the world was definitely theirs. The river was decent for spelling this out. A ten-foot wall would have been preferable.

◆◆

Before the baby, there'd been nothing between the brothers but history and a river. Afterward, there would be more of the same.

The baby had no clear notion what she'd floated herself into. She came down the river in a biscuit tin, bobbling past ducks, parked cars, and a flock of straight-backed turbines, their arms cycling like aerobic ladies. She open-eyed the sky as it swung past and, sometimes, the water. She could not yet tell up from down, but colors were available to her. She found the pallid blues familiar and also the whiteness of clouds. She could not eye the sun directly. It stung. It told her to close her eyes. Often she slept for whole miles at a time.

Where the river shuddered to avoid the big tree's roots, the water thinned and the riverbank ran thick with soft glar. The biscuit tin slurred and caught against the mud. It stuck fast. Then the baby could go no farther with the river. Shortly after this, it became night. The color of this was also familiar to the baby. Like the walls and ceiling of the previous place, but much colder and without movement of any kind. There was nothing to eat or see. So the baby slept.

Jamesie was first to notice the biscuit tin.

"The hell is that?" said he, raising a hand to tunnel his eyes.

He stood at some distance from the river, heeling himself up on the gate for a better squint. He had the dog with him—a wee yippety thing with some collie in it—and an old hurley stick he'd taken to leaning over when out and about. The wife insisted on this and the mobile in his pocket. Fully charged. "Just in case," she said, and held her long pause like a blush before adding, "At your age, 'tis best to practice caution."

The wife was bedded yet, would rise on the half hour to fix his breakfast, and afterward, lift the eggs. The wife was good to Jamesie and, once acquired, loyal as a farmyard cat. He did not greatly mind the company of her but much preferred her absence. Hence the fields and the long hours roving; the up and quickly out each morning. Not so much as a dry word in parting. No mouth kissing. Not even in bed.

Jamesie didn't immediately know it as a Family Circle biscuit tin, though he'd seen the likes of them often enough: just before Christmas and when there were visitors expected. From a field's distance, it looked like any old piece of scrap run aground in the roots. Red, it was, and chipped round the edges to reveal tarnished aluminum beneath. He looked at it hard and was reminded of fingernail polish peeling from the fingernails of certain ladies. Not the wife. Obviously. He thought he might take a closer peer and did so, sharply. The wee dog went ahead of him, chasing its nose through the damp grass. Yapping at birds.

The morning was vicious thin and early. The sun still bloody in the east and, opposite, the done moon, pale and lingering like a backward child. Jamesie felt it best to be at this hour with nothing but the cows for getting on with. He liked the sound of his own boots suckering as they lifted from the muck. The way the breath came out of him in white cauliflower puffs. And the quiet trees. *Oh,* thought he, *the comfort of quiet trees.* All this would be lessened in the company of another.

Even from the riverbank, he thought it nothing more than a common biscuit tin. Such items came down the river daily. Shampoo bottles. Plastic footballs. Crisp packets. Once the head of a child's doll staring up at him with stuck, unblinking eyes. Such shite people dumped in the river. Such ordinary shite. He was inclined to turn and leave the biscuit tin be, or stone the living piss out of it, shifting the bloody thing downriver and off his land. Then the noise began to rise off it; a noise like teeth being pulled. And the fear came on Jamesie, all up his arms and round his chest. The grip of it would not let up. He'd to sit himself down in the grass, quickly, in case he fell.

"The hell is that?" he said, out loud this time, for the benefit of the dog. This was not necessary. He already knew it was a baby, and they hadn't anywhere to put a baby. Not even a drawer or a decent-sized box. Furthermore, he could not take a baby home, for the wife was not good with surprises. Even pleasing ones.

Jamesie let himself picture the wife coming into the kitchen with her skirt-tails full of warmish eggs, her anorak zippered all the way from hip to chin. And himself standing by the range, leaning a little backward with his arms full of the youngster. It'd be awkward, like holding an outdoors cat. All itch and twitch and scrambling limbs. The child most likely howling and getting on.

"Happy birthday," he'd say to the wife, though he'd not a notion when this day usually fell, "look what I have here for you." Then the wife would drop her eggs in fright. The clear and yellow of them spreading out across the kitchen tiles, puddling under the fridge, where it wouldn't be all that easy to clean.

"Where'd you get that craitor?" she'd ask as she went for the floor cloth. Or maybe, "What would I be doing with one of them?" Which was exactly what she'd said the time he'd bought her a hostess trolley for Christmas, and duly back it had to go. To the shop. First thing on Boxing Day morning. Swapped for a new hoover with a good strong suck. "No point," said the wife, "in holding on to things we don't have need of."

The wife wouldn't want a baby. Not at her age, with the money they cost, and the racket they made, and the way the neighbors would be wondering where they'd come by a youngster and whether there was something untoward in holding on to it.

"No," said Jamesie, soldiering both feet on his side of the river, "no, we will not be acquiring a child any time soon."

He reached out over the water and, using the tip of his hurley stick, nudged the biscuit tin across the river till it wedged fast in the soft mud on his brother's side. "Now," said he, "let our Michael deal with it." He forced himself to laugh out loud because this was how he'd tell it later to the wife, at the breakfast table with a hot mug cupped in both hands. He was careful not to touch the baby with his bare skin, knowing that a child, once held, was a sticky thing. He would not be tricked into that. Oh, no! He'd sooner use a hurley stick.

Jamesie did not once think that the baby might be in need of certain items such as milk or warmer blankets; that it might require keeping. The baby was not an actual child to him. Only a noise which had been close and was now more distant. Only another bit of rubbish come bumbling down the river. He'd grown cold from standing and hungry for breakfast. He was all *ha, ha, ha* inside his head, thinking about Michael coming out to the cows and finding instead this creature, raising red hell in a Family Circle biscuit tin.

*Let my bastard of a brother take responsibility for a change,* thought Jamesie, and headed up home for his breakfast toast.

The cows were second to notice the biscuit tin.

Necks stretched and tongues lolloping out for a decent lick, they could not reach it from the riverbank and, not being naturally drawn to the consumption of red things, wouldn't risk their necks wading in. They had a notion that red was the color of great happiness, or possibly danger, and weren't certain which but knew this color was not for eating. Definitely not. They stood round the river's edge for one mean hour, cropping the grass in loose circles until the newness of the biscuit tin went old and they drifted back across the field to their babies, and their lovers, and the thorn tree, which was particularly well placed for scratching cow backs.

◆◆

During this entire time, the baby did not noise at all, not even to snuffle her nose. She understood herself in the company of larger creatures and was, for the first time, afraid. She noted a tightness to this feeling, similar but different to that of the biscuit tin.

Michael was third to notice the tin. He'd better eyes on him than Jamesie and saw the red of it screaming from the road.

"Hey-ho," said he to his wee lad, who also went by Michael, "what's that stuck in the river? Not another traffic cone, I hope."

Young Michael took off then, racing ahead of his da. All the way through the cow field, the wellies on him whipping round his ankles so he waddled like a pregnant woman or a fella wearing two left feet.

"'Tis a baby in a Family Circle biscuit tin," he said, cupping his hands about his mouth so his whole face made a megaphone.

"Is it dead?" asked Michael.

"Naw," said Young Michael. He was a farmish lad harboring neither fear nor confusion when it came to death, sexing, and all such bloody matters. "It's not dead, but it will be soon. 'Tis going blue around the lips. I'll lift it out."

"Don't touch it, son. Never touch anything you don't want to hold on to. Let me think for a wee minute."

Michael sat down on the damp grass and drooped his legs over the riverbank. He always found the thinking came quicker to him, sitting down. *What to do?* he wondered. *What to rightly do with a baby in a biscuit tin?*

The kindest thing was to keep it. To take it home to the wife, wrapped up in the inner lining of his coat, and say with big sadly eyes, "Look what came down the river in a biscuit tin, Marion. Almost dead, and none but us to care for it." To make the wife soft with the pity of it. Then take the wee mite in and feed it milk from a dropper, keep it warmly next to the Aga cooker, like a runty pig.

But Michael was not by nature a kindly man or much inclined to duty. He did not fancy the expense of another child. There were four of them already, knocking round his house—eating and drinking and costing the earth to clothe—and one more off at the agricultural college, requiring fees. This one wasn't even his by blood. "Not my responsibility," said he and, looking round, saw they were alone by the riverbank. Even the cows were off chomping elsewhere. *Only myself and the young lad to see,* thought Michael. Later, he'd remember God.

The baby looked up at Michael and his son. She didn't see them as people, only long black smudges darking against the blue. Words were not yet available to her. She couldn't speak "help." So she cried. The loud wail of her, rising up and over the fields, was like struck glass or sirens, like the Angelus bell not knowing when to stop. The thing she was trying to say was, "You are bigger, warmer, better placed. Have a bit of common decency." The thing she actually said was noise.

Michael chose not to hear. He looked down the side of the biscuit tin and over to his brother's field, where four fat heifers were grazing by the gate. *Typical,* he thought, *just typical that this baby's wound up on my side of the river when I've already the five weans bleeding me and the tractor on its final legs. And there's your man over there, sitting pretty with no children, the home house given to him, and a big, strong lump of a wife for helping round the farm. Why's it always muggins here, having to deal with whatever shite comes floating down the river?*

He wished he was home in his kitchen drinking tea, not knowing about the baby in its biscuit tin.

He wondered if enough wishing/wanting/under-breath praying might shake the biscuit tin free so it floated off down the river at a too-fast speed, with himself dashing after and never quite catching up but all the while shouting, *Come back, wee babby, come back now. I was all for helping you.* This he'd say for the benefit of Young Michael. Loudly, he'd say it, for the lad was bothered with gluey ears.

Michael knew that the thing to do in such circumstances—charitable giving, churchgoing, and the like—was to look like you were trying to help and, sadly, couldn't on account of various obstacles getting in the way.

"What should we do, Dad?" asked the young lad.

"It's not our problem, son," said Michael. "If other folks can't be arsed to look after their own weans, why should we be lumbered with them? Sure, we'd fish this child out of the river and tomorrow there'd be two of them and, by the weekend, an epidemic. Babies. Scabby dogs. Elderly ones from the nursing home. Every lazy bastard between here and Belfast would start pitching their problems into the river, expecting us eejits to deal with them. Folks need to take responsibility for their own shite."

"But it's freezing cold out here. Yon baby'll die if nobody takes it in."

"Tell you what, Mikey. Your uncle Jamesie doesn't have any weans of his own. Chances are Auntie Margaret's been after one all these years. We'll push the tin over to his side of the river and leave the babby as a wee surprise for him. Sure, it'll be good for the pair of them to have a young one about the place. 'Twill be a distraction for them. It's a wild big house for two old ones to be rattling round alone."

"Right you be, Dad," said Young Michael, and, using the toe of his welly boot, nudged the biscuit tin back across the river till it stuck firmly in the bank on Jamesie's side.

Then they turned away from the baby, and fed the cows their cow feed, and let the sheep out, and carried on with their everyday doing like there wasn't a baby in a biscuit tin turning blue at the bottom of the field. Michael would not let the guilt of this sink its teeth in. Oh, no, he would not let it catch. No other soul had noted his turning back, his line-set mouth, the way his ears deafed themselves to the baby's screams. Yes, indeed, there was a tug in his lungs like wet concrete, a heaviness which could only be shame, but with nobody there to bear witness, it would quickly lift.

Up the field he went and took soup for his lunch: vegetable broth with boiled potato chunks islanding on the surface like the faces of tiny people drowned and floating with the bloat. Read the paper. Smoked his pipe and once or twice laughed with the wife at something funny the children had said. No spare thought had he for the baby in her biscuit tin, turning blue.

The baby slept and, when she wasn't sleeping, cried and wondered why her own noise was getting farther away from her. It was less with every hour until she could not hear herself for the silence. She slept and gurned and, all day long, shuttled back and forth from one side of the river to the other as Jamesie moved her with a stick and Michael shoved her back with his foot. Then Jamesie once more with a stick and once again Michael, making Young Michael do it with a fishing rod. Side to side she went, with little licks of river splashing over the biscuit tin's edges so she was damp and dizzy from the toing and froing and could not tell where she was or which side was not wanting her now. Shortly after, it was dark. The color of this was now familiar to the baby, like the previous night and the place which had happened before. All the comfort had gone out of the blackness. All the hope of being held.

At some point during the evening, the baby fell out of the biscuit tin and went fumbling down the river to the larger sea. The sea was glad to have her. This was the way with seas, always greedy, willing to swallow anything.

In the morning, when Jamesie came down for the cows, he noticed the biscuit tin empty. *Hey-ho,* he thought, *that situation's sorted itself out,* and just a heartbeat later, *What could I not do with a biscuit tin in decent nick?* Thereafter, he entertained thoughts of storing eggs or seeds or, indeed, shop-bought biscuits still in their packets. He went hooking after the tin with a stick. There was an urgency to his grabbing which almost unbalanced him. He was bent like a snapped toothpick.

"Here now," shouted Michael, looming on the opposite side, "that's my biscuit tin. I'm for keeping photos in it. Get your thieving hands off." He bade the young lad into the river in his bare feet. "Get that biscuit tin before your uncle lays hands on it." Not caring about the current or the cold. Only wanting to own a valuable thing.

"Finders keepers," yelled Jamesie, and plowed in after Young Michael. Not a bit bothered that he'd left his wellies in the yard; that his good boots would be ruined with the wet. Then the trouble really started. The wee dog opened its mouth and howled. The cows lifted their fat heads from the grass to stare. The river ran away with itself, wanting to avoid a commotion and only carrying the fuss of it farther downstream.

This went on for many hours—the grabbing and grunting and sharp-handed trickery of the two—until one brother won and the other went home damp. Then he who finally owned the biscuit tin held it tightly against his chest, like you would a football trophy. He was relieved, greatly so, to find nothing—not so much as a smallish dent—marking the place where the baby had been.

When his wife saw the biscuit tin, she said, "Just the thing for keeping stock cubes in." He was glad he hadn't told her about the baby; the thought of it would not ruin this moment. You could never tell with women, what they'd take exception to.

# A NOTE ON PREVIOUSLY PUBLISHED STORIES

"A Certain Degree of Ownership" was short-listed for the Desperate Literature Prize for Short Fiction, 2021

A version of "Grand So" was published in *The Four Faced Liar*, 2022

"Quickly, While They Still Have Horses" was published in *The Stinging Fly*, 2018

"Pillars" was first published by Faber in *Being Various: New Irish Short Stories*, 2019

"Troubling the Water" was a commission for the Freelands Foundation, 2021

"In the Car with the Rain Coming Down" was short-listed for the BBC National Short Story Award 2020 and was read/dramatized for BBC Radio 4

"Family Circle" was a commission for the National Centre for Writing, 2018

# ACKNOWLEDGMENTS

The more books I publish, the longer the thank-you list grows. I'm very grateful for this.

Firstly, a huge thank-you to the wonderful bookish people who continue to champion my writing and encourage me. I am so honored and inspired to be working with Emily Polson and all at Scribner. It's a dream come true to have found a publisher who is so careful, considerate, and enthusiastic about my work. Thanks also to Alice Youell, Kirsty Dunseath, Irene Martinez Costa, Sorcha Judge, Milly Reid, and all the other wonders on my UK and Ireland team. Kate Johnson, the world's best agent, who's always there, always passionate and honest, and, most important, always open to every mad idea I have. I'd be lost without you, Kate. Thank you also to agents extraordinaire Rach Crawford and Emily Hayward-Whitlock.

I'd also like to thank all the amazing individuals and organizations who offered the time, space, and financial support necessary to bring these stories to fruition. Thank you to Nora Hickey M'Sichilli and all at the Centre Culturel Irlandais, Sinéad MacAodha and Literature Ireland, Peggy Hughes and everyone at the National Centre for Writing, Arts Council NI, the ARIEL residency at the Université de Lorraine, EFACIS, and the Irish Writers Centre. Thank you to the organizations who relentlessly champion literature in the North. Your hard work doesn't go unnoticed and is so appreciated. Thanks to Cathy Brown at the Seamus Heaney HomePlace, Sophie Hayles at the Crescent Arts Centre, and Glenn Patterson and Rachel Brown at the Seamus Heaney Centre at QUB.

Thank you also to all the fabulous booksellers I get to work with every week. There are far too many of you to mention, but special thanks must always go to David Torrance and the team at No Alibis, who provide a home for so many Northern Irish writers and keep us all reading furiously. Thank you to Michael Shannon for helping me realize my stories on the radio. Thank you, as always, to Joan and the team at the QFT for letting me escape into my imagination two or three times every week. I'm also incredibly grateful to have made so many new friends and supporters outside of the UK and Ireland. I'm particularly thankful for the friendship and community I've found at Sabine Wespieser Editions in France. Thank you, Sabine and Marie, for welcoming me into your publishing family.

This book, like every other book I've ever written, is made up mostly of conversations, and I'm particularly thankful for brilliant, mind-expanding conversations with Karl Geary, Michelle Gallen, Olivia Fitzsimmons, Lucy Caldwell, Clara Ministral, Monican McWilliams, Dominique Goy Blanquet, Michael Hughes, Sheena Wilkinson, Connie Voisine, Sam Thompson, Maureen Boyle, Malachi O'Doherty, Donal Ryan, Anne Griffin, Myra Zepf, Sinéad Morrissey, Sarah Hesketh, Bernie McGill, Caroline Magennis, Dawn Watson, and Victoria Kennefick. (Reading over this list, I realize how incredibly fortunate I am to have so many incredibly generous and ludicrously talented friends. Please read these people. They're wonderful human beings, and they write cracking books).

The biggest thank-you goes to my everyday people who've been there forever and ever and continue to hold me together. No matter how much I gallivant, Belfast will always be home, and I'll keep coming back to it because of these folk. Hilary Copeland, Kristen Kernaghan, Hannah Lockhart, Emma Must, Andrew Cunning, Mícheál McCann, Olwyn Dowling, Emily DeDakis, Toby Buckley, Conor Cleary, and all my lovely reader friends at Mexico and Below Book Group. You're the best. Don't go changing any time soon.

Finally, a big thank-you to my family. For support, free meals, enthusiasm, and keeping my feet firmly welded to the ground, thanks to Mum, Alan, Laurie, and my beautiful, kind, and inspiring niece and nephew, Caleb and Izzy, who'll soon be old enough to actually read these books.

# ABOUT THE AUTHOR

Jan Carson is a writer and community arts facilitator based in Belfast. Her first novel, *Malcolm Orange Disappears,* was published in 2014 to critical acclaim, followed by a short-story collection, *Children's Children* (2016), and two flash-fiction anthologies, *Postcard Stories* (2017) and *Postcard Stories 2* (2020). Her second novel, *The Fire Starters* (2019), won the EU Prize for Literature and was short-listed for the Dalkey Literary Awards Novel of the Year Award, and her third novel, *The Raptures* (2022), was short-listed for the Irish Book Awards Novel of the Year and the Kerry Group Irish Novel of the Year. Her work has appeared in numerous journals and on BBC Radio 3 and 4. She has won the *Harper's Bazaar* short-story competition and has been short-listed for the BBC National Short Story Award, An Post Irish Short Story of the Year, and the Seán Ó Faoláin Short Story Prize. Jan is a Fellow of the Royal Society of Literature.